I Listened, Momma

A Novel by Darlene Campbell

Old Seventy Creek Press 2011

OLD SEVENTY CREEK PRESS 2011

PUBLISHED IN THE UNITED STATES
BY OLD SEVENTY CREEK PRESS
RUDY THOMAS, PUBLISHER
P. O. BOX 204
ALBANY, KENTUCKY 42602

ISBN-13: 978-0615575315 (Old Seventy Creek Press)
ISBN-10: 0615575315

Cover Photo by Rachel A. Warmouth who lives in
Campbellsville, Kentucky and is the daughter of Darlene
Campbell.

PROLOGUE

Dear Reader,

Thank you so much for purchasing this novel. I would like to tell you a little about the book.

First, this book was written for my dad, William Henry Franklin, who is very much like Joe Pablo in the story. Like Joe, my dad was the grandson of a Mexican immigrant. He grew up the son of a sharecropper, who left home at fourteen to support his siblings. Then he married (actually eloped with) my momma and went to work at a saw mill to support us. With his meager earnings, he put food on our table and shoes on our feet. He was not always able to give us all the material goods he wanted to, but he gave us something far superior. He gave us the gift of dreaming, the ability to imagine. So many times I have said that Daddy taught me to dream but Momma taught me how to put wings on [my] dreams.

While the supporting characters and events in this novel are fictitious, the personalities of Chippie's parents and siblings are based on my own, and it is my heart's desire that this book teaches the one lesson my daddy always wanted me to learn: "It don't matter if you've got money or things. What matters most is that you've got family and that you stick together. That you love one another... Without love, the rest is a big fat zero."

"Love one another." If my father said that once, he said it a thousand times. This book is about love.

Secondly, this book is my stand against cancer. I hope and pray that every sufferer who reads this book will be cured of cancer forever. All royalties from this story go to fight that terrible disease. On the website for this book, http://darcampbell.angelfire.com/chippie, there is a place called *Wall of Heroes* for you to list the names of those you love who have battled or are battling cancer. If you would like to add a name to our *Wall of Heroes*, please contact us at nochipa@windstream.net. Indicate whether you or your loved one are still battling cancer, are cancer free, or have gone home. Please send us your name or your loved one's name and spread the message of hope!

Thirdly, this book is also a memorial to my wonderful grandmother, Eva Leach Turner, who believed in me and encouraged me to use my mind; to my Aunt Dorothy Turner [a cancer survivor], who has always been there for me and set an example of what it means to believe in yourself and follow your own destiny; to my Uncle Paul, who always told me I could be anything I wanted to be; and to my Aunt Edwina Garrison, whom I honestly think passed her love of painting to me. Momma used to tell me that I had inherited Edwina's talent. I pray she was right! And of course, it is for my mom, Bonnie Turner Franklin. I know that not one of my dreams would have been realized without her sacrifices, her faith, and her encouragement.

And finally, I hope to testify that there is a God and that he loves us; above all else, he loves us.

ACKNOWLEDGMENT

Thank you, Connie Hensley, for believing in me and supporting me throughout this endeavor, for reading this story and knowing in your heart that it would succeed. I suppose that's what sisters are for, but I believe you would have done it anyway!

Phillip, without your faith and support, I do not think this book would have become reality and Rachel, always you inspire me.

Brian L. Porter, you have been a great blessing to me. I am unsure what I would have done without your help.

Thank you, Savannah North and Dorothy Brouse, for your valuable insights and ideas...

CHAPTER ONE

Upper Cumberland, Kentucky 1976

My daddy was a storyteller, not the kind who traveled around to schools and got paid for it, but the kind who told real stories, ones he had lived. He could spit a story out of his heart and memory with enough detail to make you feel like you'd gone back in time. I suppose it's only fitting that my own story begins with one of his.

We were shucking corn in the barn loft down in Walkup Holler. The time was going by way slower that it ought to have until Daddy started one of his tales.

He said, "It was back in 1959. Me and Maggie June Garney had been stripping 'backer' up on the ridge."

By 'backer,' he meant tobacco; nobody I knew said it the proper way. Every winter, for the majority of his life, he had stripped tobacco for farmers scattered around the county. Stripping it meant that they took it down from the barn tiers where it had been hanging to 'cure' for a couple of months, stripped off the leaves and tied them into 'hands,' according to their grade. The grade was determined by which area of the stalk the leaves had come from. The tobacco was then hauled by pick-up truck or flat bed wagons to tobacco warehouses where it was sold to tobacco companies to be made into cigarettes, cigars, snuff and chewing tobacco.

"We were walking down by the old schoolhouse," he said. "when all at once them Dawson boys came running out from behind it, all five of them, drunk as skunks, and they lit in on me.

"Maggie June let loose a hollering like she was dying. One of them Dawson boys said, 'Shut up, little black girl, before we give you some of this too. Now get on up that holler and tell them Pablos, this is what happens to a colored when he thinks he can go with a white woman.'"

Daddy had grown up with the Garney girls. They were like his sisters, and like them, he'd been born in an old slave cabin. In the summer sun, his Mexican skin was darker than theirs, so folks called him colored.

I felt sorry for poor little Maggie June and clutched an ear of corn as if it was her and I could protect her from them mean old Dawson boys. If I were a cussing girl, I'd have used Uncle Dody Eastridge's favorite word and called them turd heads. But I wasn't prone to cussing, and Daddy would have tanned my hide right then and there if I up and said it, but that's what the Dawson boys sounded like to me...turd heads.

"Maggie's eyes got big as half dollars," Daddy said. "And she took off up that holler, yelling her head off. I hoped she'd get her daddy down there to help me, but then I remembered; he'd gone up to Danville to the backer warehouse."

"What'd they do to you?" I asked.

Daddy looked down at the corn and tore the shuck off, gritting his teeth.

"One of them had a piece of log chain in his pocket. He wrapped it around his knuckles and beat on me while the rest of them boys held me. Next part I can't remember on my own. My Granny Flor told me bout it. Her and Sam Lee was walking home that night from her girl's house.

"Sam Lee was carrying a coal oil lantern to light Granny's way. He said he saw something red in the water and Granny Flor knew right off that it was blood. Sam Lee held his lantern up and there I was, a-layin' in the water. Granny Flor said I was bleeding like a stuck hog. Her and Sam Lee packed me up to the house and she sewed me up. Later on, she told me that she put my skull back together with her own two hands. Then she doctored me up with some poultice. If it hadn't been for Granny Flor, I'd never have made it."

"I don't understand it, Daddy. How come people didn't want you and Momma to get married?" I said.

"People are set in their ways, Chippie. They get scared when somebody comes along with another way of doing things. I tell you this because everybody ain't like Mr. Walkup. But, even he can only do so much, especially when there is kinfolk a-needin' this house."

"What do you mean, Daddy?"

He tossed an ear of corn through the square opening into the crib below. "We got to move, Sis.

CHAPTER TWO

"Move away from Walkup Holler?" I said.

"To Briar Ridge," Daddy said.

I got an awful nervous feeling in my middle, like there was a chunk of something stuck between my chest and stomach.

The barn was quiet except for the two of us. The corn, the fresh cut hay in the loft, and the dried manure down in the main hall lay soft and silent. Dust particles danced in streaks pouring in through the cracks between the worn planks of the barn wall.

I looked down. I felt a big old knot in my throat and my voice was shaky when I spoke. "But why? Why would you move us up there with them mean people?"

He looked at me like he was a lawyer and I was a judge, like he was trying to convince me that what he was saying was the only way that things could be. And there was something in his voice, too, something as stubborn as a gunshot dog, hiding out on hunting day. "The Dawson boys is gone, Sissy. The youngest died of typhoid. The two oldest ones are in the state pen for killing a man. And the other one up and moved off when his daddy died. The rest of the folks on Briar Ridge won't do nothing more than talk about a person." He tore the shuck from another ear of corn and threw it down the hole into the crib.

"Is that why we're moving? Cause they're gone

and you want to go back home?"

Daddy shook his head. "Nope, it's because Pate McClean's moving back here from Louisville. He needs a place to live. Mr. Walkup is gonna let him have the house."

I looked out through the little loft window at our old white house across the field and the wooded hills rising up behind it.

It was early September and the fields were ablaze with black-eyed-Susans and golden rods. Every so often a bushy purple ironweed testified to its name and stuck up like a lone, dark island in a yellow sea.

The afternoon sun cast a golden hue, turning ordinary things like the woodshed and the chicken house into enchanted cottages from the pages of some old storybook. The pear tree, standing alone, as it had done for a hundred and ten years, had a magical glow about it.

How could we be moving? My memories were just like that pear tree, rooted in the richness of the farm, nestled in the soil among one hundred fifty acres of rolling hills.

The farm belonged to Mr. James T. Walkup whose ancestor's slaves had built the house prior to the Civil War. Once, it had been a mansion but now, with its buckling sides, peeling paint and missing border stones, it was just another reminder that the South would never rise again. But it was the perfect place to be a kid.

There was a natural spring down below our house. We called it the spring branch, which just meant that it flowed up out of a hole in the ground and formed a narrow creek, which forked and went in two directions, kind of like a tree trunk forks off into different branches. We lived on the eastern edge of cave country and at the western tip of the Appalachian Mountains. The ground was made of limestone and sandstone. Natural springs were everywhere. My fifth grade teacher had once told me that the ground beneath our state was like Swiss cheese. She called it a karst landscape and said that sink holes, caves, underground rivers, hidden streams, natural bridges and water bubbling up out of the ground, springs, were all a part of it. At any rate, the spring branch was a wondrous place. I played there, catching tadpoles, crawdads, snails and minnows. I collected these things and kept them in the old washhouse where slaves had once done the washing for Mr. Walkup's granddaddy.

That old washhouse was my 'laboratory'. It was also where my siblings and I played school, and it was the clubhouse, and a boat, and just about anything else we could come up with. Truth was that it was just an old clapboard building with rough wooden walls and a plank floor that someone had covered with a linoleum rug about thirty years ago. The rug was still there and so worn that the only thing that remained of its original pattern was an occasional splash of pink. The rest was white with brown streaks, worn there by the floorboards. It had one window in the rear wall, which Daddy had covered with the springs out of a baby crib, because a storm had blown a tree limb into the pane and broken it several years earlier.

There was not one thing about that farm I didn't love. I loved the old cemetery where I picked flowers and imagined what life was like for the people buried there since the early 1800s. I loved the big oak tree whose branches shaded that little corner of the world. I loved the cedars in the field and the steep hills. I loved the grapevines I swung on and the bluffs, and cliffs, and the buckeye trees. I loved the moss in the front yard and the little blue flowers that stuck their heads up in March, and the six big maple trees from which my dad hung our hemp swings. I loved the sky where God lived. And I loved the smell of the air after a rain and of wet leaves in the fall.

Daddy's voice startled me. "Quit studying so hard, Sis. Your face is gonna freeze like that and you'll look like a grouchy ole woman before your time. It's just got to be this way. Pate's family to Mr. Walkup, a cousin, I reckon. A man's family ought to come first. You understand that, don't you? Mr. Walkup is a good man. Got curious ways, but he's a good man. Don't be so sad, Sissy. Something good's coming out of this, something real good.

"My boss-man down at the mill, George, is giving us a place. Letting us have it for all the years I've worked for him. For a fat, rich, white man, he's all right. So, we'll be moving next week."

Daddy smiled. His smile looked more like he was gritting his teeth, stained plum near as brown as his face from years of smoking and chewing tobacco. "Did you hear me, Chippie? I said that he's given us a place, an acre of ground. My own land."

Daddy had always wanted his own place. His grandfather had come from Mexico as a teen and worked as a hired hand for the rest of his life. He would work for anybody and do anything, regardless of how hard or how dirty, just so long as it didn't require killing or stealing.

He worked tobacco crops, chopped hay, made wagon wheels, grew hemp, cut sugar cane and even whittled out wooden shoes so he could sell them.

Still Great-grandpa Oscar had made a better living than he would have in the old country. His dream had been to own land, to have a real home place. My grandfather, Willie Jose, had shared that dream and now, Daddy shared it too.

My brother, Jerry Wayne, came into the barn. His shoulder length brown hair was combed over to one side. He was wearing a pair of faded jeans that didn't quite reach his ankles and a gray T-shirt with a red thumbprint on it. It read, IMPRESS YOURSELF, BE SEEN WITH ME. That was his favorite shirt. He thought it made him look cool, and it would have if he hadn't been wearing his old pants. Of course he'd never wear those pants to school. He wouldn't want the girls to see him in them.

Jerry Wayne shoved the hair out of his eyes and yelled up to the loft. "Momma said to tell y'all to come to the house. Supper's ready."

Funny thing about Jerry Wayne, he never did show much excitement and a person wouldn't notice it in his voice, but I could tell when he was happy or excited by the way he flipped his hair with his left hand and sort of shook his head to one side. Sometimes there would be a small gleam in his eyes.

Daddy stood and slapped his thigh. "Well, hot dog. Let's go."

We headed back to the house with Jerry Wayne, wading through the field of yellow flowers. I could smell the food before we even reached the yard. Momma was a good cook. She made the best biscuits in the whole county and my Aunt Suez would drive twenty miles if she had a hankering for one of them.

We came out in the backyard by the woodshed and the sound of Momma's little black transistor radio, which she kept on top the refrigerator, drifted through the open kitchen door and greeted us with, 'Satin sheets to lie on, satin pillows to cry on.' I laughed. I'd never seen a satin sheet in my life and thought that was a silly song.

Rusty ran up, wagging his tail. The little brown mutt was half bulldog and half Chihuahua. He was Jerry Wayne's and mine to share. Daddy brought him home in his coat pocket when I was fourteen-months-old and sat him in the playpen with me. Here I was now nearly fourteen-years-old, and I couldn't remember a day in my life when Rusty hadn't been there. He met Jerry and me at the creek where the bus let us off on my first day of school, and eight years later, he was meeting six of us as we got off the bus each afternoon. He had saved Jerry Wayne's life once by grabbing a snake and killing it just before Jerry Wayne stepped on it.

Now, our kitchen was the kind of place where a body could feel cozy and free all at once. We had a big metal table with nine mismatched chairs. Some were wooden ladder-backs and some were metal-legged chairs with vinyl seats. The sink cabinet and woodwork were sea foam green with plenty of nail heads and holes to give them character. The wallpaper had little green pots and pans all over it. The linoleum rug was a small ocean of mingled brown squares, and the windows were trimmed in some lacy white curtains Momma had made.

When we entered the house Momma had the table set with macaroni, cornbread, beans, tomatoes, and beef from the cow that jumped over the bluff and killed herself. She'd gotten out of the field through a hole in the fence, and when Daddy and Jerry Wayne tried to catch her, she ran like a blind idiot, straight off a bluff and broke her neck in the holler. We couldn't drink fresh milk after that, but we had a winter's worth of beef in the freezer.

It turned out fortunate that our cow killed herself, because the hog we'd been raising for winter meat ate a nail and punctured its intestines. It was a white hog, but when Daddy went out to feed it one morning it was a thousand pounds of green pork. That big old chunk of lard had died in the night from eating that nail. Why, it was as stiff as a frozen washrag when my daddy found it that morning.

Now for supper, Momma poured us all some iced tea and we dragged our chairs up to the table. Daddy always sat at one end of the table and Momma at the other. All of us kids sat wherever we could find a spot. It was pretty crowded to have nine chairs at the table when the food was on it, too. So, some of us would sit by the stove or over at the sink or by the fireplace, which didn't work because Daddy boarded it up so he could cut a hole for a stovepipe.

Daddy took his little black cap off and hung it on the back of his chair. "Honey, when you gonna cook that mud-turtle me and Waylon caught?"

Momma rubbed her hands on a towel and took her seat. She never did wear an apron like the television moms. She never pulled her black hair back like they did either, for she always kept it cut just below her ears, because it was so thick that it made her head hurt when it got long. "I got it soaking in salt water. Figured I'd fix it tomorrow night."

"I can't wait. Ain't had no mud-turtle in a couple years." Daddy scratched his head. "Jerry Wayne, pass me that butter."

Momma reached for the biscuits. "Now, Joe, don't be scratching at the table."

Same as always, everybody in the kitchen was chattering about first one thing then another. Daddy was talking about watching reruns of Bonanza. Jerry Wayne was talking about a girl named Ginni that he saw down on Sycamore Creek, swinging on a grapevine and jumping in the swimming hole.

"That there's James Walker's girl, son," Daddy said. "They raise horses up on Briar Ridge. Years ago, when I was fourteen, I used to work for Jake Pearson up there."

Momma shook her head. "I ain't got no use for Briar Ridge. We lived up there when Chippie was a baby.

We didn't have a bite to eat in the house. It was in the dead of winter and your daddy couldn't get work cause the mill froze up. Anyway, we ran out of milk for you, Chippie." Momma looked at Daddy. "Remember that, honey?"

Daddy nodded.

"Old Meridith Goodin, that runs Goodin's store up there on the hill, wouldn't even give us two dollars credit for a gallon of milk and a pack of cigarettes."

"Them was hard times," Daddy said. "But things would be different if a man owned his own place."

"Things ain't never gonna be different," Momma said. "All's on Briar Ridge is snobs and hypocrites. Them people up there got no use for you or your family. They been making fun of the Pablos for eighty years. What makes you think an acre of ground is gonna change that?"

"A man that owns land is rich," Daddy said.

I didn't look up. "I don't care 'bout being rich. I know kids at school who are rich. They act awful. I think I'm happier than they are."

Momma smiled at me, then at Daddy. "As long as you got love, honey, you are rich."

"Love and family," Daddy said. "It don't matter where we live as long as we stick together. But some things are out of our hands and in the good Lord's. A poor man has to move when the landlord says so and he's got to move where there's a cheap house."

Lou Annie was the first to figure it out. She looked up, her thick lips parted. "We're moving, ain't we?"

"Yep. Moving to Briar Ridge," Daddy said.

All of my brothers and sisters looked the same way they did the day the dogs killed Funny Face, one of our cats. And in my heart, I felt that way, kind of numb with a big hole somewhere in my gut.

Momma wiped her hands on her dress like they were sweaty. "I reckon I'll go sign you kids up at Briar Ridge Grade Center day after tomorrow. Except Jerry Wayne. You'll still be going to high school, just riding a different bus."

Jerry Wayne pounced up out of his chair. "I don't care. I hate school, and I'm quitting soon as I have my birthday. And I don't want to move to no danged old Briar Ridge either. I like it just fine right here. Now everything's ruint. It's just ruint. That's all!" He turned and ran out the door, knocking his chair over as he went.

Momma jumped up. "Jerry Wayne, you get back in here right now."

CHAPTER THREE

I thought Momma might cry as she sat there looking at her plate. Momma was tough, but it made her cry when one of us kids was really upset, especially if it was Jerry Wayne. I suppose that was because Jerry Wayne belonged in a world where boys were valued for hunting and fishing, for knowing how to survive in the woods and build a fire with nothing but sticks and stones. Momma often said that was the kind of world that was disappearing fast.

"I just don't want him to end up working at a saw mill for the rest of his life. He needs an education. Things ain't like they used to be. You can't get by without a high school diploma nowadays," Momma said.

Daddy put a hand on Momma's arm. "Let him go, honey. He needs to get used to the idea."

Jerry Wayne hated school. He was plenty smart, but no matter how hard he tried, he never could make better than a C. He just couldn't focus on what the teachers were saying. But Jerry could fix a bicycle with nothing but an old pair of pliers. He could figure out more ways to build bridges on the dirt bank in our front yard than any boy alive. However, he sure had a fierce time with spelling and division. The very mention of school sent him into fits, even though he was already in high school and wouldn't be the one having to get used to everything being new.

"Y'all kids go on out and play," Daddy said.

I knew he wanted to talk to Momma alone for a

while. They didn't see eye to eye on Jerry Wayne's quitting school.

Daddy had said many times that he didn't think an education was so important. He felt like all the school system was good for most of the time was to take kids away from their parents nine months out of the year.

Momma had high hopes for us. Maybe she needed to prove something to her family, the Eastridges, who had never liked Daddy. They called him an ignorant Mexican. They made fun of Lou Annie, a year and a half-younger than me, and called her Fat Bam-Bam. They made fun of Carol Lee because she looked like a Filipino; of Zelphie because her hair stuck out, and she had wild blue eyes; of Willie because he was clumsy, high-tempered and bow-legged. And they made fun of me, because I was skinny and because of my name.

The Eastridges said things like, "Whoever heard of such a weird name? Jewell, I can't believe you named that child some ole Injun name?" They didn't care that I was named after my great-great-grandma on my Daddy's side. It would have been all right if I had been named after an Eastridge, something like Sarah or Elizabeth or Katherine, but Nochipa? No, that name made them feel like they had tobacco juice stains on the front of their shirts.

"Your name means 'always,'" Grandma Sadie Rose Pablo said to me one day while she was sitting on the hospital bed that Grandpa Willie Jose had moved into the living room. Grandma was fifty-years-old and dying with tuberculosis at that time. I will never forget how her hair, glossy and black like a crow's wings in the sunlight, hid her slender back. I don't know if Grandma was really beautiful or if her smile made her seem that way, but she had chosen my name. And her stories about it made me feel like a princess.

"Nochipa was the pet name your Great-grandpa Oscar called Willie's momma. He said it had been his own grandmother's name back in Old Mexico and he wanted to keep it in the family. As long as there is a Nochipa Pablo, your people will be remembered in this world."

"What about your people, Granny?"

Granny smiled. "As long as the hills stand, folks will remember the Cherokee." Then she drifted off and quoted a Bible scripture in her native language like she was prone to do. "*Ga du gi wi di gugani nahna tsvdidale wusaga aqualinigo histisgi unelanvhi agisdesgi nasgi uwoenvhi galadi a ehi*. I will lift up my eyes unto the hills," she said. "From whence comes my help? My help comes from the Lord." She would stroke my hair. "Remember that, Chippie, when you're older and life gets hard. Look out yonder at them hills and remember where your help comes from."

Grandma's folks had lost all their land. Her grandma had married a white man in order to keep her little cabin and farm, and then ended up losing it when her son came down with a fatal kidney disease.

It stung when the Eastridges made fun of my name, and of my Grandma Sadie Rose, when they mocked her ways and poked fun at her manner of worshipping the Lord. Granny Pablo worshipped God in the woods. Her Bible was worn and tattered. She prayed in her native tongue and sang old songs that I reckon only she and the Lord himself could understand.

It also stung when they made fun of me because I was so skinny. They called me things like, Ugly Duckling, Bones, and Pippi Longstocking.

Daddy's sister, Aunt Suez, who was always cold and wore long sleeves in the summer, spat in her snuff cup one day when I told her about it and said, "Don't you pay them Eastridges no mind, Chippie. You look just like my momma, and when you grow up, you're gonna to be the prettiest one of them all."

Regardless of what they thought about my name or my looks, everybody in the family said I was smart, and Granny Eastridge was the first to tell Momma that no matter what, I needed to go to college someday. Mostly because I could remember things, all kinds of things, like what color dress Granny Eastridge wore on Christmas when I was four. I could remember how many people were at my birthday party when I turned six, and the names of all the states and capitals and just about any other little detail that everybody else forgot.

Momma said I was smart and that although she hoped all her kids would do something good with their lives, she was counting on me the most. She was proud that I could draw, and whenever my birthday came, if she had a dollar, she would buy me some water paints or markers or crayons.

When I was in fifth grade, she got me a college dictionary for Christmas. She paid a whole ten dollars for it. She said it was because she wanted me to go to college one day and I would need to know all those big words. I cried when I opened it, but I never understood why I did.

When it came to me, even my daddy had a different take on things. He wanted me to have an education, because he said I had a lot of 'book smarts' and could be a teacher or something one day if I set my mind to it. Mostly, he said he hoped I'd be a writer and write down the stories of Great-grandpa Oscar, who escaped from slavers when he was just a boy, went across the Rio Grande, and then got an American soldier to bring him home after the war. I didn't know how much of the story was true but when I was nine-years-old I swore to my daddy that I'd do it, that I'd grow up and write his story.

He never said which war and nobody in the family seemed to know either, but nearly every night, my daddy gathered us around the kitchen table and told us stories about Great--grandpa Oscar Luiz Rivera Pablo.

I doubted that a little boy could cross the river all by himself, but when my daddy told a story, no matter how far-fetched it was, he meant for it to be believed. He also told us that my great-grandpa helped Daniel Boone find his way across Kentucky. I didn't have the heart to tell him that Daniel Boone had been dead for about a hundred years before Great-grandpa Oscar was born. My daddy believed that Great-grandpa Oscar single handedly decapitated six banditos who tried to rob him on his journey to Kentucky and he believed that my great-grandfather rode with a posse to bring down Frank and Jesse James. I reckon my daddy had a knack for telling stories and it didn't take much to fuel his imagination.

One of my teachers at school told me that Great-grandpa Oscar had worked for her grandfather. She had said he told her he was Indian and that he was from Mexico. He hired himself out to work because his family was poor and he didn't want to be a burden on them. Her story wasn't as exciting as my daddy's but it was more believable.

I knew Daddy just took the stories that his father told him and added to them. That was just his way. The light in his eyes kept me listening to these fantasies. Long after all the others had gone to bed, I would sit begging for one more story.

***

Zelphie and Carol Lee had their dolls on the front porch when I came out after supper. I wondered if they understood what we were leaving behind, and I felt sorry they wouldn't get to roam the hills and hollers like Jerry Wayne, Willie, and I had done. Lou Annie never was much for being outside, but she was fond of the farm.

I went around to the side yard. The roots from the maple trees made natural steps and the old rusty well pump sat where it had been for over a hundred-thirty years. I knelt down by the kitchen window near the water pipe that ran from the sink into the yard and let the dirty dishwater out into a trench that Momma and Daddy had dug.

The trench ran across the yard, under the fence,

and into the garden. Our dirty dishwater watered the garden in August when the rain didn't come as often. I sat there, watching the termites crawling over the underpinnings of the kitchen. I tore open a rotten piece of wood and watched them run around to get away from me. I enjoyed watching ants and termites. I was amazed at their tunnels, and always wondered how it felt for something so small to have so many rooms in its home.

Lou Annie came around the corner of the old washhouse. "There you are. What are you doing'?"

I shrugged. "Aw, nothing."

Lou Annie, my sister, was a year and a half younger than me. She looked like Granny Eastridge's little sister that had died long ago, the only blonde to have ever been born on either side of our family until Lou Annie came along, and I looked just like my daddy, only my skin was lighter. My hair was cut as short as a boy's and was the color of a chocolate bar. Hers was nearly white and hung to her waist. My skin was the color of caramel candy, hers ivory. I was thin and wispy as a willow sprout. My arms were lean and muscular, like a boy's arms. She was rounder, smoother, and way more huggable, like Momma. I played outside, climbing trees, riding ponies, and throwing rocks at the cottonmouths in the creek. She played inside with her dolls and watched soap operas. Yet, we had a connection. Sometimes we didn't have to talk to know what the other was feeling.

There had been times when I saw her at school and I knew the kids were picking on her because of her size. I would go to her and tell her she was beautiful, and that she should ignore those stupid kids. Sometimes I stood up for her in front of them, threatening to beat the snot out of them, even the boys, if they didn't leave my little sister alone.

Once when I was ten, I jumped into Aunt Suez's burning car to save Lou Annie's favorite dress. Daddy always told us that kinfolk have to stick together, no matter what comes or goes.

"I don't want to move," I said.

She sat down beside me. "Me neither. I love it here, but it will be nice to go to another school. Maybe I can be popular there."

Lou Annie was the only light skinned person in our family and while it seemed that the whole world loved blonde hair and blue eyes, looking that way only made things worse for her. Folks teased her about not being Daddy's real child and said that maybe the nurses switched babies at the hospital.

I smiled. "Yeah, just maybe I'll be popular, too."

"You're already popular. You're smart and all the teachers like you. I hate it when I get teachers who had you, 'cause they always expect me to make good grades and act like you. When I don't, they get mad at me. So, that's one reason I'm glad about moving, but still, I'll miss this house. It's the best house in the world."

I looked up at the house, at the stones leading into our always-flooded basement. "Yeah, it looks haunted, even though the only ghosts here are the good times we'll be leaving behind. I sure am going to miss it, Annie."

"Sissy, when I grow up, I'm gonna be a famous restaurant owner and have a bunch of restaurants. I'll be real rich, and I'll come back here and buy this house from old man Walkup."

"What about Pate?" I picked up a twig and peeled the bark from it, noting the dark rings left behind on the white wood.

Lou Annie dug her bare toes into the moss. "He's an old man. Fifty at least. He'll be dead n' gone by then."

We laughed.

"Hey, guess what I heard Momma and Daddy talking 'bout?" she said.

"What?" I touched my tongue to the twig. I liked the way maple wood tasted.

Her eyes got big as a cartoon character's. "Carlos and Joy Jane are helping us move."

"Good. I like it when Eloise comes over."

Now Eloise was my best friend from school, who also happened to be a second cousin to me, well sort of. Daddy's cousin, Carlos, had married a woman from Alaska by way of Texas, Joy Jane, who already had four children, three boys and a girl. Eloise was that girl.

Lou Annie frowned. "It's not good. You don't have that weird Daniel after you."

"No, but Robert likes me."

"He's gross," Lou Annie said.

"Ain't that the truth? He's got a beard. Beards are nasty. He's got a hairy chest, too," I said.

"How do you know?"

"One day last summer we was out by the barn feeding Spot, when all at once he said, 'Look here, Chippie'. I looked up and there he stood with his shirt undone. I swear that Robert had hair all the way down his stomach and clean down into his checkered britches. Then that turd-head asked me did I want to see what he had in his britches…"

Lou Annie slapped her bent knees. "He didn't!"

"Yes, he did. I told him that if he didn't button that doggone shirt of his and get back to feeding Spot that I was going to knock that hairy head off his shoulders and go running to the house as fast as I could, shouting out that he was a pervert. I told him that Daddy would beat the snot out of him, too."

"Then what did he do?" Lou Annie said.

"He said, 'Oh Chippie, please don't tell your Daddy. I won't do it no more."

"Robert ain't got no sense," Lou Annie said.

"He's supposed to be a genius," I said. "He took one of them IQ tests at school and scored so high that it didn't fit on the little bell-shaped graph."

"If he's a genius, I'm the president's secret child," Lou Annie teased. "I think his brain is turned to mashed taters. A tater head is all he is, a hairy tater head."

"Whoever heard of a fifteen-year-old being all hairy like that? Jerry Wayne ain't hairy."

Lou Annie laughed. "Jerry Wayne don't eat dog food neither. He's done eat so much dog food that he's turned hairy as a dog."

It was true. Robert did eat dog food. And I don't mean table scraps like we fed our dogs, either. Robert, Daniel, and Marvin, all three of Eloise's brothers ate dog food right out of the bag like other people ate popcorn. Willie and I had seen them do it while we were at their house.

I lay back in the soft moss by the old well. "If I could change things I would, Lou Annie. Sometimes I get real mad on account of no matter how big I get, I'm still too little to do anything about the stuff that really matters, like having to move when you don't want to."

Lou Annie pulled at her blue knit shorts and fidgeted a little. Then she looked up at me, her round white face taking on an exaggerated expression of importance and drama. "You know what Momma always says. What's gonna happen is gonna happen."

Just then I heard Momma yell from the kitchen. It was the sort of yell that made the hair on my arms stand straight up. Lou Annie and I jumped to our feet and went racing to the front porch. We bounded up the rock steps and flung the screen door open. We sped through the entryway and into the living room. That's when we met Momma coming from the kitchen with little Josh David under her arm. He had blood all over his mouth and chin, and it was dripping onto Momma's arm and making puddles on the floor

CHAPTER FOUR

Daddy ran in. "Sissy, watch the little uns. Josh David's done cut his mouth. We got to get him to the emergency room."

"Where's Jerry Wayne?" Momma said. Her voice shook. She was afraid and nervous.

"Right here, Momma," Jerry Wayne said. He bounded down the stairs in the hall.

Momma nodded. "Help your sister, you hear?"

"I will, Momma."

Momma handed Josh David, who started wailing, to Daddy, who ran out the door with him.

"I'll call Granny Eastridge from the hospital and get her to watch y'all kids. Be good until she gets here."

She hurried across the porch and down the steps, then over the yard and down the bank. Our station wagon's motor was making all sorts of mechanical noises and I hoped it'd get them to the hospital okay.

I knew it'd be a while before Granny got there, because she didn't drive and Grandpa would have to bring her. I thought up that we should all play school till Granny got there. Everybody was okay with that except Jerry Wayne who said he'd be upstairs talking on his CB radio if we needed anything. Willie followed Jerry up the stairs.

Jerry Wayne loved that CB. He enjoyed talking to Backer Stick Man. It was funny. Backer Stick Man was about sixty-years-old and Jerry wasn't even sixteen, yet they loved talking to each other on the CB. And Willie loved listening. Willie looked up to Jerry something fierce.

Downstairs in the big blue bedroom that Lou Annie, Zelphie, Carol Lee, and Josh David all shared, we set up school. There were two beds in that room. One sat against the left wall by the window and one sat against the right wall by the other window. An old couch, covered in laundry, sat against the wall near the hallway. The back wall where the wood stove was had the flue..

Lou Annie took Zelphie for her student and I took Carol Lee for mine. Now Carol Lee and Zelphie looked a lot alike except for the hair and eyes. Carol Lee had black eyes and silky hair. She really did look like a little girl from Asia. Zelphie had thick, bushy black hair and the biggest blue eyes imaginable. The combination gave her a bit of a frightened wild child look, but she was usually calm, except for the times when she pretended she was a motorcycle riding dare devil and started trying to jump the furniture.

We had been playing school for about half an hour when Granny Eastridge arrived. Grandpa dropped her off and didn't even come in. He never did. He didn't like Daddy and he didn't like kids, except for Zelphie. He seemed to tolerate her a bit.

Granny Eastridge took to ironing right away. She ironed skirts and shirts, pants and blouses, petticoats and bloomers. I reckon it's safe to say that she ironed until there wasn't a wrinkle in the house. Then she went to the kitchen and commenced cooking some vegetable soup, which she expected us to eat, even though we had already had supper. It smelled like butter beans.

Now, I had eaten turtle, cow tongue, hog brains, squirrels, rabbits, frog legs, all sorts of birds and plants from the woods, but I did not touch butter beans unless my last breath was leaving my body. Butter beans were just so squishy and disgusting. They tasted dry in my mouth, and I hated the way that thin coat sometimes came off and floated around in the bowl. So, when Granny called us to come and eat, we sat around the table staring at our bowls.

Granny stood there with her hands on her hips...well, sort of. Granny didn't really have hips. She was just round all over, except for her bosom, which rested on top of her stomach. Her hair was mousy brown and gray streaked and her lips turned down into a permanent frown. "What's the matter? Why ain't ya'll eating?"

"I ain't hungry, Granny," Zelphie said.

Lou Annie looked down and mumbled, "Me, neither."

"I think you burned it," Jerry Wayne said.

I didn't quite know how to read Granny's expression as my brothers and sisters left the table, but it didn't look pleasant.

Granny stuck out her bottom gum where her teeth were supposed to be. "I didn't burn it."

"Well, it's got butter beans in it. We don't like

butter beans. That's all," I said.

Tears welled up in Granny's eyes. Then she started grabbing all the bowls and dumping them back into the pot. I helped her.

Then she handed me the pot. "Here. Feed this to the dog."

I took the pot and went out back by the old washhouse. I called the dog. Rusty came out from under the smokehouse. I poured the soup on the ground for him. He sniffed it, looked at me with his head to one side, then went back under the smokehouse. That's when I realized that Granny's soup really was awful. Rusty would eat rabbit guts, yet he wouldn't so much as stick his tongue in that soup.

Granny fussed and fussed after I got back into the house. It was like Daddy always said, "When Granny Eastridge's on the warpath, about all a man can do is run and hide." So that's just what I did. I gave up trying to smooth things over with her, and scurried up to my room. That's when I heard our station wagon coming up the road.

I rushed down the stairs. "Momma's home, y'all."

We all met them at the door. Momma was laughing and Josh David, with five stitches in his lip, had a scowl on his face as Daddy closed the door behind him.

"What happened at the hospital?" Granny wanted to know right off.

"Doctor Roy took him on in and started to sew his

mouth up. Josh David hadn't said a word the whole way there. All at once, he spoke up and said, "Git yer cold hands off a-me."

Granny Eastridge frowned. "Jewell, that ain't funny. Every one of these kids needs to learn some manners. I cooked them some soup and they wouldn't eat it. Not a one of them would eat it. You're raising them like wild hoodlums. They act like heathens. These kids need to be in church."

I watched Momma stiffen. "Y'all kids go on upstairs and play until bedtime."

We obeyed, but I lagged behind, lingering near the top of the stairs. I heard Momma and Granny as they went on into the living room. My mother sounded like she had once when the newspaperman had come to take pictures of the community's 'unfortunates' who received government garden seeds and commodities. He told her she had to have her picture in the paper because our family had received garden seeds. Momma stood straight as a sycamore tree and gave him a look that would scare a snake back into its hole. "I don't got to do nothing except live and die."

I heard her with Granny and imagined her looking that same way. "Momma, I ain't got no use for religion or for church. It never done Daddy no good and I don't see what good it's done you neither. He still runs around with whores and lays out all night like he's done for thirty years."

"Jewell, honey, what're people going to think about the way you're raising these youngins? They live like the Pablo's girl. And you, you're living below your raising."

"I love you, Momma, but you know good and well that them church folks never lifted a finger to help me and Joe when we didn't have food nor money. We don't take no handouts and we would have been good for every cent we borrowed, and both of us would have worked it off in backer if we had to.

"No, Momma, far as I'm concerned, them church folks can sit right there on them pews and rot. I don't want them dragging me up to their altars if they ain't a-going to help me and Joe when the kids ain't got no food and we don't even know where Christmas is coming from...Chippie," my momma yelled. "You eavesdropping? Get your hind end upstairs before I come swat it."

I took off up the stairs and didn't get to hear the rest of the conversation.

CHAPTER FIVE

Joy Jane held my palm in her fat brown hands. She traced my lifeline with her dirt-caked nail. "Hmmm..." Joy Jane was an Eskimo. She corrected us whenever we called her an Eskimo, saying she was an Inuit, but nobody knew what an Inuit was, so we kept on calling her Eskimo. She had moved from Alaska to Texas to Kentucky, then married Carlos. She moved her four children with her. Eloise, her only daughter, was my best friend and Robert, her oldest boy, was the hairy maniac who had a crush on me. The other two boys, Daniel and Sam, were quiet and always dirty. They often wore the same clothes to school three or four days in a row. Nobody would sit by them on the school bus because they smelled. In fact, you could smell them if you sat two seats in front of them, behind them, or across the isle from them. They smelled like barn and cow, like sour milk and dirty clothes, all at once.

Joy Jane was a self-proclaimed psychic. She weighed well over four hundred pounds and was less than five feet tall. Her skin was rough and brown and her feet were the size of my hands. She walked like a penguin and when she fell down, it took all four of her kids pushing, pulling, grunting, and tugging just to get her on her feet again. Momma said that if they kept it up, they'd all have hernias by the time they were twenty.

And her house stunk to the high heavens on account of she kept animals in it- dogs, cats, birds, mice, and occasionally a small horse named Sugar. But for all her strangeness, I liked her. I thought she was funny when she got to telling us how she could read palms and see things before they happened.

Momma said that was all a bunch of foolishness. Momma believed in practical things and, according to her, all that was a bunch of mumbo jumbo, just like ghosts or, as my daddy called them, haints. Momma thought that if you couldn't see a thing, touch it, smell it, and explain it, it wasn't real. She made fun of Joy Jane whenever she heard her talking about being psychic; especially the time Joy Jane told us she'd seen a UFO back when she was living in Alaska. Momma said that she believed Joy Jane was capable of seeing anything because she was a pothead hippie who only thought she was an Indian and she sure wasn't psychic because there was no such thing. When Momma told Granny Eastridge about it, Granny said that all that junk was of the devil. Still, Momma had to be nice to her on account of Daddy who really liked his cousin, no matter how dirty his house was.

"Well, what'd you see?" I asked, half excited, half-afraid.

Eloise and Lou Annie leaned over her shoulder, watching the session, anxious to get their own palms read.

"Well," I said. "Am I ever going to get me a boyfriend?"

Joy Jane nodded, her thick black-framed glasses sliding down her brown nose. "Yes."

"Who is he? Is he blonde? Am I going to marry Kenny from school one of these days?"

"Could be, but probably not. He's got dark hair. You're standing in a field with him."

"Who is he? How will I know him?"

Joy Jane dropped my hand. She just looked at me. "You will know when the time comes."

"Huh?"

She rubbed my hand and spoke slowly, like those gypsy ladies in the movies. "You're a seer, Chippie, like me. Give it time. One day you're going to look into a mirror and see the reflection of things to come. Don't question this gift. It's from God."

I jerked my hand back. If I started seeing the future, Momma'd say I was crazy too. She might even think I was smoking pot. I decided right then and there that even if I did see stuff that was going to happen, I wouldn't tell a living soul. Besides, what could a woman as weird as Joy Jane possibly know about God?

About that time, Zelphie came out the front door. She was wearing neon green knit shorts and a Polka-dot halter-top. Her braids stuck out on both sides like they had wire running through them and she had a half-bald, naked doll, its nails colored blue with a marker, pressed against her chest.

She bounded down the front steps. "Mommy says it's time to go."

Carol Lee and Josh David came out right behind her, and then came Momma, Daddy and Carlos. The grown-ups carried the last of our moving boxes to Carlos' rusty brown pick-up truck, which already contained all our furniture.

Everybody was outside now. The house was empty, almost. Jerry Wayne was nowhere to be seen.

I followed Momma out to the truck. "Where's Jerry Wayne?"

Momma handed Papa the box she carried, then looked up toward Jerry Wayne's bedroom window. I followed her gaze. There he stood, wearing a gray shirt and staring down with the most foreboding look I'd ever seen. He looked blurry behind the screen, almost like a reflection in water.

He was so quiet, so far away, above us all, looking down. I felt chilled clean to the bone, the kind of thing that makes a body want to cry without good reason. Then Jerry Wayne was gone and that screen flickered with spots of sunlight and shadows cast by the maple trees.

Something cold touched the back of my neck and I just about jumped out of my skin.

"Hahahaha..." Robert laughed. "I scared the daylights out of you, Chippie." He had a cold can of soda in his hand. He pushed his thick glasses up on his fat nose.

I hated the way he said my name all sweet-like and drawn out. "Daggum you, Robert. If you ever hold a cold drink up to my neck again, I'm going to smack the living snot out of you." I couldn't stand him being my first cousin once removed, even if it was just by marriage. I didn't want to be kin to him in any way whatsoever. I'd rather been kin to a hole full of rattlesnakes.

"Sis. Watch your tongue," Daddy hollered. "That's plum near cussing." He walked out in the driveway and shouted toward the house. "Come on, Jerry Wayne. Get down here. Let's go."

When I first laid my eyes on our new house, I felt like bawling. It looked like a black cracker box, and didn't seem much bigger than one. It did have a porch, sort of. Compared to our old house it was just a plank walkway, with part of the planks missing. Four two-by-fours held up the little metal roof over it. I could tell right off that roof leaked. It had about fifty holes in it. There were two doors. One had a knob, the other didn't.

Lou Annie had her cat, Bug-eyes, hugged up to her when she came and stood beside me. "It's so little."

Jerry Wayne brushed past us and stepped onto the porch. "It's ugly. Covered in tarpaper. Looks like a dad-blamed chicken house."

He shoved the door open. As soon as he did, the little ones went running into the house. I heard Jerry Wayne in there telling them that since he had to live in a box, he at least got first pick of the rooms.

Momma just stood there for a few minutes, staring at that place with her mouth open. Her arms looked all limp; like she might drop the box she was holding. Daddy came over and laid a hand on her shoulder. "Well, honey, what do you think? We've got a place of our own now."

Momma looked around. The ground was a flat acre surrounded on all sides by high hills. There were big holes in the yard with stacks of mud around them. And water stood deep enough that it wet our shoes just walking to the porch.

"It's swampland," Momma said. "But I reckon it's our swampland."

"What're all these holes?" I asked.

"That's where the crawdads come out," Daddy said. "This ain't exactly Briar Ridge." He pointed to the nearest hill, a long, far-stretching hill that leveled off on the top. "That's Briar Ridge. This here little area is called Swamp Holler, on account of how people used to have to walk up this swamp before they could get up on Briar Ridge. It really is just the bottom land along the foot of Briar Ridge. Sissy, I was born and raised in this here swamp, just down the road a piece."

I looked around. The yard was filled with pools of water, insects swarming around them, and wherever there wasn't a pool of mud, there were weeds and cattails. Even if you walked in the weeds, you got muddy. I couldn't imagine what mowing that yard was going to be like. And the smell, good Lord, what a smell. It was nauseating.

"Daddy, what is that awful smell?" I asked.

"Oil," he said. "Look out yonder across the fields and you'll see the oil rigs at the foot of Briar Ridge."

"So is there oil on our property?" I asked.

"Heavens no," Momma said. "Why we'd be rich if there was oil on this acre of ground."

"There is oil here," Daddy said, "but it's full of water, seeing how this ground is so swampy."

"I bet the water's full of oil, too," Momma said.

We turned all our cats loose out of the boxes we'd brought them in, and then commenced to unpack our truck. We worked until after dark and we were all about starved to death. All day long, that crazy old Robert kept eyeballing me and winking. I was thankful for Carlos and Joy Jane's help. I loved Eloise to death and didn't mind the two younger boys, although their body odor made me gag several times that day, but I'd just as soon they left that ignorant Robert at home. So, I was thankful when they left for the night.

The house had six rooms. There were three in the front and three in the back. The three in the front were all the same size. In the back, the middle room was large and the two end rooms were tiny. All the rooms were connected so that a person could circle through the whole house and end up right where you started. Two front doors led into what appeared to be two front rooms. The room on the left end would be Momma and Daddy's bedroom. The one in the middle was the living room and the one on the right end was the kitchen.

A door full of holes led out of the kitchen onto a boxed-in porch, a tiny room. This was to be a room for Lou Annie and me. Momma said two near-grown girls ought not to have to share rooms with a lot of little kids. And I thought she was right. A second door led out of that room into the biggest room in the house. It was long and dark with only one tiny window. That room would be used for the four little ones, Willie, Zelphie, Carol Lee, and Josh David.

Jerry Wayne, because he was the oldest, got a room all to himself. He stood there looking at the tiny room and said, "Well, at least there's one good thing about this rat-infested dump. I get my own closet to live in."

It was even smaller than Lou Annie's and mine. It was just a boxed off corner at the end of the little kids' room. But at least it was private. Before the day was over, he had his big iron bed set up in there, his dresser with three drawers and a little table with his CB radio on it. Of course he had to turn side-ways to walk between the dresser and the bed every time he went into his room.

There were no closets in the house and we all had to put nails in the corners of our rooms so we would have a place to hang our clothes. That is except Jerry Wayne and Momma. They got the two dressers we owned.

I had an old trunk I kept my treasures in. A long, red dress that reminded me of gypsies; a pair of blue and white striped socks with toes in them; a pair of pants with paint splotches all over them that had too many pretty colors on them to just throw them away because of a few thin spots and holes. And of course, my water paints that Momma bought me for my birthday. She only had a dollar to spare, and she got me the one thing she thought I would treasure most, paint. She was so right in her guessing about me.

Beside our bed Lou Annie and I had a little table. I kept every gift I'd ever received on that table. A dictionary, a musical jewelry box with a dancing girl in it that Momma and Daddy got me for Christmas, a little oil lamp, and a tea set that I had gotten for my sixth birthday. Over by the door we had an old kitchen cabinet that we used to put our underwear in. On top of that cabinet was my bank, a simple glass jar with pennies in the bottom. I was always trying to save money.

We had been working about an hour when Momma sent me out back with a water bucket to the well, which had a little shed built over it. I lowered the sand bucket into the dark hole and waited to hear the bubble. Then I drew it back up.

I had learned to draw water when I was very little and knew just how to pull the rope over the pulley without blistering my hands. I knew that to get the sand bucket out a person had to keep a firm grip and not let it slip. It was letting the rope slip that could burn a person's hands and make blisters. So I always took it slow, hand over hand, until the sand bucket peeped over the top of the opening. Then I grabbed it with one hand and pulled it free of the well. A full sand bucket was heavy and it took some practice to get the water into the drinking pail without spilling it. I always spilled a little. That didn't hurt anything. I really liked drawing water. It made me feel strong.

As I brought the sand bucket up from the well, I smelled the oil so strongly that I thought I would faint. I carried the bucket to Momma and set it down.

"It stinks, Momma."

Momma poured a dipper full out and watched it puddle on the porch. "Looks like there's not only water in the oil here; there's oil in the water, too. We can't drink this water." She yelled for Daddy. He came running from the back bedroom, where he was helping Jerry Wayne set up his bed.

"We got a problem."

Daddy nodded. "Don't worry. We'll just get our drinking water over at the mill. We can still use this to take a bath in and wash our clothes in."

Momma looked like she could cry. "We'll just smell like crude oil everywhere we go," she said.

* * *

It was about ten o'clock that first night before we got all our beds set up and ready to sleep in. It was plenty hot, too. Momma came in to say good night to Lou Annie and me as we were getting our gowns on.

"Can you leave the light on?" Lou Annie asked. She was always afraid of the dark.

"No," I said. "It'll make bugs come in."

"We'll leave the kitchen light on for you," Momma said. The kitchen was right beside our room and plenty of light poured through the holes and cracks in our door.

"Momma, do you reckon Little Tom will be safe outside tonight? This is a new place. What if he gets scared and runs off?"

"That devil cat is too mean to get scared and run off," Lou Annie said.

Momma kissed me on the forehead. "Little Tom'll be just fine. He always is. Lou Annie's right. He's too mean for anything to hurt him. Now you two get some sleep 'cause tomorrow's a big day."

After Momma left the room, I turned out the light and lay still with my sheet pulled up to my chin, even though it was far too warm for cover. The light from the kitchen made the objects in our room look dark and featureless.

Lou Annie sat up in bed.

"What is it?" I asked.

She looked at the outside door. "What if somebody tries to break in on us?"

"Don't worry," I said. "I've got a butcher knife under the bed."

"For real?"

I flipped on the light, climbed out of bed, and retrieved the knife. Its chrome blade reflected the light as if it were still brand new, but it wasn't. It was old and chipped, a knife Momma had thrown away because it was useless in the kitchen. Still, it was sharp enough to cut a person. Momma didn't know I had that knife.

"Don't you worry. If anybody tries to hurt you, I'll cut them up."

"You would do that for me?" Lou Annie asked.

I nodded. "I ain't scared of nothing, and ain't nobody gonna hurt my little sister."

Lou Annie smiled.

"Now get to sleep," I told her. I put the knife back under the bed, turned out the light, and lay down.

It wasn't long 'til I heard Lou Annie breathing like kids do when they're sound asleep, sort of loud and even, but I couldn't sleep. The bullfrogs in the backyard were too loud. Maybe there was a pond behind the house somewhere. I would have to go exploring first chance I got.

Then I realized that it was more than bullfrogs keeping me awake; it was my own mind. I was anxious about going to a new school. What if they all hated me? What if I couldn't make friends and had to always sit alone?

Then there was Jerry Wayne. Every time I closed my eyes, I could see him standing behind that screen with shadows from breeze-stirred trees moving across it like ripples move across water. Why did that image haunt me so? Was it because Jerry Wayne was so hurt by this move? I sniffled, realizing that tears were silently creeping down my face. I forced myself to think about other things, to go back to wondering if there was a pond.

Then my mind drifted and I found myself thinking about Robert, that hairy boy who'd helped us move. I could still see the image of him staring at me, like I didn't have enough sense to see him, and I wondered if Robert had ever kissed a girl before. "Yuck," I said to myself. If I was wondering about Robert kissing girls, then I had definitely stayed awake too late. I needed to sleep, but it was a long time before I could tune out the frogs.

CHAPTER SIX

True to her word, Momma signed Jerry Wayne up at the county high school. He was a freshman. She signed us five middle kids up at Briar Ridge Grade Center, and lucky Josh David, being only three–years-old, didn't have to go to school. He spent his days following Momma around the house while she did her best to make it livable.

Daddy decided he'd have to go in late to the mill on our first day of school, because we didn't know which bus we would be riding. Momma didn't have a license and couldn't drive. We first went into the office where Mrs. Jessica Rainey met us. She was a skinny woman with big glasses, short curly brown hair and little flat teeth, but when she smiled, I felt good right away. I knew that if I were to get into any trouble, she'd be the one to come to.

Now Daddy couldn't write so I had to fill out the papers and let him mark them with his X. I felt so proud to be Daddy's reader like that. Mrs. Rainey bragged on my communication skills and said she could tell straight off that I was a bright child. Daddy nodded his thanks to her, and then took his leave. He needed to get back over to the mill, because he couldn't afford to lose any more pay.

We children walked down the green concrete halls with Mrs. Rainey as she took Carol Lee to first grade and introduced her to her class, then Zelphie to second, Willie to third, Lou Annie to sixth and me to eighth.

I felt sort of small as I stood there looking out

over my new class, and I mean that literally. I was used to being the smallest person in class, but that description didn't quite cut it now. There was only one girl in that class who wasn't a whole head taller than me. However, she was three times as round. And the boys, Lord have mercy, they looked like men. They were all bigger than Jerry Wayne.

The teacher got up and met me as I walked with uncertainty across the front of that room. Mrs. Rainey was right behind me, and if it hadn't been for that fact, I might have run out of that room full of giant kids.

She put one thin hand on my shoulder. "Mr. Sizemore, this is Nochipa Pablo." I heard several snickers from the students. Mrs. Rainey continued. "She has just moved here from up around Fry Creek."

Mr. Sizemore, like these students, was big. He was surely six-feet-four if not taller and brawny as well. His face was tanned and he had a sun-bleached mustache. "Well, Nachepa, it's certainly nice to have you. You may sit in the back with Lisha Faye." He pointed to a chubby girl in the back who had short black hair and wire frame glasses.

"It's Nochipa," I said. "But everybody calls me Chippie."

He smiled. "All right. Chippie it is then."

Mrs. Rainey laid my file on Mr. Sizemore's desk and left the room. I took a deep breath, clutched my notebook to my chest and walked toward Lisha Faye.

Just as I started to sit down, she slammed her

hand down in the seat. "My mother doesn't want me sitting next to anyone who might have lice. And nobody messes with my mother. She's the fifth grade teacher."

"She's a ugly old hag," the boy behind her said.

"Lisha Faye, get your hand out of that chair and let her sit down," Mr. Sizemore said, but he sounded more sleepy than angry. "Jesse, if I hear any more of that kind of talk, you're going to the office. You hear?"

Jesse snickered and slumped down in his seat. "I hear you."

I placed my notebook on my desk and hung my purse on my chair.

Mr. Sizemore said, "Now I want you all to write your spelling words ten times each. I've got to make some phone calls." Then he walked out of the room.

I found a worn spelling book in my desk, noticed that Lisha Faye turned to list 10. I did the same. Then I got to work, but no sooner had I placed my name on the paper than I felt a pinch on my behind. I jumped and turned around. The whole class giggled.

"She ain't got no butt," Jesse said in his high-pitched voice. "She's bones clear through and through." He ran his hand through his greasy blonde hair and grinned.

"She ain't got no jugs neither," a black-haired, olive-skinned boy in a red T-shirt scrawled with 'Jeremy' in white letters said. "Now, Corkie here, she's a woman. Show 'em babe."

The girl beside him stood. She was tall and slender with long brown hair, and she was developed, very developed. I could tell right away that she wasn't wearing a bra under her T-shirt. She looked at me and grinned, then stretched that shirt as tight as it would go across her chest. The boys whooped and hollered.

I did what any self-respecting decent person would do. I turned my head.

"Well, what's a matter, Chippie, you ain't used to seeing a real woman?" that dark-haired boy said again.

The class roared with laughter. I wanted to run out, to run the five miles all the way back home, to lay my head on Momma's shoulder and cry my eyes out.

"He's coming!" somebody shouted, and then I realized that a chubby blonde boy had been watching at the door.

In a flash, everyone in the room looked as if they had been writing spelling words the entire time. Mr. Sizemore never even looked at us as he entered the room. He took a seat behind his desk and started reading a paper.

We wrote spelling words for a while, then Mr. Sizemore starting calling on people to stand up and spell words without looking at them. No one could spell except Lisha Faye and a quiet girl in the back corner who had the longest, most golden hair I'd ever seen. When he called on her, I learned that her name was Brianne. In some ways she was just as pretty as Corkie, the girl who'd showed her boobs, and she was obviously way smarter.

Then he called on me. I couldn't believe he'd call on me since it was my first day. But I closed my book and waited for my word. It was *dilapidated*. I spelled it by picturing it in my mind. Instead of going to the next person, he gave me another word, *miscellaneous*. Again, I spelled it.

Everyone was staring at me. Mr. Sizemore sat back in his chair and grunted.   "How are you at math?"

"I don't like math," I said.

"But you made good grades in it at your other school?"

I nodded. "Pretty good." I didn't want to tell him that before fifth grade I couldn't even tell time, but after I went to a smaller math class, I learned fast. Until fifth grade I made C's, afterwards I made A's. I figured that maybe the math door in my head didn't open until the right teacher turned the knob. Mr. Collins had been a patient man, the right teacher.

"Tomorrow during Spelling, I want you to scoot your seat back beside Jesse and drill him on his spelling words. I also want you to coach him in Math."

I didn't want to coach that homely boy in anything. I didn't even want to be in the same room with him. But Mr. Sizemore wasn't done humiliating me and making a terrible first day even worse.

Jesse snickered. "It's 'cause I'm stupid. Heck, I don't care."

"Watch your mouth or you'll be in the office," Mr. Sizemore snapped.

Jesse chuckled. "All right. But it ain't like I never been there before."

The teacher stared at me in a funny way for a moment. "I couldn't help notice that you're sort of small, Chippie. Ever run track or cross country."

I hung my head. Oh, how I had wanted to, but my parents couldn't afford the uniform, nor could they provide me with transportation to the county meets. I was the fastest girl in my seventh grade class. Heck, I could even out run all but two boys. I didn't reply. What could I say? That I was fast but so dang poor I'd have to race in cut-offs and the town school didn't allow that.

"We're having cross country try-outs at P.E. tomorrow afternoon. Do you own a pair of shorts?"

I nodded.

"Bring them. You're trying out for the team."

I was scared. If I didn't do well, the kids in this class would have even more reason not to like me.

"Now sit down everybody and take out your Social Studies books. I want you to read Chapter Seven: Life on the Amazon, and do the questions at the end."

The kids were all whispering and mumbling. I knew that it was about me and Spelling, and Math and the cross-country try-outs.

Although there was a Math, Spelling and Health

book in my desk, there wasn't Social Studies.

"Here, share with me," Lisha Faye said, shoving her book over.

I couldn't believe it. I thought she hated me from the get go. So why was she suddenly being nice?

She must have sensed my questioning. "There aren't many of us smart kids in here," she said. "There's me, Brianne, Karen, and now...you, it looks like. We have to stick together. I was nasty to you earlier, because I didn't know you were one of us."

I smiled. "Thank you."

"I am not a nice person," she said. "But I am not like these other ignoramuses."

"Why do you sound different than everyone else? Than me?" I asked.

"I told you. My mom's the fifth grade teacher. She'd spank me if I didn't use proper English."

I couldn't believe such a thing. Shoot, my parents didn't even know proper English. Whoever heard of whipping a kid because she didn't use proper English?

Oh well, weird or not weird, it didn't matter. Lisha Faye was extending me the hand of friendship. If she had been Dracula's own daughter, I would have taken it.

At lunch, I sat beside Lisha Faye and Jesse sat across the table, three places down from me. All the while I ate, he stared at me and that braless wonder,

Corkie, kept whispering in another girl's ear. I knew she was talking about me. Every so often, they would look at me and giggle.

"Don't mind them," Lisha Faye said. "Their brains are where their bras should be, and their IQ is surpassed by their shoe sizes."

I smiled. But my smile only lasted a second. Something wet and warm hit me on the cheek. I immediately put my hand up and raked a squashed pea off.

Corkie's boyfriend, Jeremy, laughed.

"Green freckles," said the fat blonde boy, Mo-mo.

When I went to dump my tray. I felt a sharp pinch on my rear and jumped so hard that I spilled my uneaten peas and toppled my milk carton onto the floor. Someone behind me snickered then passed. I looked up just in time to see that it was Jesse.

I stomped over to where he was setting his tray in the dirty dish window. I plopped my tray down right beside his. "Keep your hands off my butt."

He laughed. "You'd have to have a butt before I could my hands on it and..." He walked away snickering.

I felt like running after him and shoving him, but I didn't. I don't know why. Maybe it was because he was much bigger than I was or maybe it was something else.

Our class stopped at the bathroom on the way back to class. The boys' bathroom was on one side of the water fountain, across from the cafeteria/gymnasium and the girls' was on the other. I was coming out a stall in the girls' bathroom when Corkie shoved me against the wall. "Don't you even speak to my boyfriend, Jeremy," she said, "or I swear I'll rip the hairs right out of your little nerdy head." Then she backed away, looking at me with daring eyes.

When she had gone, I realized I was trembling. I went to the sink to wash my hands, biting back the tears. It was my first day at school and I had managed to make an enemy out of the most popular girl in class and had become the laughing stock of eighth grade.

Lisha Faye stuck her head through the door. "What are you doing in here so long, little brown town girl? Come on. It's time for Science class."

CHAPTER SEVEN

The bus driver wouldn't pull all the way up to our house because there wasn't enough room to turn around without getting hung up in the mud, so he let us off about a hundred yards down the road where our only neighbor had an oil rig garage. Oil tanks and pump machines dotted the hillsides around our new home. We could smell oil every time we walked out the door. I hoped that we would one day get used to it and not smell it anymore.

When I got off the bus with Willie and my little sisters, I could hear snickers from the kids in the back. I knew what they were laughing at, too. *Our house*. It looked like a chicken coup. As the bus pulled away, I felt the first bit of relief I'd had since getting out of bed that morning. I hated the ugly house, but it was a haven for the moment. Besides, Momma was in there, and no matter what had happened that day, her calm nature and sunshine smile would make even the most horrid day better.

"I've made me a friend," Lou Annie said. "And for once I'm not the fattest girl in my class!" Her eyes were lit up like naked blue Christmas tree bulbs.

"Well, I hate that school," Willie said. "My teacher is mean and ugly. She makes us do Math and Spelling words all day long and puts lipstick on while we're working. I think she looks like an old crow. She's got this real long skinny nose and big-eye glasses."

"I love my teacher," Zelphie said. "She's pretty."

"Five little monkeys jumping on a bed," Carol Lee sang in my ear. I swatted her away.

"I learned it today," she said. "One fell off and broke his head."

Zelphie shoved her. "I was telling Chippie something."

"Y'all just quit fighting and take turns talking," I said. "Willie was telling about his teacher before either one of you started in. Willie, go first, then Zelphie, then Carol Lee, I'll listen to your whole song."

And that was the order we proceeded in. Willie told a little more about his skinny, stuck up teacher, Zelphie told about how her teacher was sweet and pretty and Carol Lee finished singing her monkey song 'til all five monkeys fell off the bed and called the doctor who told them, "No more jumping on that bed."

Momma was on the couch watching a soap opera when we went in the house. It was swept clean and smelled like peach cobbler. "I made you kids a treat."

"Peach cobbler!" We all shouted in unison and ran for the fridge. Momma always tried to make us an after-school treat when we had the food to spare.

"I canned peaches today. The cobbler is from the leftovers. Your daddy brought cold drinks home from the mill at dinnertime. Ya'll can each have half of one and save the rest for supper."

"Oh, thank you, Momma," I blurted out. I

wondered if those kids at school had a momma like mine who made the house cozy and clean, who cooked them peach cobblers while they were at school.

"Tell me about your first day," she said.

I let the little ones have their turns first. Willie had a note from the teacher. He'd been in trouble already for calling her an old hag. Zelphie had made Momma a card. Carol Lee had a whole satchel full of colored letter papers and had to sing her song one more time. Lou Annie kept going on and on about her new friend, Debra Jean, who was fatter than her and had acne.

"She's perfect, Momma. And she just lives over there by the country store. Can I stay all night with her sometime? Can I?"

Momma smiled. "We'll see."

"Where's Josh David?" I asked.

Momma nodded toward the bedroom. "In the backyard, building a road out of soup cans. Zelphie, you and Carol Lee change clothes and go play with him. He's been awful lonesome with everybody gone to school."

"Jerry Wayne ain't home yet?" Willie said.

"He'll be on in a minute. Now, y'all run on and play for a while. Change into your old clothes first."

"Chippie, your daddy's got a feeder pig down in the woods. The boss man gave it to him. Feeding him is going to be your job. Daddy says you get twenty-five cents a week for feeding the pig. Finish your peach cobbler, then change into some old clothes and run that bucket of scraps on the table down to the pig pen."

I headed toward the kitchen.

"Chippie," Momma said. "You didn't say anything about your day."

I set my plate in the dishpan and turned. "Momma, them kids in my room are heathens. The girls don't wear any bras, and the boys say nasty words. The girls smoke in the bathroom and write cuss words on the stalls. My teacher is making me tutor a dumb boy, and tomorrow I got to wear shorts in front of everybody and try out for cross-country. I don't fit in there, Momma. I got no friends and I don't like it."

Momma smiled. "There's an old saying. He that wants to have friends must show himself friendly. If you want to have a friend, Chippie, you've got to be one first. Reach out. It doesn't sound so bad."

"Momma, didn't you hear me? Them girls don't wear no bras. And they wear T-shirts. You can see ever thing they got right through their shirts."

"I heard you, Chippie, and you're right. You're not like them. You've got to show them girls that it pays to be smart. Let them see your talent and your good heart. When they see who you are, they'll all love you."

It didn't matter what Momma said. Her smile always made me feel like I was curled up on a blanket in the floor behind the wood stove on a cold winter night.

"You can't let them run over you, honey. Today

might have been tough, but the sun's always going to shine tomorrow. Better get the pig fed. Your Daddy will be home soon wanting to know what you think of it."

I stepped back into the kitchen and picked up the bucket of scraps. I started for the front door then turned with my left hand on the knob. "Momma, I love you." I felt all teary-eyed, but held it back.

She smiled. "I love you, too. Your pig's hungry."

Our swampy backyard ended in woods, acres of woods. A narrow dirt path led about two hundred yards from the house, winding in and out around trees and bushes. The pigpen sat at the end of this path beneath three large oak trees just past a rusty old truck that somebody must have parked there forty years ago. It had a rounded front end, was missing a glass in the passenger side, and had a broken headlight. I wondered why they parked it there. What had gone wrong with it? And were there any snakes living in it? That old truck made me feel like I was walking through a ghost town. Surely, it had once been a part of somebody's life, but the identity of that somebody was a mystery to me.

Rooting around the base of the pen was a white pig, about twenty-five pounds with big, pink-veined ears.

I leaned on the wooden slant fence. "Hello, little piggy."

He lifted his pink nose up and grunted at me. I wanted to call him Wilbur, but that was too common. I had already had an Arnold, which Daddy had slaughtered. I refused to name another pig Arnold after that. "What am I going to call you, little booger?"

I dumped his food into the trough and watched him eat. There beneath those oak trees, in the quietness of the woods, except for the pig's noisy eating, I forgot all about school. I closed my eyes and smelled the scent of the mossy ground, of the mud in the pen. Warm September wind touched my cheeks and I thought of a poem in my mind.

I turned and ran toward the house to write it down, but when I reached the backyard, Rusty came out barking at me. I started scuffling with him and forgot my words. I, then, walked past the dirt patch where my little brothers and sisters were playing and headed to the fence in our front yard where we kept the ponies, Thunder and Lightning. I took the lid off the corn barrel and tossed them in a couple of ears.

Rusty took off across the field toward the mill and beyond that, the highway.

"Rusty, you get back here," I called. That's when I saw Jerry Wayne coming across the field. I took off behind Rusty and we both ran out to meet him.

That night, Jerry Wayne played Daddy's guitar in his room and I sang for him. We wrote a song together how a person ought not to go around looking down all the time and that good times always come, if a person just waits for them and never gives up. Then we practiced singing it for Momma and Daddy.

Afterwards Jerry Wayne sat there holding his guitar on his lap, resting his arms on top of it. "High school's going to be real hard, Chippie."

"That doesn't matter. You just got four more

years left. Hang in there."

"Wanna see my books?"

I shrugged. "Sure."

"They're in my chester drawers, top one."

I started to tell Jerry Wayne that there really was no such thing as a chester drawers, that it was really called a chest-of-drawers, but I stopped myself. I knew that it hurt Jerry Wayne when folks corrected his talking. It hurt him in the same way that not having book smarts hurt him, not that he would ever cry or let on, but I could tell that it tore at something way down inside of him. So I let it go and thought that maybe when you start correcting a person's way of talking, it's kind of like painting over his photograph and you sort of lose sight of who that person really is. As far as I was concerned, Jerry Wayne could talk anyway he wanted to. But me, I would one day learn to talk both ways. I figured I could talk all proper like Lisha Faye when I was around folks who didn't understand our ways and then I could talk home-style when I was with my family.

One of Jerry Wayne's books was a literature book with a whole section of Edgar Alan Poe. I almost shouted out with excitement when I saw "Annibelle Lee". And his Science book was all about stars and planets. I wanted to start reading those books right then and there, but I didn't because Jerry Wayne looked so sad.

"See how them books are full of big words, Chippie? I ain't never gonna understand all of that stuff." He pushed the hair out of his eyes. "I don't got book smarts. I got car-fixing smarts. I want to be a mechanic.

You don't need no school for that."

I felt like hugging Jerry Wayne, but I didn't want him to think I was a sissy or a mushy girl. I thought it best to put his mind on something else for a while. So I put those books back in his drawer. "I got to try out for the cross country team tomorrow." I shrugged. "Course I ain't got no good shorts to wear. Everybody's gonna laugh at me."

Jerry Wayne put his guitar down and pulled his bottom drawer open. "Well, I done outgrew these. I reckon you can have them." He took out his red gym trunks, real track shorts, with a white J.W. on the left leg. Momma had saved up and bought them for him when he went to seventh grade and the gym teacher said they had to wear school colors to class three days a week.

I held the shorts in my hand, rubbing my fingers over the initials.

"You can rip them off if you want to."

"No, I'll leave them be. I ain't one bit ashamed to have my brother's initials on my shorts. Maybe it'll be like my lucky charm and make me run faster."

Jerry Wayne grinned. "Course it will. It'll be my magic powers, putting a spell on you. You'll run faster'n a super hero with them on. All the kids in your class will be jealous of you."

I didn't want to tell him that it would take more than fast running to make anybody there jealous of me.

I folded the shorts neatly and placed them on top

of the chest-of-drawers. "Want to sneak Rusty in the house and play with him?"

Jerry Wayne smiled. "All right. I'll open the window. You go out and call him up."

We slipped our fat little dog in through Jerry's bedroom window and played with him until Momma called me to come get the wash pan and go wash up in my room for school the next day.

My stomach had a knot in it. School. I went to the kitchen; poured hot water in the wash pan from the kettle Momma had on the stove, added some cold from the water bucket, squirted some dish soap in it and went into my room, which joined the kitchen. I pulled my door shut with the shoestring I tied in the door hole for a latch and looped it over a nail. I then stuffed all the holes with rags and began my bath. I knew better than to dawdle, because Lou Annie still had to take her bath, but I kept thinking about school and my limbs were heavy.

CHAPTER EIGHT

It was awfully hot when we went out for P.E. class. Mr. Sizemore sent the boys into the baseball field to practice. The girls that didn't play sports sat on the bleachers, talking and yelling at the boys. Then he made those on the cross-country team line up at the end of a dirt path that went winding through some woods behind the schoolhouse.

Now, it's not that the Briar Ridge School was big enough to have a lot of sports; it's just that the school board said they had to offer some girl sports. So, Mr. Sizemore set up a cross-country team and a basketball team. There was only one eighth-grade class, and most of the girls were not fit, so he had to recruit some sixth and seventh graders, too.

"This trail runs one mile," he said. "That's a half mile shorter than the one at the county meet. You girls have to pick up some speed or we won't place at all next week. Melanie, don't sit down half way through this time." Melanie was long-legged, skinny and had more freckles than a bird dog. Her mouth stuck out and she wore her black hair in a silly-looking ponytail on top of her head.

He looked at the chubby girl next to me. "Lucy, you can't walk the whole way. That won't work."

She stuck her tongue out. "I quit then. I ain't getting all sweaty and stinky." She walked over to the bleachers.

I was surprised that Mr. Sizemore didn't say anything to her.

Brianne whispered to me. "She gets to do whatever she wants. Her daddy's on the board. If Mr. Sizemore makes her mad, her daddy will get him fired."

I watched Lucy huff and puff her way over the bleachers. Her mouth was puckered and it was plain that grown-ups never told her no. I thought to myself that if she belonged to Momma, she'd change her attitude real fast.

"Get on your mark," Mr. Sizemore said. We all put one foot on the line. He held up his stopwatch. "Go!"

We took off. I started out slow. Everybody was ahead of me, but I knew to give them a few seconds, let them wear down a little, then I picked up my pace, and I kept picking it up steadily as I went. I passed Corkie; a redheaded girl named Emily; a big girl with a sour expression; and several of the sixth and seventh graders. Then I realized that only Brianne and Melanie were ahead of me. I overtook Brianne, feeling a little sad to pass her because she had been a little nice to me. I was on Melanie's heels when she grabbed her side and collapsed on the ground. The finish line was right before me. I started to stop and help her when I heard Mr. Sizemore yelling for me to keep running, so I did.

When I crossed the line, he pushed the stopwatch and grinned. "Yes, Chippie, yes. You ran that in just under six minutes. Fourteen-year-old girl and six minutes. Yes."

I didn't know what his excitement was. My side was killing me and I was sweating like a hog at killing time.

I felt a heavy hand hit me on the back. "Good running." Brianne walked past me, red-faced and gasping.

"Thanks," I said.

None of the other girls said anything. They just sprawled out on the grass and looked unhappy like they did all the time except when Mr. Sizemore was out of the room.

"What's that J.W. stand for?" Emily asked.

"It's my brother's initials."

"Boy shorts? Figures," Corkie said.

Melanie came in last, holding her side, and crying.

"Cool off, and then join the rest of the class," Mr. Sizemore said. "Chippie, I want to talk to you a second."

I went over to him and he had me walk with him toward the bleachers. "County-wide meet is next week. It's the last one of the season. Chippie, we have not placed once this year. Not one trophy, nothing. I want you to run like you just did for me, then."

"So, I'm on the team?"

Mr. Sizemore laughed. "Lil gal, you are the team." Then he put his hands in his pockets. "I want you to ignore those other girls. You understand?"

I nodded.

"Can you play basketball?"

"No, Mr. Sizemore. I am awful at basketball and softball and all other kinds of ball. All I kin do is run."

"Well, that'll have to do for now," he said.

Back in the classroom, I had to sit with Jesse. That was a most embarrassing thing. But I did what the teacher said and helped him get his Spelling pages done. Then I helped him with his Math. He made all kinds of dumb jokes and kept rubbing his nose. I tried to just ignore him. Once, he even tried to lick my face like a pup.

At bus calling time, Mr. Sizemore stepped into the hall to talk to another teacher. Mo-mo, the chubby blonde boy shouted across the room. "Hey, Jesse, got yourself a little woman back there?"

Jesse grinned. "She ain't my woman, she's my cousin."

I about died. His cousin? Yuck! I started to say that we weren't kin when he went on.

"If I was to catch somebody messing with a cousin of mine, I reckon I might mash his mouth and break his arms."

Mo-mo's eyes got big and he turned around. Jesse looked at me and grinned. "Won't nobody bother you now."

"What did you do that for?" I whispered.

"You helped me, girl. I got to help you. That's the way my pappy says things are done. Never take no handout without giving something in return." He sniffled and rubbed his nose again. "Besides, I saw you run out there today. Way I figure it, you win that track meet and this whole school ought to be owing you." He looked right at me when he said it, bright blue eyes peering out of that sunburned freckled face and long greasy bangs.

"Thank you," I said.

"I know y'all live just down the road from me in that old mill house. Me and my brothers like to go snake hunting on Saturday, you're welcome to come if your pappy lets you."

"There's an old rusty truck behind our house," I said. "I figured it might have some snakes in it."

Just then Mrs. Rainey called my bus number over the speaker. I grabbed my purse and headed out. Lisha Faye tagged me as I passed her desk. She leaned over and whispered. "Is he really your cousin? He's nasty."

"No," I said. "But I think he might be my friend." I ran out the door so I wouldn't miss the bus.

CHAPTER NINE

Mrs. Idy Jo Page, our new neighbor, came to our house that first Saturday after we moved in, to welcome us to the neighborhood. The *neighborhood* consisted of her house, our house, her husband's oil rig garage, a saw mill, a country store, and George's house. George was Daddy's boss. There was also an empty white house at the end of our road that no one had lived in for many years. Idy Jo's husband, Tiny Elmer, had inherited it from his daddy.

Mrs. Idy Jo Page came across the road, which was really a dirt lane with grass growing in the middle of it, with her cake pan in hand. She was a short, dark-haired woman in her early forties. She wore a gingham yellow dress and gold frame glasses on a dainty chain. She walked with tiny steps, and a straight back, which signified right off that she was a lady, not just a regular woman.

Momma saw her out the window and opened the door.

"Howdy, Mrs. Pablo. I'm Idy Jo Page, your neighbor and I wanted to make y'all feel welcome. I brought you a cake, lemon. Hope you like it."

"Thank you, Mrs. Page," Momma said.

Now we didn't normally take handouts, but someone wanting to welcome you to the neighborhood was a special occasion and to refuse it would mean we were refusing her friendship, and Momma would never do that. She had been raised an Eastridge, and she knew all the things to say.

Momma invited her in and served her iced tea in our best glasses, the clear plastic ones we got from collecting oatmeal boxes. She let all of us kids have a piece of cake and sent us outside to eat it, so they could talk grown-up stuff.

After Mrs. Idy Jo left, Momma collected all our dishes off the porch, and then called me into the house.

I bounded through the door. "Yeah, Momma."

She was back in my bedroom. "Come in here."

Momma had laid my short-sleeved pink sweater and green skirt, the very best outfit I had, on the bed.

"Chippie, Idy Jo Page wants you to go to church with her in the morning. You know I ain't big on religion, but she's a good woman, and since we got to live right beside her, you go on with her. It'll be good for you."

I swallowed. Church? I hadn't been since I was five-years-old and went to a Bible school.

"Why did she pick me out of all us kids?"

"Cause she once had a girl the same age you are right now...fell offen a horse and died. She saw you in the yard and said you reminded her so much of her girl that she wanted to do something special for you." She looked at me, put her hand on my shoulder. "I want you to go, Chippie. Make Granny Eastridge proud. Make me and Daddy proud."

"All right, Momma. If you want me to go, then I'll

go."

She smiled and hugged me. "You're a good girl, Nochipa Lynn Pablo."

"Well." I said. "Um, seeing how I am a good girl, I suppose it'll be all right if I go down to Jesse's tomorrow to shoot some hoops."

"So long as you ain't sweet on him. His momma's my second cousin, once removed."

"Yuck." I couldn't believe my ears. "He's my cousin for real? Oh, Momma, have you ever seen how homely Jesse is? Ain't no girl in her right mind ever going to get struck on him. And just to think he is my cousin, after all."

"Course, you'll have to take Willie with you. You know how he loves to play ball and I won't have you leaving him here while you're off doing one of his favorite things."

I didn't know how I was going to keep Willie from tattling that we were going to the creek to look for snakes, but just maybe if he enjoyed himself, he'd keep quiet about it so he could go back next time.

"I don't mind if Willie comes," I said.

Willie and I had a great time shooting ball with Jesse and his two brothers. He had one sister, who was too young to play with us. Then Jesse showed us the animal pelts he had tanned and tacked on the outbuilding wall. And his stuffed albino squirrel. We went down to the creek and threw rocks at snakes. Willie promised he wouldn't tell Momma so long as I brought him with me every time I went to Jesse's house.

Jesse's momma, a thin frail woman with blonde curly hair, cooked us up a dinner of macaroni, salmon patties, pinto beans, cornbread, and fried potatoes. Of course it was nowhere near as good as Momma's cooking, but I thanked her for it, covered it up in pepper, and ate it anyway. We washed our meal down with red kool-aid.

The next morning, I woke up with knots the size of basketballs in my chest. I put the clothes on Momma had picked out for me and went to the kitchen for breakfast. As usual, Momma's little black transistor radio sat on top of the refrigerator. "All the Gold in California" was playing and as usual, everybody at the table rattled on, but I had no idea why. I was just so nervous about going to church.

After breakfast, Momma put some clips she'd been saving for a special occasion in my hair and said, "You'd better get going. She'll be leaving any minute now." She opened the front door and gave me a gentle shove.

I started across the driveway, heading toward that little dirt lane. Then I stopped. I stood there, fighting back the tears. What if those church folks, who were surely all as old as Granny Eastridge, said mean things to me because I had not grown up in church and didn't know anything about the Bible? I didn't know what to expect, and I was scared of riding with Idy Jo Page. She was a stranger to me.

I started to go back to the house, and then I thought of Momma. I couldn't let her down, so I wiped my eyes and stiffened myself up. Then I went across that dirt road and knocked on Idy Jo's door.

She was wearing a blue skirt and white blouse when she opened up. "Hello, Chippie. My car's behind the house. Go on and get in. I'll grab my purse and we'll go."

Her car was nice, finer than any vehicle I had ever ridden in. It was beige with leather seats, and it smelled clean, not like oil or gasoline as our old station wagon always did. It didn't have a single rust spot on it and the wheels all matched.

We didn't talk much on the way to church. It took about five minutes to get to where we were going. Sadie Hill Church was a small but pretty brick building on a hill in the middle of a graveyard, overlooking a big holler. There was a country store down the road and a little white house across the highway. The parsonage, a small brick house, sat at the edge of the cemetery.

My nerves were so bad by now that my skinny knees were bumping each other. Idy Jo just kept smiling at me but didn't say much. I got out of the car and followed her to the church house steps. Some men were standing there, smoking and talking about tobacco crops. Idy Jo exchanged pleasantries with them and told them I was Joe Pablo's little girl. They nodded their recognition.

I don't know exactly what I expected when I walked in that place, but the moment I stepped through those white wood doors, I sensed something. It was as strange as the feeling I had gotten when I saw Jerry Wayne, blurry behind the screen, the day we moved. It was as if I was meant to be there, as if I had been waiting my whole life for this day.

Sunlight poured through green tinted windows

touching the wooden interior with gold. The choir, all seated up front, were singing "Love Lifted Me" and then I felt it, warmth, love, just as real as when Momma kissed me good night or made after school treats for us. I felt it, but I couldn't quite tell where it was coming from.

I watched Idy Jo take a red hymnal from the back of the pew, so I took one, too. She opened it and started singing. I didn't know how to read music, but I turned to the page and followed along with every song. I glanced over my shoulder once and saw some boys from school, sitting on the backbench, snickering, but I didn't care. The music and the warmth I felt were more important than what those kids thought of me. I made a decision, right then and there, that every time there was church, I was coming, and I was going to learn every song in that red book.

As I sat there, caught up in the singing, I saw out of the corner of my eye, movement in the back, and then felt something on my neck. I glanced over my shoulder and saw Jesse, along with a row full of other boys. He was grinning. Just then a paper wad fell off my neck onto the pew. I turned around, wondering why Jesse enjoyed hitting me in the head with paper wads.

After the singing, we were dismissed to Sunday school. I sat next to the only other girl in the room. She had short curly brown hair, acne, and the biggest bosom I'd ever seen on a real live person. She wore a blue peasant-style dress. Her features were pudgy and her eyes small.

"I'm Deanna," she whispered.

78

"I'm Chippie."

Our teacher came in, an attractive lady in her early twenties. "Good morning, everyone. I'd like to welcome two new members to our class today." She sounded educated and intelligent. Her words didn't sound northern, but they didn't sound like everyone else either. "Looks like we are finally getting some girls in our Sunday school class. I'd like you all to welcome Chippie."

"I already know her," Jesse said. "Except I ain't never seen you in a dress, Chip. You almost look like a real girl."

The pretty teacher ignored his silliness and continued. "And this is Deanna."

"Well, hello Dolly!" Jesse blurted out. He put his hands out in front of his chest to indicate the size of her boobs.

Deanna's face turned red, like she had a sunburn.

"Let's not have any of that," the teacher scolded. "Girls, I am Ms. Jamie and want to say that I'm so glad you are here. Deanna is the daughter of our new pastor, Rev. Carlson."

She then passed out the new Sunday school books.

There were three boys sitting with Jesse. I recognized two of them. There was Ray Dean Kurtsinger, a quiet, dark-haired boy from my class at school, and there was Jesse's second older brother, Daniel, tanned with brown hair and very even features. The other boy was light skinned with black hair and almond-shaped eyes. I had never seen him before, but thought he looked like the man on the cover of the kung fu magazine down at the five-and-ten-cents store on the square.

As we got into the lesson, the boy with the unique eyes read fluently and answered every question the teacher asked. I figured out that he wasn't Asian, after all, because he talked just like the rest of us.

"Good Lord, he's smart," I said to Deanna afterwards when we were going out the door back to the sanctuary.

"Yes," she said. "He's nineteen-years-old! Too old for us."

"What's his name?"

"Clint Kurtsinger. He's Ray Dean's brother."

"Gosh, they don't look alike. Hey, how come I never see you at school?"

Deanna shrugged. "My dad just took over the church last week, and my Mom, my sister and I didn't get moved here until yesterday. I'll be at school tomorrow. I hate being a preacher's kid. We're always moving and I can't keep friends."

I liked her, despite the fact that she looked kind of like an over grown cabbage with hair and eyes. "I'll be friends with you. And if I am, Jesse will be, too."

We stepped back into the sanctuary and I sat beside her on her pew.

"I think he is so cute," she said

I looked back at Jesse, his greasy hair falling down in his eyes, his checkered shirt and freckled nose. I didn't see the 'cute' she spoke of.

"Well, I guess every girl's got their own idea of good-looking."

"I'm telling you, Chippie, that boy's cute and I aim to make him like me."

I didn't say it, but I thought that was a crazy sort of notion.

CHAPTER TEN

Sunday night it rained. We discovered that our house leaked in the living room and Momma set a dishpan under it. Then it leaked in the kitchen. She used the coal-packer in there. Lou Annie sat on the bed and got wet. So, we had to put a lard bucket in the middle of it. Momma and Daddy's room had three leaks. We scraped up every container we could find to catch the water.

Daddy said he'd fix the roof first thing after work Monday, and we all sat down to watch our favorite show, a program about three cousins who lived in Georgia and went around acting like modern day Robin Hoods. No sooner had it come on than we heard a commotion outside-Rusty barking, the ponies running and neighing.

Daddy jerked the door open and flipped on the porch light. There was my pig, racing around the lot behind the ponies and behind the pig was Rusty, and being half pug bulldog and half Chihuahua, he was no bigger than that runt pig.

"Lou Annie, stay in here with these babies," Momma said. "Jerry Wayne, Chippie, Willie...y'all come on. Me and your daddy's gonna need you to help catch the pig."

We spent the next hour in the pouring rain, chasing that little white critter. Then we spent another hour helping Daddy find the place where he got out of his pen and fixing it. Jerry Wayne found the loose board and held it while Daddy put the nails in. Willie held the light, and I held the pig. He squirmed and squealed, almost getting away more than once. Rusty ran around in circles, wagging his tail and barking like he had done some great thing by chasing that pig. Momma went to the house to make Daddy some coffee.

Once we had gotten the little fellow in his pen, Daddy was pretty mad. He cussed and cussed about having to fix a hog pen in the pouring rain at night and Jerry Wayne was going on about having to miss an all-new episode of *The Duke Boys*.

On the way back to the house, Willie said, "That stupid pig ain't nothing but a headache."

"That's the truth, son," Daddy said.

"Well, then," I said. "I reckon I'll call him Headache."

Willie laughed. "A pig named Headache."

"I'd like to know what y'all thank is so danged funny," Momma said when we got back to the house.

Daddy hung his cap on the back of a chair in the kitchen. "Sis has named the pig." He sat down and lit a cigarette.

Willie jumped over the threshold. "Headache, Momma."

Momma took the teakettle from the stove to pour Daddy some instant coffee. "Hold on, Willie, I'll get ye some aspirins."

"No," I said. "The pig is named Headache."

Momma laughed so hard she nearly spilled the

coffee water. "That was a sight. The pig chasing the ponies. The dog chasing the pig. We're going to have to tie Rusty. Not only did he chase the pig tonight, but Idy Jo said he chased Tiny Elmer's car all way to the end of the road. I'm afraid he'll get out on that highway and get hit."

"I'll tie him up tomorrow," Daddy said.

Momma handed me the coffee pot. "Chippie, refill this, for in the morning."

I took it over to the water bucket and placed three dippers full in it.

Momma got a gallon jug of milk out and poured some in Daddy's coffee until it overflowed the cup, ran down the sides and filled up the saucer, just the way he liked it.

"Honey, you want some blackberry jam and biscuit with that coffee?"

Daddy stirred his peanut butter colored drink. "No, thank you, Sugarfoot, I don't care for any. I got good news for you kids. George's giving your Momma the old sink out of his house and a used well pump. Carlos is coming over day after tomorrow and we're going to put them in. Y'all won't have to carry water up from the mill anymore. We're going to have running water in the house."

All of us children had been taking turns carrying water from the mill where Daddy worked after school, and Jerry Wayne, who got off the bus there, brought a jug home with him every day.

I was thrilled with the news. Most kids I knew had

running water in their homes. They had bathrooms and telephones and colored televisions. We had never had a phone or an indoor bathroom. We did have a television, a black and white, a nineteen-inch one that Uncle Dody Eastridge gave us, but the picture tube was going bad, and there were always streaks going across the screen. We had a new TV once, but Willie thought he was the *bionic man* and dropped it when he was five-years-old.

Momma looked up at the little clock sitting on top of the refrigerator. "It's done past ten o'clock. Get that mud wiped off, put on some clean clothes, and get to bed. Tomorrow's your big track meet, Chippie. You need your rest."

Lou Annie stayed out of our room long enough for me to wash myself and put on my nightgown. I had to put a cut-off milk jug under one of the leaks so I could use the wash pan. I opened the backdoor and tossed my dirty water out. Tom, my cat, ran in. I was sure that Tom and Rusty could both understand everything I said. So, I spent time talking to them. Tom was a rough cat and would attack other animals. He tried to kill other cats. He had even been known to chase dogs. He weighed about twenty-five pounds, was yellow-striped, and had a black spot on his neck. I had found him at Grandpa Pablo's when I was ten. He had been a crippled kitten then. Now he was a four-legged terror.

Lou Annie knocked on the door. "You done with your bath, Chippie?"

"Come on in," I said.

She stuck her head in. "You got that mean ole cat in

here? He's the devil."

"He ain't neither. He's just smarter than other cats."

Lou Annie got her pillow off the bed. "I'm scared of him and I ain't sleeping in here lessen you put him back out."

"All right," I snapped. "I swear, Lou Annie, you are a big scaredy cat."

"You ain't supposed to swear," she said.

I rolled my eyes, gathered Tom in my arms, and put him out the back door. Lou Annie grinned like a possum in a persimmon tree as she changed into her pink pajamas. They had white ponies all over them.

I took out the Sunday school book I had gotten from the teacher at church and started reading the lesson for the next week.

"What are you doing?" Lou Annie asked.

"I got this at church and I'm getting ready for next week."

Lou Annie laughed. "You must have loved it."

I hugged the little book. "I did."

I told her all about the kids at church and about my young pretty teacher. I told her about Deanna and the stained-glass windows.

"I wish I could go."

"Then I'm going to ask Idy Jo if you can ride with us. She's got a big car. There is sure room for one more kid. That is if you don't mind the back seat."

Lou Annie didn't answer. I looked down and saw that she was asleep. I continued reading my lesson. It was about a man named Solomon who was offered anything he wanted by God and all he asked for was wisdom, the ability to know right from wrong. As I read the lesson and answered the questions at the end, I felt strange inside.

I had always talked to God my whole life, the way Granny Pablo did. She said it didn't matter where a body was, he still heard you, even though Granny Eastridge said that you needed to go to church. I believed what Granny Pablo said, that God was a spirit and everywhere all the time, and that he loved me, but I liked church and understood why Granny Eastridge went. It just felt good. That night I whispered so I wouldn't wake Lou Annie, "God, make me wise like Solomon. I don't care 'bout being rich and famous, but I wish you'd make me wise way beyond my years just like you did him."

I felt calm, assured that I would receive what I had asked for. I had heard things at church that morning that sounded beautiful, and I wanted to know more, so I added one thing more. "And, Lord, show me what getting saved is. Cause I might want to do that, too. Anyway, good night, God, and I do love you. Amen."

I lay down, excited about church and Solomon, and about the county track meet I was to run in, but I dreamed about Tom. His tail got infected, and he was sick. I had seven dollars and begged Momma and Daddy to take him to the vet. The vet gave him medicine and he lived. Then I heard Momma's voice.

I opened my eyes and there she was, her head sticking through the door. "Get up, girls. Time for school."

While we were getting dressed, I told Lou Annie about my dream.

"That ain't going to happen," she said. "We ain't never took a cat or dog to the vet."

She was right. The only time we had ever seen a vet was when the hog swallowed the nail. Momma and Daddy couldn't pay human doctor bills, let alone animal ones. I shrugged it off as a crazy dream brought on by the previous night's activities. Besides, I didn't have seven pennies, let alone seven dollars.

* * *

School had been going much better since Jesse and Lisha Faye had buddied up with me. No one bothered me or teased me about being little anymore, because Jesse had taken a shine to me. He was fifteen-years-old and could whip anybody in the school if he had to. He'd been held back. For the most part, he was easy-going and just liked to make everybody laugh.

I felt sorry for Deanna that morning, her first day of eighth grade. The boys called her Dolly. I was worried that she might have her feelings hurt so bad she'd never want to come back to school. Jesse asked her if he could stand under her boobs to get out of the rain. I whacked him in the stomach for it and told her he always said stuff like that and not to pay him any mind.

Later on in the bathroom she said, "I don't care what he says to me, so long as he talks to me. Ask him if he'll go with me."

I was washing my hands. I couldn't believe what I heard. She was all bubbly, not one bit upset over the horrible things the boys said to her. She seemed to get some kind of energy boost from it. "That's crazy," I said, half way aggravated at her for not being mad at them all. "You don't ask a boy to go with you. You wait until he asks you."

"He might not ask," she said.

I turned off the water. "He won't respect you that way, Deanna. I know him."

"I don't want him to respect me, just to kiss me."

"Gross," I said. I rolled out some paper towel and dried my hands. "That's gross. Nobody wants to kiss Jesse."

"I do. Ask him to go with me."

I got out of all my afternoon classes that day for the track meet. We rode the bus to town where we met up with one-hundred-fifty kids from all over the county, all running for the top eight places.

My stomach was so queasy that I thought I was going to puke before they even fired the pistol. My heart just about jumped to the moon when that gun went off.

I took off, using the same strategy I always did in practice, marking myself a pace, gradually building up, and passing people as I went. The only thing crippling me was that I had only had two weeks practice. Everyone else had been privileged to two months' worth.

As I rounded a wooded bend, I saw Melanie, laid out on the ground, holding her side. She was so fast, she could have beaten anybody, but she always wore herself out half way through the race. I passed Brianne. She didn't say anything, but her eyes told me that I wasn't moving fast enough yet. I looked toward the finish line, just a half mile away from me at the time. There were eleven people in front of me.

I am not sure what happened, but I put my head down like a charging bull. It felt like I was leaving my legs behind. My lungs were bursting, my eyes watering and my nose burning. I saw someone's legs as I passed them, then another person's. I didn't look up for fear of losing my speed. I passed a third person. I got a stitch in my side. I started losing speed. It was hurting so badly.

I looked up and saw I was less than an eighth of a mile from the finish line. As I crossed, someone stuck a stick in my hand. It had a number eight, in blue ink, written on one end.

I started to collapse, but Mr. Sizemore grabbed my elbow. "Walk around, Chippie. Cool down first. You don't want to get sick. You did well. Real good. We placed. For the first time ever, we placed."

We waited around while they gave out trophies. Only the top three places got one. Then they passed out green, white and pale pink ribbons for fourth through eighth place. I received a pink one. It was just an honorable mention, but I had earned it. I slipped my wrist through the little braided string at the top and headed back to the bus. My side was still hurting.

Back on the bus, I waited as others loaded for our trip to our own school. The coach from the town school stepped on and looked straight at me. "You used to come to school here. Didn't you?"

"Yes, Coach Bryson," I said.

"You're a good runner. Why didn't you try out for my girl's cross-country team?"

I shrugged. I didn't want to tell him in front of my classmates that it was because I couldn't afford the uniform. "I guess I was just shy."

He stared at me a moment more. "You're a traitor, little girl. If you ever move back, you're running for me." He started to get off the bus.

Mr. Sizemore, who was sitting in the driver's seat, said, "Looks like I stole that one right out from under your nose, Sam."

Coach Bryson grinned. "If only I had known. I would have trained her like a race horse."

I wasn't sure I liked being compared to a horse, but I think he meant well. I felt awfully proud that afternoon and had a lot to tell my family when I got home. Of course, Jerry Wayne said it was all because I wore his shorts and they brought me luck.

CHAPTER ELEVEN

The bus jerked to a stop and Jeremy, the good-looking olive-skinned boy that dated Corkie, made his way to the front. He punched me on the shoulder as he passed.

"Oh, sorry, Chippie."

He winked and I felt uneasy. He had never said anything decent to me and I knew it wasn't genuine. Then again, he had never spoken when she wasn't with him, either.

Jesse squinted and looked out the window. "What's that all about?"

I shrugged. "I don't know." Then I rested my chin on the back of the bus seat. "So, anyway, Deanna wants to know if you'll go with her."

He grunted. Then he was quieter than I'd ever heard. He was that way for at least a mile. When he looked back at me; something about his eyes, glazed over from malnutrition and lack of sleep, seemed plumb sad to me. "Why'd you ask me such a thing?"

I shrugged. "She won't let me be. That's why. I can't even go to the bathroom in peace, without her going on over how cute you are and begging me to fix y'all up." I felt so bad for asking. He didn't say it, but I knew he had never had a girlfriend.

"She's got the biggest jugs in the county. People would laugh at me, going with her."

I don't know why I did it, but I play punched him on the shoulder. "Ain't nobody going to laugh at you. You're the only person in our room that nobody will mess with."

"'Cause I'm big and stupid," he said, and then laughed like he was playing. I knew he wasn't.

"No. It's 'cause you ain't afraid to be who you are," I said.

"Then why are you asking for her, Chippie? I don't want to go with some big ole jugs woman that's got a cabbage head for hair. I want to go with y-"

He turned back toward the window.

My stomach churned. He hadn't said it. He didn't have to. I felt sick inside, not because Jesse was an illiterate boy who wore clothes that looked like something my Grandpa Pablo would wear, or because he had enough grease in his hair to cook eggs. It was because he had been kind to me, even when everyone knew he was never kind. It was because he had wanted to be fair with me, no matter what everyone else had said about me. Or maybe it was because there was something I could not put a name to that looked out of his eyes, some kind of home-brewed code of honor that he lived by.

The kids at school were always going steady, kissing behind the old outhouses, arguing, breaking up, but friends like Jesse and I, we didn't do that. I knew right then that I'd rather have one friend like him than a whole bus load of good-looking boys offering to go steady with me if I'd do their homework or let them put their hands up my shirt when the teacher was out of the room. The way I figured it, what Corkie and those other girls had with their guys was pretty cheap, but a friend like Jesse only came along maybe once in a lifetime.

He was better than a girl to do things with because he wasn't afraid of snakes or the dark. He didn't give out when we went walking in the woods or mind how sweaty I got playing ball. He didn't care if I had freckles or never wore makeup or if my clothes even matched. And he didn't complain about getting horsehair on his pants when we rode ponies.

I never understood why some girls always wanted to talk about cute boys and movie stars, or why they hung posters all over their walls. With Jesse, I didn't have to deal with that kind of stuff.

Jesse lived walking distance from us and had become so much like my brothers that Momma regularly started setting him an extra plate on Saturday evenings for supper.

His voice broke through my thoughts. "Of course no smart girl, cross-country winner would ever want to go out with me."

"That ain't so," I said.

He jerked his head around and grinned. "What do you mean?"

"If I weren't your cousin, maybe I would be your girlfriend."

"You really mean that, Chippie?"

"Course I do." I thought in my mind that maybe I was lying, but there was no way to prove it, since he really

94

was a little bit kin to me.

He smiled. "You ain't like the rest of 'em. That's why I liked you right from the get-go."

"Why'd you tease me so much that first day then?"

"Don't you know?"

I drew back. "No. I don't. Now dang it, Jesse Alan, you better tell me."

"It's 'cause you're pretty."

"Corkie and Shelly are pretty," I said. "All the boys like them."

"It ain't 'cause they're pretty. Believe me. It's like cars. Pappy drives an ugly old truck, got the hood tied down with wire. It's the best he can get, and he can get in it whenever he wants to, so he acts like it's something, but you ought to see his eyeballs pop out when he looks at the hotrod magazine down at Thomas Mann's garage. He knows them cars ain't easy to come by. He ain't got no hope of getting one so he goes on about how great his truck is. Some girls are like old cheap trucks, and others are like fine cars. You ain't no truck. If I go with Deanna, it's 'cause she's a cheap junker, Chippie. It's 'cause she might let me see if them things of hers are real or not. It ain't special and I ain't going to ever love that cabbage head. Only girl I like is you. But you won't go with me 'cause you're my cousin? Right?"

"Right," I said.

"But it's way down the line. Something like third or fourth cousins, Chip. Fourth cousins get married all the time."

"My momma would whoop me until my legs bled if I was to go with my cousin. She says that's what happened to Daddy's Uncle Beaty and Aunt Mable. They were fourth cousins and married. All their kids turned out with a rare blood disease and died, except two and they're afflicted. One of them still wears diapers and he's thirty-five-years-old."

Jesse's eyes got huge. "Good Lord! No wonder your momma's so strict on not dating anybody that's one bit kin. All right. Tell Jugs I'll go with her. And I'll tell her right up front that I put kinfolk," he winked, "above girlfriends any day of the week."

* * *

In late October I joined the BETA club, which was a club for junior high students who had a grade point average of 88% or above. There were only eight kids in the club, three of them from eighth grade, the rest from sixth and seventh. Of course BETA was supposed to be for top eighth grade students, but since we only had four, counting me, that wasn't much fun, so sixth and seventh graders were recruited.

Miss Lindy McCaughey, the young and pretty first grade teacher who wore her strawberry blonde hair so long that it reached half way to her knees, was our sponsor. She told us that we needed to come up with some way to raise money for our club. Lisha Faye suggested we sell candy bars, so we did. But since most of us were from poor families, we had no way of selling them and went in the hole on the project. At our November meeting, Miss McCaughey said we had to come up with another fundraiser or we wouldn't be able to do anything at all to make our year special. I suggested a talent show.

Lisha Faye rolled her eyes. "That's a cheap idea." She was against anything that didn't require her mother's touch or her daddy's money.

Miss McCaughey chewed her pen top. "Yes, it is cheap. That's the beauty of it. Go on, Chippie. What else?"

I shrugged. "Well. We could involve kids from sixth, seventh, and eighth grades to put on acts of whatever they're good at. The little kids could come to the show and pay a quarter or fifty cents each to get in. But we could make our real money off the parents. They would pay a dollar to get in. If we put on a good enough show, they'd get their money's worth."

Miss McCaughey stood up. "That is a very good idea. Before next week's meeting I want each of you to bring in an idea for your act. I want you to recruit your classmates to be in the show. You may do group acts or individual ones."

For the next month we worked every afternoon practicing our acts for the talent show. Corkie and her little posse of popular girls wouldn't have anything to do with us. Jesse and his rough friends didn't want to be in the show, but he was behind me doing it all the way.

That left nine from my class to be in the show. Lisha Faye, Brianne, and Melanie worked together to put on a skit. Mickey, a chubby blonde boy in my class, played the guitar and sang an Elvis tune. Karen and two seventh graders did a dance. Chester, a skinny kid with red hair and freckles, did a stand up comedy routine. And I chose to twirl a baton. I had been using a whittled stick at home. Then, one afternoon, Momma told me that Daddy was taking me into town on Saturday. I could spend the money I had been saving from feeding Headache at the five-and-ten-cents store on the town square to buy a baton. I was thrilled.

I spent the whole weekend just rubbing that shiny little piece of metal, and wiping the white knob ends with a wet cloth. I practiced until I could do my routine without stumbling or dropping it.

Lisha Faye said I needed some great music to perform to, so she brought a cassette tape of some sort of space disco stuff. Miss McCaughey played it and was pleased with the way it went with my routine. She then went into the P.E. equipment room and brought out a green and gold cheerleader's outfit.

"I'd like you to wear this, Chippie. It just seems that with what you're doing, you need a uniform of some kind, like in the marching bands you see on television. Go try it on."

I took the suit into the bathroom and put it on. It was a little big, but felt pretty good. When I came out to show Miss McCaughey, the BETA kids had all been dismissed and sent back to class. Jeremy was in the gym helping the janitor wash tables as punishment for smoking behind the outhouse, a common offense.

"My, that does look good," Miss McCaughey said. "All right, thank you, Chippie. You can get your clothes back on and take that on home with you. Have your momma wash it by hand after the performance."

She then went on back to her first grade class to relieve her aide and make sure they got on their buses safely. I walked back toward the girl's locker bathroom to change. I had to go right past Jeremy.

There were no grownups within earshot. "Hot danged, Chippie. You look good in that little dress. Come over here, why don't you?"

"What for?"

"I need your help with my homework. I got to write five hundred sentences on top of cleaning these tables. Why don't you help me out?"

"That's cheating, Jeremy. If I got caught, I'd be in as much trouble as you."

"Cheating? It ain't a test, girl."

"But it's not right. I have to do what's right."

He snickered. "What? You think you're too good to do my work?"

"No, but it's not right."

"What do you care about right? You're Mexican. My old man says your people are all lazy and dirty. I know your family's poor as chicken crap, too. So, I'll give you five dollars."

"I don't want your money," I said. My jaws were so tight I could feel them tremble. I turned and walked to the bathroom.

"Dirty little Mexican," I heard him say as I pushed open the bathroom door.

Alone in the girls' bathroom, I locked the door, sat on the toilet and cried. I stayed until I stopped shaking, until the janitor started to come in and I had to holler that I was in there. I changed clothes and went back to class then, not looking up at Jeremy as I passed by him. I felt safe, knowing the janitor was just a shout away.

I took the uniform home, so proud of it that I thought I'd bust before I could show it to Momma. Lou Annie begged all the way home on the bus for me to let her try it on just one time, but I knew that Lou Annie would stretch it out of shape or pop it at the seams. It was hard to tell her no, but I did. I didn't fault Lou Annie any. Once I had tried on a pair of Zelphie's pants that someone had given her and popped them out myself. I was so ashamed that I just hid them.

Momma was excited to see that outfit. She washed my white socks out right away and told me to clean up my tennis shoes so that I would look neat in 'em. That night, I slept with sponge rollers in my hair, because she wanted me to have bouncy hair.

The next afternoon, two days before Thanksgiving, we had our talent show. I wore white ribbons in my hair, which had grown to my shoulders since school started, white shoes and socks, and the green and gold cheerleader's uniform. I stared at myself in the bathroom mirror. I had never thought of myself as pretty, but the girl in the mirror wasn't me. She wasn't Chippie. She looked like some kid from an after school special or a real baton girl from a real marching band.

As I walked down the hall with the other performers toward the stage entrance to the gym, it hit me. A sick nervousness rushed in on me. My legs shook. My hands perspired, but mostly my heart beat so hard, I thought I was going to pass out. I stood behind the curtain and watched as my classmates, all as nervous as I went through their skits, songs, dances, and so on. Some of them messed up terribly. Some of them performed flawlessly. Then I heard Miss McCaughey call my name over the microphone.

I stepped out, stood feet together, head down until the music started, then I launched into the routine, concentrating too hard to feel my nervousness anymore. In three minutes, I was done. I had practiced an entire month for a flawless three minutes. I ended in splits with my baton upright in front of me. The crowd stood and clapped. That's when I saw Momma and Daddy toward the back. Daddy had taken off work and lost a half-day's pay just so Momma could see my show.

I nearly cried in front of all those people. Now, I understood why I had felt so proud. Momma had put as much work into those three minutes as I had. She believed in me enough to come in the middle of the day. And Daddy, he loved Momma so much he'd do just anything she asked of him. I smiled at them. I was sure that I was the luckiest girl in the whole world.

As I walked back to the classroom after the show, I thought about Momma and how much I loved her. I remembered how I had cried every day of my first grade year just from missing her. I remembered how I had only wanted to feel her soft, warm arms around me, and I thought of how no matter what happened, she made it all right again. That's when a strange understanding spread over me, a knowing that I couldn't shake, and I nearly fainted. Momma wouldn't always be there.

I entered the classroom. Mr. Sizemore was out of the room. He was out a great deal. He always had important coaching business to take care of and phone calls to make. My classmates who hadn't been in the show were carrying on like they always did, standing on the desks, telling dirty jokes, pinching each other, and indulging in just plain ornery foolishness.

I ignored them and went to my locker. I was standing there with the door open when suddenly someone slammed it on my hand then jerked it open again. I was more stunned than hurt. There was Corkie, face red, lips smelted into an angry scowl.

"You little hussy," she shouted at me. "You danged little hussy. You got up there and twisted your butt all over the place. You ought to be ashamed of the way you acted." She grabbed the baton out of my hand, tore the end off and threw it; then she shoved me into the lockers. I came up with my left fist and struck her right in the face, her wire frame glasses flew off and she staggered, but my locker door kept her from falling. The whole class went silent.

Corkie shrieked, "Dang you!" She picked up her glasses and ran out of the room crying. I just stood there, staring after her, shaking, unsure what was happening.

Then Jeremy came up to me. "Why'd you hit her like that?"

I looked at my new baton, torn apart and thrown in

the floor. "She tore up my baton...and...shoved me...and..."

"Like this?" He pushed me against the locker. "Listen, dirty little Mexican piece of trash, you don't go hitting on my woman, you hear?"

When Corkie had attacked me, I was stunned, hurt. Now, I was angry. I waded up both my fists and started punching him in the chest and in the belly. I couldn't get past his blocks for his face. He was much taller than I. He grabbed my wrists, pushed me away, and went after Corkie.

Jesse hadn't been in the room. I don't know where he was, bathroom, I suppose. Lisha Faye came in just in time to see a bit of it, but Deanna was there. She saw the whole thing. Both those girls, my friends, gave me a look of sympathy as I walked past them and headed out the door. I went to the bathroom on the first grade hall to change into my regular school clothes. I didn't want to run into Corkie.

Why did that girl hate me so much? She didn't even know me. I had always believed I was a good person.

When I got home that afternoon, Momma had made brownies for us all and was bragging on me the minute I walked in the door. I almost broke down in front of my whole family.

"What on earth is wrong with you?" Momma said. "I was so proud I could have popped today."

Lou Annie and Willie were sitting on the couch. Zelphie, Carol Lee, and little Josh David were in the kitchen eating brownies. Jerry Wayne came in the door at that very moment. I told them everything. How Corkie had shut the door on my hand and shoved me. And about how Jeremy kept calling me a dirty Mexican and had shoved me, too.

"I hit her, Momma. Then I hit him, too."

"And where in the sam hill was the teacher? Why didn't he do something about it?"

"He was out of the room. And I couldn't tell on them. If you tell on people at school, nobody likes you and they call you a squealer."

"Come here," Momma said.

I went to her and she put those wonderful arms around me.

"Now, listen here, young'un. I don't want you crying over this. All your life, you've been sticking up for Lou Annie and the little ones, but you don't stick up for yourself too good, not without having all these guilty feelings. You did what you had to do, Chippie. Sometimes you just have to stand up to bullies."

"But Daddy always says that it takes more courage to walk away than to fight. I didn't walk away. I just started hitting."

"Your Daddy's right, but it's kind of hard to walk away when you're shoved into a locker, now, ain't it?"

That night Daddy called me into the kitchen where he was drinking his nightly cup of extra strong instant coffee and eating a left over biscuit from supper.

"Sis, I heard you had a rough day after your show."

I nodded.

"Well, I'm proud of you. Now, I'm going to tell you something. I've had to fight a many of times. A body's got to stand up for himself and his family. That girl had no right doing that to you, and if that boy ever lays a finger on you again, I'm going over to his daddy's place and I'm going to set that bunch straight. Now give me some night sugars and go on to bed." I gave Daddy a kiss and went into my bedroom.

I hurried out of my clothes and into my nightgown, then shot under the covers. Lou Annie stuck her head in the door.

"I'm sleeping with Zelphie tonight. Momma told me to."

"Okay, just turn out my light then," I mumbled.

She closed my door and the light from the kitchen poured through the holes and cracks in it.

I lay there beneath the same patchwork quilt I'd slept under since I was six-years-old. It was made from the scraps of clothes Lou Annie, Jerry Wayne, and I had worn when we were little babies. The backside was brown and said Kitty Hawk all over it and had pictures of little white airplanes on it. That quilt was so warm, so soft, just like Momma, just like my whole family.

I cried myself to sleep, not because of the fight, but because there had never been a night in my life that I hadn't kissed my Daddy goodnight and felt Momma's big soft arms around my neck. Because Lou Annie, although she was the messiest kid that ever walked, understood that sometimes I needed to be all by myself. And Jerry Wayne, though he had never told me he loved me, was never ashamed of me in front of his teenage friends. Then there was Willie, who could destroy a fortified city with a match, and Zelphie who thought she was the greatest daredevil on earth, and Carol Lee who pouted every day, and Josh David who would eat anything I cooked even if I got the salt and sugar mixed up. Sweet Little Josh David would come up and touch my hand when I least expected it. With thoughts of them, I fell asleep and dreamed that I was helping Jerry Wayne put a fence up back in Walkup Holler.

CHAPTER TWELVE

Corkie did not speak to me at all when I went back to school and every time Jeremy looked at me, he gave me a bad finger sign. I just ignored them. When we let out for Christmas break, they still hated me, but even Jeremy was afraid of Jesse. I made sure that I was always with Jesse, even when he was with Deanna. Deanna and Jesse were still going together, even though Jesse told me daily that he couldn't stand her. I finally figured out that he really did like her, but didn't want to lose his tough guy image by letting on like he did. She didn't care. She was so desperate for a boyfriend that she would have jumped off the Empire State Building naked if he had asked her to.

Just before Christmas, Eloise's family, including her weird brothers, came to visit. They hadn't been around much since they had helped us move. We had a great time and they stayed for dinner. Joy Jane talked some of her newest psychic visions. Premonitions, she called them. She then said we ought never to ignore our dreams. Momma went out to use the bathroom, which was a fine new outhouse now.

Joy Jane turned to me and said, "Chippie, little girl, it's getting about time for the gifts to kick in for you."

Eloise grinned. "It's a good thing. Wish I had the gift, too."

Joy Jane smiled. "Everyone has it, but it is stronger in some than others."

As Momma came back into the room, we changed

the subject. Joy Jane and Momma drank coffee and talked. Daddy and Carlos were down at the pigpen, trying to fix it so Headache would stay in, but all of us knew it would do no good. Headache lived up to his name and rooted his way out every time it rained.

"We're moving," Joy Jane said. "Back to Texas."

I was stung. I would miss Eloise something fierce, although, I confess that I didn't much expect to miss her brothers. As best friends do, Eloise and I promised to write each other, cried, hugged and all of the usual sad goodbye things, but I did not want to sadden her too much. After all, she was headed off for a grand adventure in Texas, a faraway place that I had only seen in the movies.

* * *

As usual, we were without money and Christmas time was upon us. Daddy's check from the mill was barely enough to keep food on the table. It was a tradition that we children would go with him to cut the tree. Lou Annie never went. It was too cold, and there was too much walking involved to suit her.

We got a tree so fat that it took Daddy and me pulling on the top end while Momma and Jerry Wayne pushed on the back part just to squeeze it through the front door. That night we decorated it. When Momma turned out the lights, I sat there just staring at it, thinking about how when Jesus was born into the world, there surely weren't any Christmas trees. I wondered what it was like all those years ago, and if it were quiet in the stable that night.

I watched my Momma and Daddy. I knew they

hadn't bought any presents yet. They had nothing to buy with. Christmas was hard on them, because they wanted so much to give us nice gifts, but never could. I knew that many times Daddy had borrowed money or worked extra jobs in order to spend ten or fifteen dollars each on us. That was a big amount of money for a family of seven children. My parents never received gifts for Christmas, which made me terribly sad.

Daddy was sitting on the floor behind the living room stove, whittling cedar, and Momma was in the kitchen, cleaning up. I went into the back bedroom where the little ones were playing. There was music coming from Jerry Wayne's room, 'Down on the Corner, out in the street, Willie and the poor' boys'.

"Jerry Wayne?" I stuck my head in the door.

He looked up. "Yeah?"

"Let's have a family pow wow...just us kids though. I got an idea."

I ushered Willie and the three little ones in from their room, then peeped in the living room where Lou Annie was partaking of her favorite past time, television. "Come here."

Daddy didn't pay us any mind, because we were always going off in the back room for something or another. We had our secret meeting in Jerry Wayne's room.

I started. "Momma and Daddy never get any Christmas presents."

"Cause we're just kids," Lou Annie said. "We ain't got no money."

"I wish we could give them something, though," I said.

Jerry Wayne flipped his hair over to the side. "Well, they do like music."

"Yeah," Lou Annie said. "We could sing for them."

My heart lightened. Yes, we could sing for them. It wasn't much, but they would surely like it. "But it should be really special."

"We could put on a show for them," Jerry Wayne said.

And that's just what we did. Lou Annie and I went into the living room and announced that we would be putting on a special performance for Mr. and Mrs. Joe Pablo in honor of Christmas time. Momma and Daddy got tickled. They sat on our orange vinyl couch with its torn cushions and clapped as I went back into the bedroom and Lou Annie introduced the first performer.

"Ladies and Gentlemen," she said, like the room was full of people. "I'd like y'all to give a big round of applause for country music star, Jerry Wayne Pablo, who is sure to be the next all time Grand Ole Opry star."

Jerry Wayne walked out of Momma and Daddy's bedroom into the living room with Daddy's guitar strapped around his neck, just like the singers on the Saturday night Grand Ole Opry show did. He sang about prison blues, making his voice really deep and trying to sound as much like his favorite country music singer as he could.

Then he spoke. "I'd like to thank y'all for coming out to our show tonight and now I'd like to introduce the Pablo Sisters singing 'Barbara Ellen.'"

Lou Annie and I came out and sang our song. Then Lou Annie sang one called "In the Pines" and I did "Pretty Saro."

Then Zelphie came out as a dare devil, whom she modeled after that motorcycle guy who was always jumping over cars and breaking his bones. She jumped over some chairs.

Willie sang the "Crawdad Song" and Carol Lee did an imitation of her favorite cartoon character. Finally, little Josh David banged on Daddy's guitar and sang "B-I-N-G-O."

We wrapped up the show with all of us singing "We Wish you a Merry Christmas." I don't suppose Momma and Daddy had ever had such a fine Christmas present before, and I doubt they ever did after.

Two days before Christmas, Daddy gave us all something he had made, the things he had whittled from cedar.

He sat in his chair behind the living room stove, with his cap hanging on the back of it. "I'll just tell you kids right now, I don't expect we're going to have much of a Christmas, but I've made you all something that I hope you'll keep just in case me and your Momma ain't able to come up with something by Christmas morning. It ain't much, but it's all I got right now."

He called us over one at a time and gave us a gift carved from cedar-a football charm on a chain for Josh David, a little bat for Willie, a cross for Jerry Wayne and for all four of us girls, the same thing, a cedar heart with a little metal hook to hang it on a chain or a leather strap.

I rubbed my fingers over the smooth pinkish wood. "I don't care if I don't get another thing. This is a good present, Daddy, and I love you." I hugged him. He smelled like tobacco, a wood stove, and coffee.

The next day, Christmas Eve, a brown station wagon pulled into our driveway and two gray-haired ladies, one in a long navy coat and the other in beige, got out and came toward the house.

Momma was looking out the window. "That fine car, them nice coats. Looks like religious people, trying to convert us again. Wonder what they're a-wanting on Christmas Eve." Normally, she made us all pretend we weren't home when salesmen and religious recruiters came around, but this time she didn't. She just answered the door.

The lady in the navy coat, who was tall and thin, stretched out her hand. "Mrs. Pablo, I'm Edna Mae Crawhorn from the church in town. Your mother and I have gotten to be dear friends over the past couple of years and she told me you had seven children. My son is a member of the CJ's club. Every year the CJ's and our church select a family to bless at Christmas. This year we have chosen you. We have quite a few gifts in the car to bestow upon your children if you will permit us." She spoke even more properly than Lisha Faye. I figured she must be a teacher.

112

I found myself whispering under my breath. "Please, Momma." Momma was awful proud and didn't want to take anything that might be looked upon as a handout.

She looked at all of us, who in turn, were looking at her with pleading expressions. "We don't take handouts."

"Oh, but Mrs. Pablo, it wouldn't be a handout," Mrs. Crawhorn said. "It's a gift, which is different than a handout. See, the Lord Jesus said that when we had given to the least of these, we had given unto him, and surely he meant to give unto children in saying that. He said that unless we give, we will not receive. You might say that we are obeying orders and if you refuse our gift, we will be letting the Lord down."

Momma thought on that for a moment. "Well, I reckon if the Lord says you have to give, then I wouldn't want to be the one to make you disobey him and miss out on heaven."

The two ladies smiled. "Bless you, Mrs. Pablo. We can't thank you enough for helping us out that way. We'll just unload the trunk and—"

"No you won't," Momma said. "Jerry Wayne, Willie, you boys get your shoes on and pack them presents in for these ladies."

"All right, Momma," my brothers said in unison and with considerable enthusiasm.

On Christmas morning, we had more gifts to open than we had ever opened in our lives. I looked at the Christmas tree and thought of Baby Jesus. "Thank you," I whispered. "Thank you, very much."

CHAPTER THIRTEEN

January brought our first snow in twelve months, and Jerry Wayne's sixteenth birthday. He got one dollar for his birthday. In the dead of winter, that was all Momma could spare.

He refused to go back to school when second semester started up, and true to his word, he quit. Momma didn't cry. She'd done all that back in September when he first said he was quitting. She did put Jerry Wayne to work though. He split wood, carried water, fed the ponies, the dog, the cats, helped Momma do laundry, ricked wood into the neatest pattern-all orderly, like when a little kid stacks wooden blocks to make steps. He did practically all the chores while we were at school every day. Of course, he never fed Headache and he never went near Tom. Nobody went near that cat except me. Like Lou Annie, Jerry Wayne believed he was the devil.

The second semester went by pretty quick with most of the usual things like Deanna and Jesse committing fornication behind the schoolhouse, me helping him pass the eighth grade, and Corkie, who had taken to calling me bad names every chance she got. She wrote bad things about me on my desk, on my locker, and all over the bathroom stalls. I ignored her and pretended it didn't bother me, that I didn't see it. Eventually, she went back to the silent stare. Then there were snow days, and basketball.

Now, admittedly, I was the shortest girl on our team, but I played anyway, because Mr. Sizemore kept telling me that he needed just one more player. And the girls on the team were awful. They could hit the basket but they would not pass the ball. When they guarded, they always fouled, because they thought it was okay to just elbow, bump, and knock the opponents out of the way. The town school referee was not in agreement with that. The girls were always getting mad and quitting.

I was number 35. Momma was so proud of me that she took my picture in my green and white uniform with her 126 Camera. However, she could not attend any of the games. The day games would mean Daddy taking off work and with winter upon us, we simply couldn't afford to lose any hours off his paycheck, and the night games were at the other end of the county and we couldn't afford the gas to go.

Now, Jerry Wayne got a job doing odd chores for a farmer up on Briar Ridge. At first, Daddy would drive him up there before going to the mill, but pretty soon Jerry Wayne saved up enough money, three hundred dollars, to buy a car.

It was a little red Nova, covered in rusty spots. On a pretty day toward the end of January, when it was up in the sixties, Jerry Wayne went to the five-and-ten-cent store and bought some blue spray paint. Willie and I helped Jerry Wayne paint his car.

It was the last game of the season, held at night in a tiny school of seventy kids at the far end of the county. Mr. Sizemore used a school bus to come around and pick up us players at our houses, because like mine, many of the parents were too poor to get out to the games. However, there would always be a few proud parents there, because this last game was a double one.

The boys would play first, then us girls. Boys' games always brought out more spectators than girls' games. Mr. Sizemore said that even though it was traditional that girls go first, that since a lot of people had to get up early to do their milking and go into the factories, we should get the boys' game over with, then those who wanted could stay behind for the girls'.

I sat on the bench through the boys' game, and then just as the girls' game started, I looked up in the seats on the stage where the parents sat watching, and there was Jerry Wayne. I wanted to hug him. If ever I have loved anyone, I loved my brother in that moment. He had spent his own money that he worked for to buy gas and drive himself to my game.

I knew Momma would have come with him, if it wasn't for her having to help Lou Annie on her Science homework and having to get the little ones bathed and in the bed. Daddy wasn't any good with that kind of stuff and he couldn't help any of us with our homework because he couldn't read.

The game went on, but I still sat on the bench. I kept looking at Jerry Wayne, thinking that maybe he would be ashamed of me if I didn't get put in the game. I was not one to beg the coach to put me in. I was terrible at basketball, and we both knew it. I was a lousy guard during practice, and rarely did anyone pass me the ball. I had not even scored one point all season. I hadn't been in long enough. I spent most of my time on the bench just so there would be enough players to have a team. Still, Mr. Sizemore assured me that because I was willing to do that,

I would enjoy the same benefits--I never figured out what those were--as all the other players.

Toward the end of the game, with just seconds left on the clock, Shelly twisted her ankle and Mr. Sizemore did the unthinkable-he put me in the game.

Briana, our best player, tied the score. Then after the other team had taken the ball out and passed it back in, I somehow managed to intercept a pass and found myself holding the ball. All I could think of was that I needed to get rid of it. I was just past half court and terrified. On an impulse, I shot the thing. The buzzer went off as the ball swished through the net, not even touching the rim of the goal. The game was over. Mr. Sizemore jumped to his feet, shouting. I thought he was mad at first, and then I realized what had happened. We had won the game by two points, the only two points I had scored all season.

Our team jump and squealed, all the girls high-fiving each other. Afterwards, our team gathered in the hall, still giving each other high-fives and talking all at once. Then Jerry Wayne came out there.

"Good game, Chippie. Want a ride home?"

"Yeah," I said, proud that he had seen me. "But I have to ask Mr. Sizemore first."

While I was asking my teacher, Jerry Wayne acquainted himself with my classmates and not one of them was shy around him.

On the way home, it was cold in his car because the heater didn't work right. Still I was glad to ride with him.

That's when he surprised me. "Chippie, you know that red-haired girl in your class?"

"You mean Emily Snider?"

"Yep. I asked her to go with me."

My mouth fell open. She was one of the popular girls, one of Corkie's friends.

"She said yes," he went on. "She's fifteen you know. She got held back a year."

So started the courtship of my big brother and a red-headed girl named Emily, who happened to be a friend of Corkie's... In the following days, no one gave me any trouble at school. Corkie laid off me and gave me some space. She still didn't like me, but my brother was handsome and had his own car, unlike all the boys in our class, even Jeremy.

* * *

There were a few notable events at home that spring. One sunny day on spring break, Momma made all of us kids gather the brush and rubble off our yard. We piled it high and she set fire to it. Daddy picked up some hot dogs at the store by the mill on his way home and we had a hot dog roast that afternoon. After all the brush had burned, Momma raked the ashes until they were smooth. Then she gave each of us a pack of flower seeds she had picked up in town.

"Why are we planting seeds in the ashes?" I asked.

"Ashes will fertilize them. We are turning what was ugly into something beautiful."

In a few weeks, our backyard was alive with blazing orange and yellows. I think all of us developed a love for flowers after that.

Another notable event was when we went dry land fish hunting. Now this is something we did every year in April. Daddy's old friend, Ben Lee Garney, had lived and died up on Dehoney Hill. He was buried up there and his two spinster daughters still lived in the house that their grandparents had built.

Ben Lee had been a black man who loved my Daddy like a son. He had been great friends with my Grandpa Pablo and had helped my grandfather's family during The Depression. He and my grandfather were friends for nearly seventy years. They had grown up working for the same farmers, eating in the same back room or the boss man's house because in those days it wasn't proper for coloreds to eat with the white folks. Grandpa Pablo, being very brown, wasn't considered white. Since he did the same work as the coloreds, for the same white people, he was expected to behave according to the same customs.

Daddy had told us many times how the Garney girls, though black, were like his own sisters, and the truth be told, he loved them like kinfolk and would fight any man who tried to harm them. He had promised Ben Lee to look after them the night the old man passed away. He had played his guitar for his friend that night and held his hand as he died. Daddy could never tell the story without crying, yet sometimes he insisted on telling it.

Once a year, he took all of us up on Ben Lee's land to hunt dry land fish, which were mushrooms. We all knew exactly what they looked like and just where to find them. They were usually grayish or brown, sometimes black, and they resembled miniature cedar trees with little holes all over them. We would gather them into bread sacks and bring them home, where Momma would slice them, wash them and let them sit in salt-water over night. Then she would roll them in flour and fry them for breakfast. She always served them with gravy and biscuits.

This particular year as we brought our fungi treasures out of the woods, a terrible thunderstorm set in and we had to run furiously, all the while getting soaked. It rained so hard that we just sat there in the car waiting for it to pass before heading home.

"Well, it would catch us in a rainstorm," Daddy said.

Momma laughed. "Ain't no storm going to last forever. The sun's always going to shine again."

That saying of hers always made me feel good. I found myself laughing. We had an enormous amount of dry land fish and we were all together, in one car, wet and waiting out the storm. I laughed until Momma said, "Chippie, quit being so silly."

I didn't mind getting scolded. I could never tell them why I was laughing, why I was happy, mostly because I didn't really know myself at the time.

* * *

For my eighth-grade graduation, Momma made me a white lace dress and Granny Eastridge gave me a green Bible. At the ceremony, I walked beside Jesse as my escort as all girls had to walk beside a boy classmate if possible. It only seemed right that Jesse and I should graduate together. His grades were still horrible, but they were passing.

Momma brought her camera to the ceremony and took lots of pictures of me, and of Jerry Wayne who posed under the entrance arch with all of my friends. She took pictures of my brothers and sisters. Then she took one of Jesse and Deanna, because they were my closest friends. Lisha Faye's mother wouldn't let her pose with any of us, but I knew it wasn't Lisha Faye's fault. Her mother was just a weird control freak.

When we got home that night, I was walking through the kitchen toward my bedroom door when Jerry Wayne hollered at me.

"Chippie, here. I didn't want to give you this in front of everyone."

He handed me a little box, wrapped in white notebook paper.

"It ain't rocks, is it?" I said that because one time at Christmas, he and Willie had wrapped up granite rocks in a corn flake box and given them to me as a joke.

"No, this time it's a real present. I bought with my farming money."

I tore it open and in the box, dangling from a gold chain was a little butterfly with lacy gold wings.

He shrugged. "Butterflies make me think of you. I hope you like it."

I just touched those wings with my index finger as if they were made of crystal. "It's the most beautiful necklace I've ever seen." Without thinking, I just grabbed a hold of him and hugged him really tight.

"Thank you, Jerry Wayne. Thank you so much. I'll cherish this forever and ever."

He grinned. "You're welcome." Then he turned and walked through the living room. As he reached Momma and Daddy's bedroom door, he looked over his shoulder.

"I'm proud of you, Chippie. One day, you're going to be something."

"You already are something," I said. "You're the best brother in the whole world." He smiled at me, then ducked behind the quilt that hung over the door. I stood there, holding that necklace, staring after him. For a second, I felt like shouting for him to come back. It was as if he had disappeared from me forever, and I never wanted to let him go.

CHAPTER FOURTEEN

The week after I graduated eighth grade, Granny Eastridge took sick. Now, she had struggled with sugar diabetes for years, since the last of her nine children was born. Granny had been a thin thirteen-year-old of ninety-eight pounds when she married Grandpa Eastridge, but that had been so long ago. She was sixty-five and tipped the scales at about two hundred pounds. Granny was only four feet, eleven inches tall.

The doctors were constantly fussing at her about her weight, her blood pressure, and mostly because of her addiction to sweets. She would hide candy and eat it when no one was looking. Then she would lie and say she'd not had any. Whenever Granny was caught in a lie, she broke right down and cried in front of everyone, because lying was a sin. But that sugar was the devil in her life and he had his hand around her throat.

We were watching the Friday night movie on one of the three channels we could receive, when Uncle Dody Eastridge, one of Momma's brothers, pulled into our yard, driving his fine white car. He didn't come to visit often, as we always seemed to live on a badly managed gravel road that might damage whatever delicate machine he happened to be driving at the time.

He jumped out of the car, pushing his black hair out of his eyes. "Jewell," he shouted before we even got out of the house. His voice was high-pitched and he wasn't the cool, high and mighty Eastridge that he usually was.

Momma yanked the door open, "What on earth's wrong, Dody?" Then before he could answer, she cried,

"Oh, it's Momma, ain't it?"

Momma and Daddy got into the car with him immediately. She stuck her head out the window and said, "Chippie, watch the babies." Then Uncle Dody jerked the car in reverse, spun gravel, and they were gone.

It was late when they got home that night, past eleven, and all the kids were asleep except Jerry Wayne, Lou Annie, and I. Uncle Dody let Momma and Daddy out, then left without coming in.

My parents entered quietly and for a moment I was afraid Granny was dead. Then Momma sat down and said, "Kids, your Granny's bad off. Her sugar went so high that she almost died tonight, but Doc Roy's got it under control. He says that she is not to be left alone for one minute, because she can't be trusted to lay off the candy and to give herself insulin shots when she's supposed to. Somebody's going to have to start staying with her."

We sat quietly. We didn't know what she was getting at. I was just glad that Granny was still alive. I had been mightily scared when Uncle Dody came up like that earlier, and I had felt knots in my stomach the whole time we waited on them to get home. I think Lou Annie and Jerry Wayne felt the same. We hardly talked, just watched the little ones and watched television.

"The trouble is," Daddy put in, "is that your Aunts, Darla and Poodle Bug, live far off from here and everybody else in your Momma's family's got jobs they can't leave to watch Granny."

"Daddy just ain't able or dependable enough to look after her proper. Besides, she gets awful mad at him when he tries to make her lay off the sweets. She throws things at him, which makes him mad. Then he goes whoring down at the wash house with White City trash."

"Don't talk like that in front of the kids," Daddy said.

But he didn't need to protect us. We knew what White City trash was. It was where people who had moved in here from other places congregated in trailer parks and run-down houses on the outskirts of town. They let their kids run dirty, used cuss words, hung out at the boot legger's and drank whiskey all the time. They also slept with anybody, regardless of color or kinship. At least that's what I'd heard Granny Eastridge say one time while we were breaking beans for canning.

"They're white trailer trash," she had said, then cried because there was a rumor that one of them was going around town saying she was having Grandpa's baby, that it was conceived at the wash house where Grandpa worked, right in the back of Grandpa Eastridge's van. Grandpa was seventy-years-old, and Granny was immensely disgraced. She pretty much hated Grandpa but believed divorce was a sin, so she stayed with him. Nobody could ever prove any truth to that rumor and Momma wasn't even sure there was such a rumor, but Granny Eastridge believed there was one and when Granny believed a thing, it was so no matter what anybody else said.

"Well, it's come down to this. Somebody's got to stay with Granny," Momma said, "and all my brothers and sisters have talked it over. They're willing to pay us if you kids will take turns staying. I mean, just you three oldest

126

ones and maybe Zelphie. Daddy really likes Zelphie and she's a good girl, even if she is young. She'd be good company for him when Momma's having one of her mad fits, which brings me to another thing. Your Granny's got a terrible temper, but she holds it in around children, because she likes them so much."

"She don't like me," Lou Annie said. "Granny Eastridge hates me. She tells me I'm fat."

"That's just because she's afraid of you being like her one day. She is afraid of you getting health problems," Momma said.

So, after that night, it was settled. Four of us Pablo children, Jerry Wayne, Lou Annie, Zelphie, and I, took turns staying with Grandma and Grandpa Eastridge, because nobody else could. As it turned out, Jerry Wayne and Granny Eastridge hit it off real well. Granny loved having "a man around the house" to do all the things Grandpa didn't mess with, like helping her do the laundry, washing the porch, running across the street to the country store and checking on the neighbors, then reporting back to her what they were up to.

When I stayed, I was sent to the garden to pull weeds, to feed the dog, to water the horse, and most of all to help Granny with the canning, which she wasn't supposed to do, according to the doctor, but Granny Eastridge was stubborn.

First, she would send me to the garden to pick whatever she wanted to can that day. If it were beans, then I would also have to sit under the shade tree in the backyard and break them. During this time, she would tell me stories of how it was when she was a kid and talk about how shameful it was that women didn't wear dresses anymore and how terrible that my hair was almost as short as a boy's. Then she would go on about how I was so skinny that I looked like a child from Ethiopia. Before long, I figured that Granny used the excuse that I needed fattening so she could bake a cake or something, which I know she sneaked and ate from when I was out in the garden.

Sometimes she would ask me to recite all fifty states and capitals, and spell terrible hard words. She enjoyed this because she had been considered a child genius and had gone to high school at eleven. She often said, "If you don't go and get yourself knocked up before you get out of high school, you just might amount to something. She always went on about how she was sure Jerry Wayne was really going to go far in life and that just maybe two of Jewel's kids might make it in society. No one had told Granny that Jerry had quit school. He couldn't stand the thought of her being disappointed in him. So, we all kept his secret.

Jar washing was my most specialized job at Granny's house. She had me wash jars almost every time I came, because she couldn't get her hand in them. But she would heat the dishwater until it was so hot that it burned my hands and made them red. She would also put a ton of soap in the water, so the jars were slick, too. I was so afraid of breaking them.

Lou Annie always came back crying when she stayed with Granny Eastridge, because Granny constantly fussed at her for being too fat and wouldn't let her have a piece of cake. She made her eat diabetic candy and refused to allow her sugar for her tea. Lou Annie couldn't stand tea that wasn't sweet. After a few trips, she begged Momma to stop sending her. Eventually Momma did, and the other three of us just went more frequently.

Not only did we stay with Granny Eastridge a lot that May, but Jerry Wayne worked for farmers all over Briar Ridge, setting tobacco. One day, he took me with him. At first, the farmer didn't want to hire me because I looked so young, not a day over twelve, he said.

"She's fourteen," Jerry Wayne said.

So, the farmer, Short Huber, put me to pulling tobacco plants. I did this every day and at night, my legs hurt from squatting and bending all day. After a few days though, the hurting stopped. One day, he was short-handed and needed one more person to ride the setter. His wife showed me how to place the plants in the holders and so began my tobacco setting career.

After that farmers all over Briar Ridge were asking for the two Pablo kids to come work for them. Whenever we weren't staying with Granny Eastridge, Jerry Wayne and I were in the fields working. We were as brown as molasses and the sun bleached my hair to a reddish color. We made three dollars and fifteen cents an hour.

Jerry Wayne made enough money to have a telephone put in our house so he could call his girlfriend. It was a big black wall phone with a rotary dial. It hung in Momma and Daddy's room.

I made enough to help Momma and Daddy buy groceries and to put back for our school clothes in the fall. As far as having money, our family had never had it so good.

By late June, all the tobacco setting was done and we were back to just staying at Granny Eastridge's. One night during Jerry Wayne's turn, the phone rang. Momma answered.

We all got quiet when the phone rang, still marveling at its power to unite people.

"We'll be right there," I heard Momma say. Then she hung up the receiver and turned to Daddy. "That was Jerry Wayne." She burst into tears. "It's Momma. Jerry Wayne came back from taking out her trash and found her passed out on the floor. She's up at the hospital in the emergency room."

Once again, Lou Annie and I were left in charge of our little brothers and sisters. We waited up late on our parents. Hardly anyone spoke. We just sat watching television, but not really watching it either. Finally, all the three youngest ones were asleep, and it was just Lou Annie, Willie, and I awake.

Then it came to me, a knowing I could not explain. I knew that I would never wash jars for Granny Eastridge again, that she would never tell me to read my Bible every day, or that I was so skinny that she mistook me for the scarecrow in the garden.

Lou Annie broke the silence. "I had a dream last night," her voice was so quiet that it was almost as if she were just mumbling to herself, "about Granny...."

"She ain't coming home," I said.

Lou Annie lowered her eyes. "No, she ain't coming home."

Willie didn't say a word. He was too sad and scared. He sat like a frightened kitten in the corner behind the stove that was being used as a summertime table.

Just then Jerry Wayne's car pulled up. Momma was crying when they walked in the door. She went into the bedroom.

Jerry Wayne was crying, too. He ran off through the kitchen, into my bedroom and out the back door.

Daddy stood with his hand on the door lentil, like it was holding him up. "Your granny's gone, kids."

CHAPTER FIFTEEN

For some reason, Momma took us all to the funeral home to sit in on the decision making process. All eight of her brothers and sisters were there. The Eastridges had never been a close family, but news of Granny's death brought my aunts from Memphis and Nashville. It brought Grandpa's 'other' child, the one he'd had with the woman he married before he met Granny, down from Hazard. I'd never seen her before.

Grandpa hadn't been with his first wife long; just long enough to have a baby. Then he got in a fight with a man from Knoxville and accidentally killed him. As a result, Grandpa Eastridge went to prison for a while when he was a very young man. While he was in there, his young bride found herself a new husband. When he got out, he married Granny who had been only about thirteen at the time.

I never understood the course of events that brought Granny Eastridge and Grandpa Eastridge together. I only knew that it had something to do with Granny's family moving back here from Chicago and that when she spoke of living there, her eyes would fill with tears and she would say no more. So, whatever happened to Granny in Chicago must have hurt her so much that she married the first man she came across once she got back to Kentucky.

My grandparents' staying together was even more mysterious than Granny's hidden past and the details about her courtship with Grandpa Eastridge. They were as opposite as any two human beings could be. He was tall, thin, and strong. Granny was short, round, and weak from her constant sicknesses.

Granny always wanted to know what everybody in the community was doing. She wanted to know who got married and who was expecting a baby and whose son was in jail. She wanted to be around people so much that she couldn't stand to be alone. Grandpa never talked to anybody. He couldn't care less if anybody ever got married or had a baby, and the only sons he worried about being in jail were his own, because one of them had a drinking problem from time to time and would go around town firing off his pistol.

He sure didn't want any visitors and, if he ever had a pain in his life, no one knew about it. If there had ever been any love in their relationship, no one, not even their own children, had ever seen it demonstrated. I suppose their marriage was more like some sort of arrangement that they both agreed to maintain. They did have one thing in common. Neither of them smiled much.

The funeral home was a big, white house, left over from pre-Civil War days that sat on the edge of town. It was as pretty as a calendar picture inside and out, but it smelled like chemicals. Chandeliers hung from beamed ceilings and a winding staircase led to the family's living quarters upstairs. I wondered how in the world it would feel to live upstairs in a house, even if it was as fancy as this one, while there were dead people downstairs. The furniture was old as the house and made me think of castles I'd seen in fairy tales. I figured all those delicate little benches and couches with their plush seats weren't really for sitting on, and that was why there were metal folding chairs.

After making arrangements for Granny's funeral, we all went over to Grandpa's house to wait for them to lay her out. It was a strange time with all the Eastridges talking and crying and remembering all the times Granny had spanked them, and Grandpa Eastridge just walked around the yard, saying nothing. I didn't know what was in Grandpa's heart, but I knew he had never loved Granny, at least not the way Daddy loved Momma.

I went out on the porch where Jerry Wayne sat watching cars go up and down the road, because Granny's house was near town and a road ran right in front of it. I sat down beside him, and for some reason, neither one of us said a thing. We just sat there on the front steps, watching those cars. Then Jerry Wayne got up and left me sitting there. He headed over to the used car lot, on the property adjoining Granny's. I knew he was hurting, and that made me sadder than knowing that Granny was gone.

Lou Annie came out of the house and sat beside me. She put her chubby little white hand on my arm. "It's my fault," she said. "I am fat and not smart and could never do anything to suit Granny. She was so upset about me not being good that it killed her."

I put both my arms around her. She buried her face in my shoulder and cried. I sat there stroking her hair. "It's not your fault, Annie. It ain't never been your fault. Granny was sick and getting old. At church, the preacher says all us got to die one day."

"That ain't fair," Lou Annie sobbed. "Why are people born just so they can die? It just ain't fair at all. Do you think Granny went to Heaven?"

"Of course she did. She's right up there with Grandma Pablo."

"I still wish Granny had liked me better," she said.

I didn't know what to say. "Me, too."

It was the first time I'd been to a funeral home since I was six-years-old, since Grandma Pablo died. I could remember it mostly because of the pictures. We had pictures of her in her casket and of all her children standing around in their best clothes, looking mournful. Now here we were, all in *our* best clothes, standing around Granny's metallic pink casket, getting our pictures taken by teary-eyed amateur photographers. Momma took pictures of all of her brothers and sisters, each standing alone, crying at Granny's casket. They all took one of her. Then Daddy took one of Momma with her whole family standing by the casket crying.

The days dragged by. We spent hours at the funeral home and hardly went home to eat. After three days, we had Granny's funeral. Her preacher stood before us all and cleared his throat. He was a chunky man with red thinning hair and he wore a navy suit.

"Mrs. Eastridge was a fine woman," he said. "In the twenty-four years that I've been a pastor in this town, she's rarely missed a service although she never owned a car or had a driver's license. That's a credit to Mr. Eastridge, who brought her so faithfully. Mrs. Eastridge loved the Lord and she loved his children. Many a times she baked cakes and cookies for Bible school. She was always one to help out whenever a helping hand was needed. I heard her talk often about how she wanted to know that her loved ones were saved and on their way to Heaven. If Mrs. Eastridge left a legacy behind, it'd be this: that she loved God, loved her family, and loved her neighbor as herself, true to the words of Jesus himself."

The preacher said a lot of other pretty words about Granny and about her life. Then the ladies who had brought us Christmas presents played the organ and sang "I'll Fly Away" and "Amazing Grace." Then they had us walk out in rows by the casket and we followed the hearse to the graveyard in our cars.

It was a sunny day. That didn't seem right. It seemed like it should be cold and rainy for a funeral, not blue and bright like all was right with the world. After we all took a rose from Granny's casket, we walked quietly back to our cars and went to Grandpa's house where Momma's brothers and sisters argued over who would get what of Granny's things.

In the days that followed, they argued more, until some weren't speaking to others, and I wondered how such a loving person like Momma came from such a selfish bunch of people. Yet, they weren't always selfish and they weren't always grouchy. I grew to love my Aunt Darla with her Memphis talk, her sports car, her movie star hair and her eight-track player. She wore stylish clothes and make-up. She carried a shoulder strap purse and wore high-heeled sandals. She took me out for a soda and gave me her dresses that wouldn't fit her anymore. The only problem was that they really didn't fit. She was much taller than I.

I told her I loved the dresses. When she went back to Memphis, I put them in my old trunk. I kept my treasures in there, treasures like my striped toe-socks that had too many holes in them to wear anymore. This is where I kept my red dress that dragged along the floor, which I liked to put on and stand in front of the mirror when no one was around, so I could pretend I was a gypsy princess. Now there were the dresses Aunt Darla gave me, dresses that Granny Eastridge would have said were hussified, meaning they showed too much leg.

July came and there was work to be done in the tobacco fields again. Jerry Wayne and I were hired to drop sticks and break suckers. Now dropping sticks was a job and a half. The boss would bring a pick-up load of tobacco sticks out to the field, which was maybe an acre, sometimes two or three acres. Those tobacco sticks resembled giant toothpicks with one blunt end and one sharp end. We would gather as many sticks as we could carry in our arms and walk down the rows of tobacco, placing a stick at every fifth plant.

The hardest part was that the plants were higher than my head and not a bit of breeze could reach me in there amongst those giant plants. It was nearly a hundred degrees most days and I would sweat so much that my shirt looked like someone drenched me with a garden hose. Another thing about scattering tobacco sticks was that the bundles of sticks were so hard to carry and got heavy. They pinched my arms until I had big pink welts from my wrists to my shoulders. Scattering those sticks was an important part of raising a tobacco crop. When cutting time came, one person would use a sharp knife, like a machete, to whack the huge stalk down. Then he would hand it to the his partner who would come along behind him, pick up that stick, place a sharp steele 'spear' tip on it and skewer that big old stalk of tobacco. One stick could hold up to five stalks of tobacco and could weigh up to eighty pounds. Most weighed about forty or fifty.

Breaking the suckers out was a little easier. We would just walk along the rows and break off any extra shoots coming off the main stalks. We would also break the blooms off the top, which was called topping. This was a type of pruning to make the leaves grow wider and healthier so the tobacco would be heavier and bring more money at the market in the fall. At the end of every other row, we would have to drink water to keep from getting heat stroke.

Daddy didn't like the idea of us working in tobacco, of us doing grown men's work. Every night as we sat around the super table he'd say things like, "Y'all drink plenty of water out there. I worry about you kids a lot."

And I know he did. Sometimes at night, when he thought I was asleep, he would come into my room and lay his hand on my back just to see if I was breathing. I know he did that with my brothers and sisters, too.

After Granny Eastridge died, Lou Annie got afraid to sleep in our room anymore, because of that outside door. Even though I kept a butcher knife under the bed and swore I'd kill a burglar if he tried to hurt her and that I wasn't afraid of anything in the whole world. She said she believed me, but she wanted to hug up to the little ones in their room.

So, most nights, it was just Little Tom and me. I would let him in at night after I read my green Bible from Granny Eastridge or read over my Sunday school lesson. I'd stroke Tom's fur and tell him he was the best cat in the whole world, even though I knew he really wasn't. He was always fighting and attacked anybody who looked him in the eye.

I would lie there those nights, without a fan, with my head near the open window, listening to night things, my arms and legs tired from my work in the tobacco patches. Sometimes I'd look over at the little green cupboard, which had been left over from Momma's kitchen cabinets, where I kept a gallon pickle bologna jug. In that jug was my money, the money I had been saving all summer to help Momma buy school clothes.

One night, I finished my Bible reading, my favorite story, the one of Jonathan and David. I laid the Bible on the table and wondered what it would be like to have a friend like Jonathan, who loved me more than his own soul, who would give up being a prince just to be my friend if he had to. I thought of Jesse. He could be a friend like that, and almost was, but not quite. And of course, Eloise had moved off to Texas. Deanna was a silly girl, like lots of girls. Then I thought of Jerry Wayne, my own brother. Could a person's own brother be a best friend? Yes, surely, he was, and Lou Annie, and Zelphie, and Willie, my own brothers and sisters. They were my Jonathans and I was their David.

I went to the door and called Tom. He didn't come. I called and called. Finally, I gave up and went to sleep. The next day as soon as I came home from the tobacco patch, I pounced in the front door. "Momma, have you seen Tom today?"

She was working a puzzle with Josh David. "No, haven't seen that monster. Night before last when you and Lou Annie were in your room playing that crazy old rock album of hers, the cats got in a fight up in house rafters. I hit the ceiling with the broom and haven't heard from either of them since."

I went outside and called again. He didn't come. Then I walked through the woods, looking for my cat. Nobody would help me, because they were all afraid Tom would jump out of a tree onto their heads or something. I called and called.

Tom never came.

On Saturday, Jerry Wayne and I took the day off to go yard sale shopping with Momma. I bought clothes for everyone. Then we went to the dollar store and bought shoes, too. I had seven dollars left over when we got back home. All of us had new clothes, new tablets, and the little ones even had new crayons. I had never been prouder in my whole life.

I took my bag of new clothes in my room and was trying on my jeans again. They were boy jeans, but I liked boy jeans because they sort of hung on my hips and didn't bunch up around my waist and get in the way when I was active. I stood in front of my mirror and looked at them. I liked them a lot. That's when I heard a hoarse meow.

I jerked open the outside door. Tom lay on the step, a big gash in his tail, his eyes pleading me for help. I scooped him up in my arms and ran through the house.

"Momma, Momma."

"What in the world is wrong with you, Chippie?" she came through the living room.

I didn't have to answer. She saw the shape Tom was in.

"Oh, Chippie," she said. "You best let your Daddy put him out of his misery. Ain't no sense in him suffering like that."

"What's happened to him, Momma?"

"Must be from a big fight. Looks like Tom got the worst of it."

"We've got to take him to the doctor, Momma. We can't just let Little Tom die."

"Oh, Chippie," she said. "We can't afford to take our cats to the vet. You know that. Ain't no telling how much it'll cost."

"I've got seven dollars left."

"You'd give up all your money to save that cat?"

"It ain't right to let something die when you have the power to save it."

Daddy came in from outside as I stood there pleading my case. "Oh, Chippie. This is ridiculous. Poor people like us got no business taking animals to the doctor like a rich man."

"Please, Daddy. Would you want somebody to just leave you lying on the back step if your leg was cut and bleeding and all infected?"

"But it's a cat."

"Didn't Grandma Pablo always tell us that every

creature's got a soul and a right to live unless you need it for food? Don't you think she'd want me to try to save Tom? Please, Daddy. Please." I was nearly crying.

My daddy shook his head. "Dag-blame-it, Chippie Lynn Pablo, you can talk a man right out of having any sense. Put him in a box and tie it up."

"Then go get your money," Momma said.

I ran into the kitchen and grabbed a box out of the trash. It was easy to place Tom in there. He didn't have the strength to fight. "Please, God, don't let Tom die," I kept saying as I stuffed an old shirt in there for him to lie on then tied the box shut with a shoe string.

Daddy put Tom in the truck while I fetched my seven dollars. As he pulled out of the driveway, I remembered the dream I'd had about Tom months earlier and I knew exactly how much his visit would cost...seven dollars.

CHAPTER SIXTEEN

I suppose everybody's got something or another in their past that they're ashamed to tell. In comparison to all that happened with Granny Eastridge and the terrible things I have seen in my time since then, mine seems a might small now, but it wasn't. Demons tend to feed on the young, the naive, and the foolish. I was all of those. When I speak of having my own personal demon, it's not a figure of speech.

My private shame had to do with my cousin, Damien Pablo. Damien was an awfully good name for him, because it sounded like a demon, which is what I thought he was. And anyone who'd known him since the day he was born was inclined to agree with me on that, anyone, that is, except his grandpa who spoiled him rotten and bought him whatever he wanted.

Damien's daddy, Jim Elee Pablo, and my daddy were brothers. Now Uncle Jim Elee had named his first boy Damien after his wife's rich grandfather that used to own thirteen slaves. His wife, Mary Lou Ellen MacCraken III, bragged all the time about how her grandpappy had owned thirteen slaves down in Alabama during the Civil War. Momma said that she didn't even believe there were any MacCrakens in Alabama.

She was the kind of woman that wore red lipstick just to go to the hen house looking for eggs. She always wore one of those criss-cross brassiere under her double-knit dresses, which she said was quite fashionable, and wore a girdle to make her belly look trimmer. She was just mighty struck on her good looks, which Momma said had well faded after her third baby came.

It wasn't that Momma didn't like her sister-in-law. It was just that she felt Mary Lou Ellen was a foolish and vain woman, going on about fashion and high heels when she ought to have been hoeing out her garden and sewing school clothes for her kids. Momma didn't care for the way that Mary Lou Ellen would put her Christmas tree up in November and then stayed on the road, going here and there, until the following June, nor did she like the way that Mary Lou Ellen once locked a poor hunting dog in an out-building and forgot to feed him for days and days.

When she remembered she had a dog and wondered why she hadn't heard him barking, she sent Damien out there with some old cornbread and he found the poor thing, dead and half rotted. He made a joke of it and bragged on and on of how he took a stick and whacked its head off. Daddy said that Granny Pablo would have turned over in her grave to hear how one of her own had starved an animal to death.

He said that Mary Lou Ellen and Damien both would be held accountable on Judgment Day for what they had done. But my uncle told Daddy he was wrong in speaking to his wife in such a way. So for two years, our families didn't see each other and there was a quarrel between Daddy and his brother. Eventually, Uncle Jim Elee had become a born again Christian and asked Daddy to forgive him and they made amends with one another. Not long after that, Uncle Jim Elee said he believed the Lord had called him to preach and everyone else was inclined to agree with him.

Being a preacher kept Uncle Jim Elee and Aunt Mary Lou Ellen on the road. He went from town to town doing revival meetings, brush arbor meetings, camp meetings, and tent meetings. He prayed until his face was blood red and his clothes soaked in sweat. Uncle Jim Elee cast out devils and laid hands on the sick, but he couldn't do much at all with his wife and children. I think the biggest devils in his life wore red lipstick and rode bicycles.

Now Uncle Jim Elee and Mary Lou Ellen had two other children besides Damien. They're not important for me to tell about right now, except to say that all of them were spoiled worse than a jar of milk that had been left in the sun for two weeks and so mean that no one anywhere was glad to see them coming. Their mother loved them while they were babies, but as soon as a new baby was born, she didn't like the old ones anymore and just let them run wild. But she worried fiercely over which Bible looked better with her purse and where to buy new white shoes for summer.

I came nearest to absolute shame as I have ever known one day in July when Damien was spending the night with Jerry Wayne. He was already seventeen, a bit older than Jerry Wayne and much bigger, but still, once in a while, he took a notion to spend the night at our house.

It was late afternoon and I had gone down to the hog pen to look for Headache who, as usual, was out and running scott free. I had on a pair of checkered cotton shorts and a red blouse. I called for Headache to come. I heard a rustle in the woods and turned, thinking it might be Headache or that maybe Tom had followed me, which he had taken to doing every since I had sent him to the vet to get his tail sewed up. Rusty had followed me in the past, but now he was tied up so he couldn't chase Headache all over creation.

Instead of seeing my cat or my pig, I saw my cousin, standing between two trees at the edge of the woods.

"Hidy, Chippie," he said. He grinned like he was the devil and had just claimed an eternal soul.

"Hidy," I said.

"What're you doing out here all by yourself?"

"Looking for my pig."

"You're looking hot is what you're doing," he said.

I shrugged. "Not too bad. I don't mind summertime."

He came close to me and leaned against a tree. Damien had never shown much interest in me at all. He usually just hung out with Jerry Wayne. I didn't see how Jerry Wayne stood him. They were nothing a-like.

Damien had already been in jail more than once for stealing and fighting in town. His Daddy just wanted to disown him and his momma plainly told my momma that she hated Damien and wished he had never been born. She said he was a disgrace on her good family name and on the Lord God Almighty, too. Damien had been eleven when she said it and she said it right in front of him. He just got meaner and meaner after that. But for some reason, Jerry Wayne tolerated him whenever they came to visit.

Damien grinned. "Let me ask you something, Chippie."

"All right. Ask."

146

"Do you think I'm good-looking?"

I shrugged. "You're my cousin. I never thought about whether or not you're good-looking." He was tall with long hair that he wore down to his chin where it curled under, kind of like one of the lead singers in a rock band he liked. Only thing Damien had a big wide mouth that took up most of his face as far as I was concerned. He always had nicer clothes than us and could afford just about anything he wanted, but whenever I looked at him all I could see was mean.

"Thanks," he said. "I've been watching you for a while now, watching you walk in them cute little rag pool shorts of yours." Then he pushed me right up against that tree and kissed me so hard that my mouth hurt. I had never been so scared in my life. I couldn't even move. He held my wrists in such a way that my arms were pinned against the tree bark. They burned. When he lifted his mouth off mine, he clamped his hand over my mouth, somehow got behind me and pulled me down to the ground.

"I want to see what's in them shorts, and then I'm going to get me some of it."

I kicked and squirmed, now frantic of him. His hand had somehow gotten into my shorts and opened the button. He was saying all manner of vulgar things to me, whispering.

Just then I heard a voice drifting through the woods-someone shouting for me. Jerry Wayne. It was Jerry Wayne. It startled Damien, too, because he loosened his grip. When he did, I bit his hand. I bit it as hard as I could. Then he jerked it back and hollered. I jumped up, fastening my button as I ran. I met Jerry Wayne coming down through the woods.

"Momma sent me down here to tell you Headache's at the house." I wanted to tell him what Damien had done, but I was so afraid. Damien was bigger than Jerry Wayne and I wondered what might happen if he fought my brother. The thought of him doing something awful to Jerry Wayne was worse than the memory of what he had tried to do to me.

* * *

Damien took to visiting us more and more often over the next few weeks. I had to put tape over all the cracks in my bedroom door as I caught him peeping in more than once while I was getting ready for bed. Whenever I went to the outhouse, I had to make sure he wasn't anywhere around, for he would look in on me. It was an awful feeling, like I was dirty all over and no amount of washing would ever make me clean. He didn't seem to bother Lou Annie as she was pretty heavy set and he thought he was too good for 'fat girls,' and he didn't bother my younger sisters, but he became a nightmare for me. As the days went by, I found I could tell no one at all, but I wish with all my heart I had.

Late July and early August brings fields full of black-eyed-Susans, low levels of water in the ponds, dusty roads, scattered thunderstorms, June bugs, and hot days. We had experienced a week of days when the temperatures were in the mid to upper nineties. Jerry Wayne and I had scattered tobacco sticks all week for local farmers. My arms had pink welts on them from where the sticks had

148

pinched my hide. Of course, they didn't really look pink because I was so brown from all that time in the sun. My hair which was naturally a shade from black had become so bleached out that it was the color of a block of caramel candy, same color as my face, even though I wore a little white cap that one of the farmer's wives gave me.

It was Sunday morning and I had decided to stay home from church, mainly because Momma said I needed to rest up from all my hard work. She said it bothered her to see her kids working out in the heat. She must have been right, because I didn't wake up with the sun as I had done practically every day of my life. Instead, I woke up to the sound of country music coming from the kitchen where Momma was frying bacon. I sniffed and just lay back on my pillow taking in the peacefulness of the moment. I put my hands behind my head and smiled. I had a good life. Light streamed in through the windows on my outside door. I lay there, under my sheet, staring at the dust particles, dancing in the light.

Then I heard Jerry Wayne's voice in the kitchen.

"Momma." His voice was higher than normal.

I sprang up, grabbed my shorts from the floor where I'd left them the night before and went into the kitchen. Something was wrong. I pushed the door open. Jerry Wayne's brown face had gone plumb pale. "What's wrong?" I said.

Jerry Wayne looked down. "Rusty's dead, Chippie."

I gripped the back of a chair. I don't think a truck could have hit me any harder than those words did. Then I dashed back into my room and out the backdoor. I had to see for myself. Jerry Wayne and Momma were right behind me.

Daddy was standing, hands on his hips and looking down, by Rusty's little white doghouse.

I knelt beside the small body. This dog had been my friend for as long as I could remember. He was a part of all my memories, how could he be gone? Then I realized, poor Rusty, his teeth had fallen out over the years and the fur around his face had slowly turned from tan to white. Why had I not noticed before? Or had I? Maybe I could just never admit to myself that he was getting old, that he would not live forever.

Jerry Wayne squatted beside me. He never said a word and neither did I. I unfastened Rusty's collar. Somehow it didn't seem right that he ought to have to be buried in a collar, like he would be tied in Heaven. And I did believe he would go to Heaven, no matter what any preacher anywhere said about animals not going to Heaven.

As soon as I took the collar off, Jerry Wayne scooped Rusty up in his arms and started down the path that led through the woods. I walked beside him and Daddy followed with a shovel in his hands.

Jerry Wayne said, "Pick a spot, Chippie."

We walked past the old truck and the pigpen. I found a spot on a little hill about fifty feet from the pigpen. It was under an oak tree and over-looking a little pond. Daddy dug the hole, and I kissed my dog one last time on his head as my brother lowered him into the ground.

"Goodbye, Rusty," I said. "Goodbye."

Jerry Wayne did not cry, yet I knew he was hurting inside. I didn't cry either. Somehow I had to keep myself brave because that was what Jerry Wayne needed of me, that I should be brave, that I should be strong, just like him.

After we buried Rusty, Daddy talked. I think he must have loved that dog, too.

"You kids don't remember how I brought him home in my coat pocket and sat him down in the playpen with you, Chippie. I said he was yours, yours and Jerry Wayne's to share. I said to your momma, 'Honey, these kids can have this here pup, but I want to name him myself. Let's call him Rusty, cause he's the color of iron rust.' And that's how y'all's dog got his name, kids.

"You were fourteen-months-old when I got that dog. Jerry Wayne was just over two-years-old. Them's a lot of years for a dog. He was getting awful old. We treated him good and he was a good dog, had a good life. Y'all ought not to be too sad."

"I'm just going to miss him," Jerry Wayne said.

"I love him," I said.

As we started for the house, Jerry Wayne looked back at the gravesite. "I've been thinking and I think that I'll be going back to high school this fall. Granny Eastridge never knew that I quit and I was thinking that maybe I'd go back for her."

Daddy put his hand on Jerry Wayne's shoulder.

"Your momma's going to be glad to hear that."

"We'll be in the same grade," I said. "I'll help you with your lessons, Jerry Wayne."

He grinned. "I know you will."

Despite losing Rusty, there was some rejoicing that day as Momma was so happy about Jerry Wayne going back to school that she hummed and sang all day. I spent the afternoon making a cross for Rusty's grave. I selected two pieces of wood from the kindling pile, nailed them together, and painted 'Rusty, We Love You' on it in pink and blue letters.

It didn't turn out as nice as I had hoped, but all my brothers and sisters were pleased with it. I took my younger siblings and showed them where we had laid Rusty to rest. Then I conducted a funeral service and preached of all the wonderful dog deeds Rusty had done like saving Jerry Wayne from a copperhead and always barking at strangers.

For the next few days, I went to Rusty's grave whenever I fed Headache. I knelt by the little wooden cross and talked to Rusty, telling him what everyone was up to and that I loved him. Sometimes I talked to God, too. There wasn't much to tell him. I figured he already knew everything, so mostly I just ask him to help me with stuff. Sometimes I just sat by that graveside and thought.

A thing nagged at me, some knowing that I couldn't quite name, a feeling that once sadness had touched a family with its poison finger that it would just keep spreading and spreading until it infected everything. It was the kind of knowing that tormented me and drove me to spend hours alone down in the woods, to paint pictures of graveyards and barren trees, and to walk around biting my lip and fighting back tears that I couldn't understand a reason for having in the first place.

"What's wrong with you, Chippie?" Momma said one night as I was getting into my bed.

I shook my head. "I don't know, Momma. I just feel sad and I don't know why."

She looked over at a painting I had done of the graveyard that I had played in back at our old house. I had painted the big oak tree, the broken headstones, and angels flying above the cemetery.

"That's morbid, Chippie. I don't want you painting no more graveyards."

"It's beautiful to me," I said. "I miss that place, Momma. I feel like if we hadn't left there Granny never would have died and Rusty wouldn't have either. I feel like we'd be riding our ponies and picking blackberries forever."

Momma didn't always tuck me in at fourteen-years-old, but tonight she had wanted to talk to me. She brushed my hair back from my face. "Oh, Chippie, life's got bigger things for you than riding your ponies and picking blackberries. You always were a funny kid, always feeling and dreaming and pretending stuff. You're special, smart and I want you to promise me something right now. I want you to promise that you'll use all these talents of yours to make something of yourself. I'm proud of you. Your brothers and sisters are good kids, but they're all looking to you to lead the way for them, show them that a Pablo can do anything you set your mind to." She kissed me on the cheek. "Now get some sleep, young-un."

Momma turned out my light and closed my door. She had always made me feel warm all over whenever she showed me love like that. But this night, the sad feeling didn't leave me. It only got worse. Then I realized what it was. I worried that there would come a day in the future when Momma and Daddy were gone and I was grown. I wondered if all my brothers and sisters would still be alive and, if we were, would we drift apart? That was the worse thing I could think of and that was the thing that just tore me up inside. One day, I would not have Momma in my life. She would grow older and die as Rusty and Granny Eastridge had done.

I cried until I fell asleep.

* * *

High school had been in session for two days. I had found it to be a wonderful place compared to Briar Ridge Elementary School. All my friends from eighth grade were there; even Jesse, who swore that he wasn't going to high school. The county social office said he had to go until his sixteenth birthday, which wasn't until November.

I immediately joined the Art club and took more than the sixteen credits required. I talked the counselor into letting me take eighteen. I was so excited about the art classes that on the second day of school, I meant to spend my lunchtime in the art room drawing. The teacher, Mrs. Sneed, a gray-haired lady in her mid-thirties with the figure of a pencil and the face of a Christmas tree angel, told me to go eat lunch. I liked Mrs. Sneed right away. She talked like a city slicker and grinned like a little gray possum.

The best thing about high school was that Jerry Wayne was in my homeroom. I was fourteen. He was sixteen, but we were starting high school together and had already talked about how we would graduate together, how we would be the first Pablos in history to get high school diplomas. We would set a new standard and we would do it together.

Jerry Wayne would watch my back and not let anyone make fun of me for being a geek and I would make sure he never made below a 'C' on his report card. It was a beautiful arrangement. Other than homeroom, the only class we had together was Math, which Jerry Wayne was taking for the second time.

For my extra credit class, I took Spanish. That night when Daddy was sitting at the table, having his nightly coffee, I went into my room and took my schedule out of my tablet. I held it for a moment, imagining the day when I would speak Spanish as well as I spoke English, when I could speak the language my family hadn't used in eighty years. I stepped back through the kitchen door and eased into a chair at the table.

"What are you grinning about, Sis?"

"Daddy." I laid the paper on the table in front of me, even though I knew he couldn't read it. "I'm going to learn how to speak Spanish."

"What're you talking about?"

"Mexican, Daddy. I'm going to speak Mexican just like Great-grandpa did."

Daddy set his coffee down and gritted his teeth. "Sissy..." He shook his head.

I didn't understand what the problem was. I fumbled with my paper, drawing it closer to myself.

"You don't understand. We been treated like colored folks my whole life. I want better than that for you kids. That's why we don't speak Mexican. I don't want you speaking Mexican just like Momma's people didn't want me speaking it when I was little. My Uncle Henry spanked me for saying words I heard from Grandpa until I learned the difference. I forgot them Mexican words. Forgot every one of them and here you are wanting to go dig them up again."

I stood up, tears in my eyes. I didn't know why I was crying; why my heart felt like it was coming up into my mouth. I clutched my schedule to my chest. "They had no right to do that. They were Cherokee. They should've understood how a person needs to know."

"Yeah, they were Indian and because some of them were like you and wouldn't keep quiet about it, they lost everything they had," Daddy said. "They lost it cause they weren't white, Sissy. If you ain't white and you got no land, you get no respect from anybody. You kids got a chance to have better than I ever had, and I don't want you getting notions in your head 'bout telling everybody you're Mexican. I can't help being Mexican, but you don't have to be. Your skin ain't black like mine. You can be anything you want to be."

I felt my face scrunch up. My voice came out quivery and my legs were shaky. "I am Mexican, and I'm proud that I am," I said. "'Cause I'm your daughter. If you're Mexican then I am too. I can't be something different than you, and I'm white too, 'cause Momma is. And I'm Cherokee 'cause Grandma was. If I was black like your Uncle Ben Lee Garney and his girls, then I'd be proud I was black. I'd learn everything I could about Africa. I'd be a proud black person. I'm going to speak Spanish and I'm going to speak it good."

Daddy made a fist. I thought he was going to pound the table. Instead, he brought it down with control and silence. "Sis, don't go on with such foolishness."

I straightened and made myself taller, as if the action would give me more courage, make my words stronger. "It ain't foolishness, Daddy. You're going to see. I'm going to make you proud of being Mexican. One day when people hear the name of Pablo, they're going to say it with respect."

"Aw, Sissy," Daddy said. "You're so dag-gum stubborn, just like your Momma. If any kid can make something of herself, it's you. Go on and learn your Mexican talk, but don't be using it over at the store in front of people."

I nodded. "You'll be proud of me."

Daddy took a drink of coffee then set it down again. "You know what would really make me proud? You getting a high school education and writing it all down. The whole story of my life and your grandpa's life and your great grandpa's, if you wrote a book about us Pablos for a time in the future when it don't matter too much if a person's got Mexican blood or not."

I stood at my door. "I will, Daddy. I'll write a story that'll make us proud."

CHAPTER SEVENTEEN

Near the end of August, the church had a revival. Deanna's daddy didn't preach it though. He called in an evangelist. This evangelist was the roundest man I'd seen in my life. His face was shaped like a basketball with a button nose. He wore his red-brown hair in a bowl hair cut with bangs he couldn't keep out of his eyes. A pair of thick black-rimmed glasses made his eyes look bigger than any human's should, but there was something about him, something kind.

It was hot out, yet I wore long sleeves and a denim skirt to the meeting on Saturday night, a perfect fall outfit. The shirt was a soft white cotton button-up with little blue clouds all over it. I'd bought that outfit with some of my tobacco money and was extremely pleased with my taste. So, I pushed the sleeves up and wore it anyway.

I sat by Deanna and Jesse as I always did. Clint Kurtsinger, the boy with Asian eyes, and Jesse's brothers sat behind us. It was all Deanna and Jesse could do to keep their hands off of each other. It wasn't that Jesse liked Deanna. He liked making out with her, because she knew no limit. She knew no shame. Sometimes, I was ashamed for her. I thought if my dad was a preacher, I wouldn't do the things she did. One time she told me that she hated her mom and dad, and didn't want to be like them when she grew up.

I couldn't imagine hating my parents. I felt sorry for her Momma and Daddy. Deanna's Momma was a thin lady in her mid-thirties, who was battling breast cancer. Every time I looked at that woman, my heart hurt. I couldn't understand how Deanna could be so carefree, knowing that her Momma might die. But in my opinion, though, Deanna was my friend, I was firmly convinced that she was what Jerry Wayne meant when he talked about airhead girls.

That night the evangelist said something about having to make a public profession of faith to please God and go to Heaven. Neither Granny Eastridge nor Grandma Pablo had ever said such a thing and I was sure they were in Heaven. But this man knew so much about the Bible and all the stories in it. He could quote the words of Jesus. Then I realized I had never made a "public profession of faith". So, near the end of his sermon, my heart beat faster and faster. My face was sweating and my hands, too.

Then he had the choir sing, 'Just as I am'. I wanted to go. I wanted to show God that I really did love him. But there was Deanna and Jesse, looking all googly-eyed at each other, and the Kurtsinger boys sitting right behind me. I clutched the wooden pew, brown and shiny from a hundred years of varnish and backs swiping against it. I wrestled within myself. What would all my friends at school say if they knew I'd got religion? But I felt as if I was a little iron nail and the altar was a giant loadstone.

I swallowed and pecked Deanna on the shoulder. "I'm going up," I said. Then I bolted from my seat and headed to the altar where that fat little preacher with the bowl haircut met me.

I knelt at the altar railing. "Now, honey," he said. "What's your name?"

"Chippie," I said.

"Well, Chippie, all you got to do is confess your sins

to the Lord and he will wash your crimson stains as white as snow."

I couldn't think of any sins at the moment, so I just said, "Lord forgive me of all the bad things I've done."

"Now, repeat after me," he said. "Lord, you said in your word that if we confessed Jesus with our mouths."

I repeated his words.

He went on. "And believed in our hearts that God had raised him from the dead. Do you believe, Chippie? If you do, repeat what I just said."

I nodded and then repeated his words.

"Then you shall be saved," he said.

"Then you shall be saved," I said.

"Now, Chippie, you are saved, born again, a new creation in Christ. Do you believe that?"

"Yes, sir, I do," I said.

Then the minister had me stand up and he called for the church to come up and welcome me into the family of God. I didn't look at the people, especially not my friends in the back rows who never came down that isle. I just stood there, not letting the tears that were trying to sneak out of my eyes get on my face. I did not want to cry in front of all of those people. I kept saying on the inside to God that I loved him and I wanted to do something good with my life.

In the car, on the way home, Idy Jo Page said, "That

was a real smart thing you did tonight, Chippie. And brave, too."

When I got home, I went in and found that only Momma was still up. I guess the meeting had gone on later than I thought. She'd been waiting on me there on our orange vinyl couch. "'Bout time you got home."

She stood to give me a good night kiss as I crossed the threshold between the living room and the kitchen.

"I got saved tonight, Momma."

She looked at me in a way I couldn't determine, kind of distant and uncomfortable. "Saved from what, baby? I didn't know you were lost."

I did not know how to answer her, so I said, "Good night, Mommy, I love you."

       * * *

High school got into full swing. I loved my Art class so much that I spent my lunch breaks painting instead of eating. Sometimes the teacher ran me out and made me go eat, but she must have seen my love of art, because most days she just left me alone and let me paint. I made the highest grades in my Art class and nearly missed the bus everyday, because I tried to squeeze in every last second of painting. It was so different than Briar Ridge Elementary School, a whole new world, one that I just loved.

I didn't sign up for cross-country or track. I knew I couldn't afford the uniform, so I just didn't even mention it to my parents. I would sometimes watch the drill team practice and wish I could be a part of that, but then again, there was the uniform thing. I didn't have to worry about the likes of Corkie and Jeremy, who had given me so much trouble in eighth grade, either. They ran with a different crowd than I did. Our paths rarely crossed.

One afternoon as I was getting on the bus, Deanna handed me a note from Jesse. In Jesse's hen scratch writing it read, "Deer Chipe, Clint K. wants to no if you will go wit him."

I folded it up and handed it back to Deanna. "That's a mean joke to play on me. You tell Jesse I said so."

"It's not a joke," she said. "Clint's got a big crush on you. He's been seeing you at church and wants to go with you. So, what do you say?"

"It's not a joke?"

"No, not a joke."

I thought about Clint, the boy with Asian eyes, who knew all the answers in Sunday school, the boy who was completely out of high school with a car of his own and a job down at the sawmill. He liked me? A fourteen-year-old freshman? I was way too young for him. And he was so much better looking than me. Why would a good-looking boy, who wasn't mean or perverted like Damien, want to go with me?

I shrugged. "I don't know what to say."
"Just say yes," Deanna said.

I took a pencil from one of my notebooks and wrote 'yes' on Jesse's little note.

The following Saturday Jesse and Clint pulled up in my driveway in a 68 Chevy. I started out the door, wearing bibbed overalls and pigtails.

"Chippie," Momma said from the kitchen. "Why's that Kurtsinger boy here?"

I hung my head, a little embarrassed. "Momma, he asked me to go with him."

"Go where?"

"Nowhere, Momma. You know...to GO with him."

"You mean he wants to court?"

"That's what y'all called it, Momma, now we say that people are going together."

She looked at me and scowled. "Well, you sure didn't fix up none for the boy."

Again, I was nervous and stuck my hands in my pockets. "Um, I just figured that if he liked me looking as bad as I can look, then he must really like me."

Momma laughed. "Good point."

Me and Clint sat on his car hood and talked, then taking Willie and Jerry Wayne along with us, went up to Briar Ridge and played a game of basketball on the court, something all the local kids did when school was not in session.

That next day, Sunday evening, September 7, I sat by Clint Kurtsinger at church. I wore my favorite white sundress and my hair down, because I liked the way it felt on my bare shoulders. It was a special service as a southern gospel group from Edmonton had come to sing to us and there was no preaching. The group was made up of a family. There was a girl, not much older than me, who could sing as well as any country star I had ever heard, and so could her momma. They had received a record offer from a company in Nashville, but turned it down because they wanted to use their gifts and talents for the Lord.

After church, Clint walked me out to Idy Jo's car while we waited on her to finish talking to her lady friends. He gave me a blue ring with two hearts on it. I knew it came from the five and ten cent store and was a very cheap ring, but it meant so much that he cared enough about me to buy me something. The only boy who had ever bought me a present was Jerry Wayne.

"It's beautiful," I said, putting it on.

"This means you're my girl," he said. "I have to go into town in the morning to get some things for Momma. Want me to stop by your house and give you a ride to school?"

"Yeah," I said. "Let me ask Momma first."

So, it was a plan. If my parents gave the okay, I could ride to school with Clint, instead of Jerry Wayne.

Soon as I got home, I let in to asking Momma and Daddy. I reasoned and pleaded until Momma finally said, "Go ask your daddy." And Daddy said, "Go ask your Momma." Of course, when they started doing that the thing was settled. Clint was going to get to take me to school.

Jerry Wayne wasn't home when I got there. He had gone swimming with Damien and J.R, a second cousin that had moved down from Indiana. Daddy and Jerry Wayne had a big fight that morning over it, because Daddy had a terrible fear of water. Jerry Wayne got so mad at Daddy that he kicked his tire and said he was going anyway. I felt uneasy about him going, too, but I was so excited about having a real boyfriend that I ignored the queasiness in my gut.

After getting my parents' okay to ride with Clint, I started picking out the clothes I would wear to school the next day. I was in my room, rummaging through the cupboard I used as a closet, when the phone rang.

The moment it rang, a knot came up in my chest. I started walking through the little kids' room to Momma and Daddy's room to answer the phone when I heard Daddy say, "Hello," in the loud, slow way he always used on the phone. Daddy had lived his whole life without a phone and it was a wondrous contraption for him. He always held the receiver as if it were made of clay.

I stood in the doorway, watching, listening, and trying to figure out who was on the other end.

"Yeah, this here's Joe Pablo."

A long silence. Whoever it was, they were saying something that was draining the color from Daddy's face.

"No," Daddy said in such a way that it sounded like a dog that had just been shot in the leg. He dropped the receiver, let it just dangle on its long cord. And I knew it was something terrible.

"Oh God, honey, Jerry Wayne's drowned. Oh God, our baby's dead. Our baby's dead." He paced the floor, saying over and over, "Oh God, our baby's dead."

Momma clutched herself and fell against the door just like somebody had stabbed her right in the heart.

I can't describe how I felt in that moment. Sort of like the walls of my house had fallen down and I discovered I was standing where there was no ground, nor sky, nor right or left. I felt I was tumbling into darkness and there was nothing tangible to grab hold of.

I had never seen my Daddy go to pieces like that, but he was screaming and crying and shaking and holding Momma who was wailing, "No!" Then all the kids started crying, too. They were walking around the house aimlessly, wailing. Everyone was crying, everyone but me. I stood there, unable to move or think or speak.

Somehow Daddy managed to get us all from the house to the car and he drove as fast as he could into town. I remember Momma saying at one point, "Slow down, honey, or we're going to end up going off one of these bluffs and killing the whole family."

There wasn't much talking after that, just more crying. So much crying. It was like my hands and head and body were all detached from me and the real Chippie had just got up and left, run away and deserted me when I needed her most.

Momma and Daddy dropped us off at Grandpa Eastridge's house. Everything was a blur. No one's words registered well in my mind, but somehow I came to understand that my parents had to go identify the body.

Grandpa Eastridge held Momma. All he said in his coarse and little used voice was, "Of course your kids can stay here."

We stayed up a long time waiting for Momma and Daddy to come back. Lou Annie, Willie and I stood on the porch, watching the highway. I found myself staring at the sky. There were billions of stars. They would have been brighter if we hadn't been so close to town and the streetlights hadn't been on.

I stood with my hand on the porch post and found myself whispering, "Please, God, you can do anything. Don't let that be Jerry Wayne up there dead in the funeral home. Let him just get up. Bring him back to life. Raise him up from the dead. Please, God, please." I kept on saying this, but inside I knew that it was meant to be that Jerry Wayne had to die, and I hated that knowing.

Lou Annie came over to me and I held her. She talked, but I had no idea what she said. I just held her. For the moment, she was the only thing real in my whole world. When Momma and Daddy came back, they gathered all of us kids into Grandpa Eastridge's kitchen. Some of us sat on the floor, some of us on chairs, and some of us stood. I leaned up against the wall behind the woodstove.

"Jerry Wayne's dead," Momma said, her tears starting up again. "But we got to pull together to get through this."

"In the morning, they're going to have him out," Daddy said. "Sissy, you've got the most level head of anybody right now. Go in there. Get on the phone and call up your aunts and uncles."

I walked into the living room, a tall room papered in yellow flowered wallpaper. A burgundy couch sat against one wall, a chair against another, and a table with a television and a phone sat near the front door. I stared at the shiny black phone. I wanted to throw it away. I wondered if, for the rest of my life, if I'd jump every time the phone rang. I wondered if I would always fear death was on the other end.

Then I thought of Jerry Wayne, how he had bought our phone and been so proud of it. I took the cool receiver in my hand and dialed a number. First, I called Aunt Kate, then Aunt Suez, then went on down the list, until they had all been called. Each time, I numbly said, "Hello, this is Chippie. Jerry Wayne's dead. He drowned this afternoon in Coffee's Hole while him and Damien and J.R. Sherman was swimming." Then I would have to answer their questions as best as I could.

We left Grandpa Eastridge's afterwards and went to visit J.R.'s momma, Wilma Jean Sherman. Her man had left her all alone up in Indiana. She had moved back home to Kentucky and lived in a white four-room house down in White City. She was sitting on the couch, bawling when we got there.

J.R. didn't say a word. He just sat on the couch, his long brown hair concealing his face. He was very tall and thin. His clothes were stained and torn. There was something soft and pitiful about him, like an owl that had lost its ability to see in the dark. I didn't think he looked like white trash, just kind of poor and skinny, like the rest of us. I wish I had been able to become his friend under a different set of circumstances.

As we sat there in the wee early morning hours, the obituaries came over the radio, and the announcer told about Jerry Wayne drowning. He named off all of us kids and Momma and Daddy and Grandpa Eastridge as survivors. The crying started up again and I just went out to get some air.

I didn't hear the screen door slam shut behind me and turned around to see why. J.R. was standing there holding it. He followed me out. I sat on the curb. He came and sat beside me.

"It's my fault," he said in his Indiana accent.

I shook my head, "No, it's not anybody's fault. It just happened. But I wish I could have been there. Maybe I could've saved Jerry Wayne."

J.R. broke down and cried. "I'm glad you weren't there. I'm glad you didn't have to see. I was too scared, Chippie. I froze. I couldn't do a thing but stand there. I was too scared, and Damien, he was too drunk and mad."

"Drunk? Was Jerry Wayne drunk, too?"

J.R. shook his head. "No, Damien brought the liquor and planned on getting Jerry Wayne drunk, then beating him up. But Jerry Wayne wouldn't drink any of it. He knew Damien was up to something and jumped in the water ahead of us."

"Why?"

"'Cause Damien found out this girl he's been seeing liked Jerry Wayne." He shook his head. "I shouldn't have told you that." He took my hand and squeezed it. "I'm sorry, Chippie. I'm so sorry. Will you ever forgive me? It should have been me that drowned."

He dropped his head into his hands and cried like a little six-year-old boy. I don't know what made me do it, but I put my arms around him and held him until he had cried all the tears his body had. I felt sorry for him, and at the same time, I wished that it had been Damien that drowned in Coffee's Hole and not Jerry Wayne.

The days that followed went by like a blur. Momma and Daddy insisted that Jerry Wayne would be laid out in a real funeral home, not in the house. Our parents took all of us kids to pick out Jerry Wayne's casket. They said he was our brother and that Jerry Wayne would want us all to have a say in things, even down to little Josh David.

The funeral home director knew we had no money. He knew we could never pay for the funeral. He told Momma and Daddy that they could take as long as they needed to pay it off. They could just pay five dollars a month or whatever they could afford. He was a kind man, soft-spoken, with a big nose, white hair, thick glasses and a dark blue suit. I liked him.

The local men's shop, run by Clint Kurtsinger's uncle, donated clothes for Jerry Wayne's funeral. Momma requested that Jerry Wayne be buried in blue jeans and a blue-checkered western style shirt. He had always liked western style shirts. Some ladies from the Methodist church bought clothes for the rest of us to wear to the funeral. We had never had such fine clothes in our lives. It was a strange time, all of us agreeing on everything, seeing Momma crying all the time and Daddy, who was always laughing and talking, saying nary a word.

After the funeral home closed down for the night, Idy Jo and Tiny Elmer came over and just stood in the driveway with Momma and Daddy. They talked about how they had lost their little girl. Idy Jo cried. Then she brought over cakes and potato salad.

"Y'all got to eat something, Jewell," she said. "Starving won't bring Jerry Wayne back, and your little ones are hungry." Momma said she was right and told us kids to go in the house and eat. We went in, but we didn't eat. Normally, we would have loved cake, but now it just didn't matter much, not without Jerry Wayne to eat it with us.

I kept thinking, wondering if Jerry Wayne was scared or if he suffered or felt any pain. I kept thinking about my brother lying at the bottom of that creek, lost all afternoon and about how the man on the radio said the rescue squad had to drag the creek bottom for him. A whirlpool, the newsman had said. I didn't even know a creek could have a whirlpool. Now they were calling Coffee's swimming hole, Deadman's Hole. I hated that name and I hated that place for killing Jerry Wayne.

All our relatives came to the funeral. They came from Indiana, Tennessee, and Arkansas, but most came from the same place they had been born, the farms and hills of southern Kentucky. The high school took up a collection for us, and red-haired Emily brought it to the funeral home and gave it to me.

I called Clint Kurtsinger from the funeral home about four o'clock in the afternoon. I knew he'd had time to get off from work by then.

"Did you hear about Jerry Wayne?" I said.

"Momma told me that it was on the radio," he said.

"I wish you'd come down here," I told him. "Seeing how you're my boyfriend and all."

"Funeral homes make me nervous, Chippie."

"Well," I said. "They make everybody nervous, but when somebody dies, you just have to go to them."

"All right, I'll be there," he said. Then I heard his momma talking in the background.

"I don't want you goin', Clint. I am sorry for what's happened to them," she said, "but you don't need to be a-seein' that Mexican girl."

I got so upset that I hung up on Clint. Then he showed up there at the funeral home, telling me he was sorry for what his momma had said and that he'd be there to help my family anyway he could. My momma heard him say it and she hugged him for it.

Clint stayed with me until after dark. The moments he was there made the nightmare a little easier to live in. We sat on the front steps of the funeral home and talked. Then I stood up on the porch railing, the moonlight falling on my skin. It looked silver like a fairy's wings. And I was wearing a purple dress with puffy sleeves. Clint reached up and put his hands on my waist, then lifted me off the railing like I was a little doll. He spun me around and sat me down. Then he bent right down and kissed me. It was just like a fairy tale. I was a girl in a world of troubles and he was a knight coming to my rescue to carry me off to some place where nobody ever died.

He didn't have to come to the funeral home or be with me in such a sad time, yet there he was. Surely a person wouldn't do that unless he loved me. "I love you," I said, before I even realized what had popped out of my mouth.

"I love you, too," he said. Then the sound of someone approaching closed the door on that magical land of knights and princesses. Momma came around the corner of the building.

"There you are," she said. "Chippie, I want you to go get something to eat."

"I'll take her up to the Burger Queen," Clint said.

Momma smiled. "Take good care of her, Clint. You're a good boy."

The funeral was the hardest part, sitting there as Deanna's father tried to preach the funeral of a teenage boy through his own tears and the whole room was filled with sobs and wails. So many people came that they had to stand in the hallway. We had so many relatives. All of Jerry Wayne's friends came. All the kids from my eighth grade class at Briar Ridge came.

Everywhere I looked there were tears. Everyone was crying, everyone but me. Jerry Wayne was my brother and my best friend. He was my hero and a part of every memory I'd had since the day I was born, yet I couldn't cry. I went into the ladies' bathroom and locked the door. I stood, staring at myself in the mirror, wondering where my tears were. I looked like a girl, but surely only a monster couldn't cry at her own beloved brother's funeral. Why was I so numb inside?

Momma knocked on the door. "Chippie?"

I opened it. "Yeah, Momma."

"You okay, honey?"

"Just wondering is all. Why can't I cry?"

Momma stroked my hair. "Chippie, it's okay. Some people give their flowers before the funeral. Jerry Wayne wasn't much for crying neither. You're strong, Chippie, and we all need that right now. We're going to need it tomorrow and the next day and when Christmas comes without Jerry Wayne...and..."

She couldn't say anymore. I put my arm around my Momma's waist and walked with her back to the parlor, back to where the sad music was playing and words were still being spoken, back to say good-bye to Jerry Wayne.

That night, I sat alone in my room. I took out my little blue diary that Granny Eastridge had given me for graduation and took a pen in my hand. When I tried to write, the only things that would come were a terrible lump in my throat and an empty feeling in my chest. I could not write, not that night nor the next one. I locked the blue diary, placing it in the bottom of my closet. I didn't know if I would ever be able to write again or if the lump in my chest would stop the feelings and thoughts from flowing out to my hand for the rest of my life.

CHAPTER EIGHTEEN

The wake of my brother's death was much like the aftermath of a tornado in that it left debris all over our lives, just lying there in silent despair. Daddy cried nearly all the time. When he wasn't at work, he was walking the woods. He muttered over and over. "A man ought not to outlive his boy. It ain't right. It ain't right at all."

He'd sometimes stare at a black and white photo of him and Momma. It had been taken just before I was born. Jerry Wayne, who was two-years-old at the time stood in the background. He had sneaked into the picture and was in there by accident. Daddy would look at that and mumble things under his breath.

Momma didn't want to talk about Jerry Wayne at all. She couldn't bring herself to go into his bedroom or sort out the laundry he had left behind. Jerry Wayne was born just a year and half after she married Daddy. She'd been seventeen.

Three days after the funeral, I did the only thing I knew to do. I went to school. Momma said we didn't have to go until we were ready. But I figured that if I was going to be numb inside, I'd just as soon be numb at school.

Nobody spoke much to me during the morning classes. Every so often someone would say, "I'm so sorry to hear." People's faces were strained and sad to see. Both teachers and students were bothered by Jerry Wayne's death. When I walked down the hall, a hush fell over the kids standing at their lockers. Looking at me reminded everybody of Jerry Wayne.

During my afternoon break, I went behind the

school where a catwalk ran from the schoolhouse, a red brick building, up to the agriculture building. Kids hung out here between classes, smoking, talking, and just relaxing. I found a quiet place where steps led down into the school basement. I sat down.

I had tried to just keep moving through the grayness of the day, of everything; just keep moving and not think. But now I thought. I thought about how I used to ride to school with Jerry Wayne. I remembered how he came to my basketball games and how he had faced that wild dog. I thought of how his hair always fell in his eyes and how pretty his brown eyes had been. I recalled how Jerry Wayne didn't want to move to Briar Ridge. "I miss you," I whispered. "I miss you so much." A tear slid down my cheek. I was crying, not for Jerry Wayne, but for me, for my life without him in it.

Then I realized there was someone sitting beside me. I looked up and there was Jesse. Why he was there and where he had come from, I did not know, but he was there. He never said a word. He just took my hand in his and held it. We sat there a long time, neither one speaking, just holding hands. The afternoon bell rang, and I stood.

"You okay?" he said.

"I will be." I wanted to tell him how much him sitting there had meant to me, how much his being my friend meant to me, but I couldn't find the words. "Thank you," I said, then headed off to my Algebra class.

Two weeks passed and my fifteenth birthday rolled around. Late September in southern Kentucky usually brings temperatures in the eighties and late afternoons of golden sunshine with sharp shadows, so Momma planned to have me a birthday party at the state park, just outside of town. Parties weren't something I was used to having, because we rarely had money for them, but we needed something away from the sadness, something to remind us that we were still alive. She planned it for Saturday afternoon. She and Lou Annie called all our cousins, aunts and uncles.

When I woke up Saturday morning, it was forty-five degrees, not a normal September morning and not a good day for an outdoor party. Momma went ahead with her plans anyway. The temperature never climbed higher than the mid-fifties all day, so everyone showed up at the park wearing jackets. Still, they showed up. I don't know if they came for me, for Jerry Wayne, or for themselves, but my cousins on both sides of the family came. My aunts and uncles came, Eastridges and Pablos.

Momma put on a smile and served cake, yet sadness hung over her and over Daddy who stood off to himself under an oak tree.

Clint Kurtsinger came. He picked up Jesse and Deanna on the way. Before the meal was served, the four of us walked over little wooden bridges, talking, then we played a little Frisbee. I was terrible with it, but my three friends didn't seem to mind.

After blowing out my candles and eating some cake, I opened my gifts, a necklace from Uncle Dody Eastridge, a bracelet from Aunt Pinky, and cards from the Pablos. I knew they couldn't afford gifts and that was okay with me. There was a small neatly wrapped package from

Aunt Darla Eastridge. She had mailed it all the way from Memphis.

"Well, open it," Momma said, smiling. She obviously knew what was in the package.

I cautiously tore at the paper, Jesse and Deanna looking over one shoulder, Clint over the other, and all my relatives watching.

I removed the lid from the box, and then quickly pushed it back down. I was too late. Everyone had seen the lacey red panties.

"Aw, come on, Chippie, everybody wears panties," Momma said. "Hold them up. Show us what they look like."

I couldn't believe Momma was saying that, and she was laughing, really laughing. For the first time since Jerry Wayne's death, everyone was light-hearted. In spite of my embarrassment, I quickly held them up. Red lace bikini panties, and then I stuffed them back in the box and slammed the lid on them, much to Momma's delight.

After a while, the relatives started to drift, one family leaving at a time, until it was just us, Momma, Daddy and the six of us kids. We cleaned up our belongings, piled in the station wagon, and went home.

* * *

Sunday morning, my whole family went to church. After the service, my daddy walked up to the altar and told the preacher he wanted to be saved so he could be in Heaven with his boy when he died. My daddy knelt down at the altar that morning and dedicated his life to the Lord.

In the weeks that followed, Daddy went to church every Sunday morning and night. He went on Wednesday, too. He went to the Methodist church. Then he started going to the Church of God in town and to the Holiness church over in Jabez, and he went to the tent meetings and the brush arbor meetings, where Christians gathered around a large bonfire and listened to sermons way into the night. There would be singing and people crying out, repenting of their sins and turning their lives over to God. He went to every gospel singing he could find and dinners on the ground down at the Baptist Church. A dinner on the ground was an event where folks would come from all over, bringing dishes of food, fried chicken, green beans, pintos, corn bread, potato salad, baked beans, fried green tomatoes, peach cobbler and just about any other mouth-watering dish you could think of. Some women from the church would cover long tables with sheets or cloths and set it all out. People would line up and pile their plates high, then go sit on the ground and eat. After everyone had their fill, some singers would get up and sing, then a preacher would preach, then another preacher and sometimes it would go on four or five hours. Daddy even went up to the Nazarene a few times. Wherever there was a meeting, that's where my daddy could be found. He was rarely at home after dark. When he wasn't in church, he was out at the graveyard, one hand on Jerry Wayne's tombstone, the other on the ground, talking to the Lord.

At home, he didn't talk about fixing up the house like he used to. He didn't talk about the mill or picking up corn for his boss. He talked about church and the people that went there. He talked about being baptized and filled with the Holy Ghost. Momma got to where she didn't want to sit up and drink coffee with him anymore. She took to playing cards way into the night with Lou Annie and one of Jesse's brothers.

All this time, I dated Clint Kurtsinger. I played basketball up at Briar Ridge Elementary with him, Willie and Jesse on Saturdays while Deanna sat on the car hood watching. She never played ball on account of how her triple D-size chest got in her way so much. Besides, she wasn't very coordinated. I was not a good player, but I was fast and sneaky. This kept Jesse and Clint on their toes and made them laugh. Plus, we played with street rules, meaning that we made our own.

I guess in the grief of losing Jerry Wayne, my parents didn't worry too much about me. Once, Momma even told Clint that she was glad I had somebody around to take my mind off things. Clint liked Momma's cooking and would come over to eat her pinto beans and chili just about every Saturday night. He also liked to watch television and talk religion with Daddy. So, my folks took a real shine to him, even if he did look like a boy from China. I loved how he wore a bandana around his head when we played basketball. I thought it made him look like Bruce Lee.

One Saturday evening in mid November after our regular basketball game, Clint dropped Jesse and Deanna off, then took me on home. It was nearly dark when I got home, although it was just about five o'clock. As I pushed open the front door, heat from the wood stove rushed into my face. The smell of joule meat, which came off the fat sagging jaws of the hog frying in the kitchen, told me supper was soon coming. I smelled strong coffee, too. Momma was kneading biscuit dough on the table. I thought of how she used to hum while she kneaded the dough. She hadn't hummed since early September.

Daddy brought an armload of wood in the front door, kicking the mud off his boots onto the threshold as he did. He dumped it down in the wood box behind the stove. At the very moment he raised up, Lou Annie came waltzing into the living room. She had come from the back, from Jerry Wayne's room, and she was wearing one of his shirts, a lavender western style shirt with pearl white snaps that Momma had made him the week before he died.

She had the shirt tucked in her jeans and they looked tight. It wasn't because she tried to be indecent. It was just that she had always had a slight weight problem and clothes never fit her for long before they got too little. Lou Annie had outgrown nearly everything she had, and there was no one to give her hand-me-downs. All of mine went to little Zelphie who was almost as big as me.

"Where'd you get that shirt?" Daddy said.

"It's Jerry Wayne's," Lou Annie said. "I don't think he'd want his clothes just to lie in there and rot."

Daddy gritted his teeth and pointed his finger. "You get in yonder and take my boy's clothes off right now. You ain't got no right wearing my boy's clothes."

I don't know which shocked me more, Daddy's words or Lou Annie's face. She burst into tears.

"Honey," Momma said, coming from the kitchen. "She's right. Jerry Wayne always shared ever-"

"Get them clothes off." Daddy yelled. "They're Jerry Wayne's."

I had never seen Daddy act like that, but he hadn't acted one bit like himself since the day Jerry Wayne died.

Lou Annie turned and ran into the other room, sobbing loudly as she went. I took after her immediately. I understood how it must have shocked Daddy to see her wearing Jerry Wayne's shirt, but Lou Annie was just a girl. She meant no harm.

I held her that day while she cried. And I knew that nothing in our house would ever be the same.

The following week Damien's family came up. I was back in Jerry Wayne's room, looking through his notebooks, just reading his homework, some of it we'd done together. I loved the way he wrote with a left-hand slant.

I looked up and there stood Damien in the doorway.

"Hey, Chippie," he said.

"What do you want?" I didn't care if he knew I didn't want to talk to him.

"Well other than pulling up your shirt and seeing what's under it-"

"If you touch my shirt, I'll knock your head off," I said. And I meant it.

"Be cool, Chippie, I just wanted to talk."

I closed the notebook. I didn't want that moron looking at my brother's stuff. He didn't have enough sense to be sad or understand what it's like to lose someone.

"I know you think I killed Jerry Wayne, but I didn't. I swear it. I tried to save him."

I had trouble believing Damien could try to save anyone and J.R. hadn't mentioned it.

"You got to believe me, Chippie. I didn't kill Jerry Wayne."

"Did you try to get them drunk?"

He slammed the wall. "Aw hell, Chippie. J.R. told you that, didn't he?"

"What if he did?"

"J.R.'s an idiot. He was so tore up he don't know what happened. We both were. I swear to you, Chippie. I never would have hurt Jerry Wayne."

"But you were planning to beat him up."

"I wasn't planning to kill 'im. Him drowning wasn't my fault."

But you tried to hurt me. I reckon that wasn't your fault either, I thought. Then I remembered how I had feared for Jerry Wayne. Nobody knew what J.R. had said. Nobody but me. If I told anybody, it would drive a wedge between our entire families. I would wait. If he really had been to blame, one day I would discover the truth.

"Chippie, please believe me. I don't want you thinking I'm a killer. I have done a lot of bad things. I know that, but I'm not a killer. Don't hate me. Please don't hate me." He looked like he was going to cry. I didn't want to see that. I didn't like him and I sure didn't want him crying on my shoulder.

"All right," I said. "I don't hate you. I don't like you, but I don't reckon I hate you either." Maybe he wasn't a killer. Maybe he was just a pervert, a thief and a liar. I didn't know. One thing for sure was that he was pretty pathetic. "Let's go in yonder where Momma and Daddy are." I didn't want to be in the room alone with him anymore.

He went into the kitchen and sat at the table with the grown-ups. I sat in a chair in a corner of the living room, picked up a notebook, and started drawing a picture of mountains and trees. Lou Annie was on the couch, watching television.

Damien's momma came in the front door. She'd been to the outhouse. She noticed me sitting over there, not talking, just drawing. She stood and watched for a while, puckering up her red lips, her hands on her hips. She stepped into the kitchen doorway, blocking my good light.

"Jewell, this kid'll never amount to anything. All she ever does is sit in the corner and scribble. That drawing ain't never gonna get her anywhere."

"You're wrong," Momma said. "She's got a gift. And one of these days, it's going to make her rich and famous. You just wait and see. Besides, Chippie's got a lot of book sense. I know she'll make something out of herself."

I wanted to hug Momma for that.

"Well, maybe," my aunt said. "But I don't see how it'll be, and Lou Annie." She looked at my sister with contempt. "Lou Annie gets fatter and fatter. Y'all need to quit feeding her so much."

Daddy looked through the door at Lou Annie curled up on the couch, her white legs sticking out from under her, because she was wearing shorts.

"Get up and put some clothes on."

Lou Annie got up and stomped off into the bedroom. I don't know what the adults said after that. I put my work down and quietly disappeared into my room. I went through the door into the little kids' room where they were all playing with their dolls and trucks.

I found Lou Annie in Jerry Wayne's big old iron bed, the quilt over her head. She was crying. I sat down on the bed beside her.

"It's me," I said. "Please don't be sad, Annie."

"I can take old lipstick face poking fun at me and I can handle the kids at school, but I can't take it from my own Daddy. He's started treating me just like Granny Eastridge used to. And you know why? It's 'cause I'm different. 'Cause I got blonde hair and 'cause I'm big-boned. I ain't that fat. I only wear a size fourteen. Lots of people wear a size fourteen. No, it ain't my weight. It's 'cause I look like the Eastridges, Sissy, and Daddy don't like the Eastridges. So, I reckon he don't like me neither. I am the black sheep in this family, too Pablo for the Eastridges and too Eastridge for the Pablos."

I put my hand on her shoulder. "He loves you. He's just hurting right now. We all are."

She sat up. "That's just it. Jerry Wayne's been gone over two months now. It's almost Thanksgiving and the rest of us have to go on like we don't hurt, but Daddy, he still sits around moping and feeling sorry for himself. He's forgot he's still got six more kids."

"Adults have a way about them," I said. "They can hurt you when you're a teenager and not even realize what they've done. Then I reckon that when they're hurting, well, maybe grown ups are just kids in bigger, hairier bodies."

"One of these days, I'm gonna show 'em all, Chippie. I got dreams, you know."

"Yes, I know."

"Remember how we used to play Cindy and Kathy when we were little?"

"Yeah. I used to be Cindy. I always liked that name. And I always played like I was a famous singer, traveling all over the world."

"Yeah, and I was Kathy, owner of a fine restaurant."

"You said you were going to invent chocolate biscuits in a way that no one would have to go to the trouble of getting the chocolate gravy recipe right."

"That's right and that's my dream."

"Chocolate biscuits?"

"No, silly. To own a fine restaurant. One of them kind that serves wine with the food and has a real band on the stage. I'll have famous singers come and sing nice music. Rich people will pay lots to see people like her and to eat my special food inventions."

"Well, maybe I'll be a famous singer and come sing in your-"

"No, you can't be no singer. You got to be a world famous artist and design the inside of my restaurant and I'll have your pictures all over the wall."

Carol Lee poked her head in the door. "What are y'all talking 'bout?"

"About me being a famous restaurant owner," Lou Annie said.

"And me being the best artist in the world."

"Well," Carol Lee said, putting her little brown hands on her hips. "Know what I'm going to be? I'm going to be a...a..." She twisted her mouth. "I'm going to be on a cartoon."

Lou Annie and I double over laughing at her idea of success.

"Yeah." She threw her hands out in wild gesture. "I'll give people presents that blow up in their faces!" Then she skipped back to her dolls.

CHAPTER NINETEEN

Thanksgiving came and went. Momma fixed a turkey dinner, complete with all the trimmings-cornbread dressing, mashed potatoes, cranberry sauce, and hot biscuits. But this year there was an empty seat in our kitchen, a chair nobody sat in, over by the sink. A strange quietness, not silence, hung over us. It was almost as visible as the swirling smoke that drifted out and rose to the ceiling every time Momma opened the oven door to check on things. That light smoke stayed in our house and played around above our heads. So did the quiet.

Any kind of quietness would have been foreign in our small house of nine people before September. I wondered when the quiet days would end and if every Thanksgiving for the rest of our lives would seem empty like this one. For the first time ever, I dreaded Christmas. I think we all did. How would we go to Granny Eastridge's this year with her not there? How would we stand Christmas morning without Jerry Wayne, or how would it be to get the tree without him? I soon found out.

In mid-December, Daddy called me into the living room where he sat behind the stove rolling cigarettes on a cigarette machine he had used for as long as I could remember. It was a sure sign that we were flat broke whenever Daddy started making cigarettes out of a small hand of tobacco leaves he kept in a dark corner of his bedroom and little scraps of paper. He was desperate for a smoke.

"You want me to roll your cigarettes?" I asked. Daddy handed me the machine. I could always roll a good cigarette and was a good hand at cutting papers for Daddy's machine.

"Sissy," he said. "A man came by here this morning and offered me a hundred dollars for Headache."

I nearly dropped the cigarette machine. "Daddy, I can't sell him. They'll eat him!"

Daddy shook his head. "No, he don't want him for eating. He says Headache never has grown much because he's one of those kinds of pigs that won't grow. The man said Headache will never get big enough to eat. He's bred to be a pet pig. Who ever heard tell of such a thing! Anyway, he's got more money than sense, I reckon. Wants to buy him so he can breed him with a girl pig just like him... Their babies won't never get bigger than fifty pounds. He says people keep them kind of pigs in the house. He promised me he didn't want to kill or eat your pig, Sis. We need that money awful bad. We need it for Christmas."

I nodded. "Okay, Daddy." What could I say? What could any decent girl say to her Daddy who was heartbroken and needing money to buy his little ones Christmas presents? So I had said, "Okay" and I never mentioned it again.

That Saturday morning, a gray pick-up with wooden racks on the bed pulled into our driveway. Daddy went out to meet our visitor and I went, too. A short man in bibbed overalls and a checkered wool jacket got out. He had a cigar in his mouth and wore a red cap with a feed store logo on it. A few tuffs of gray hair stuck out from under the cap.

"Hidy, Joe," the man said. His cigar dangled out one corner of his mouth when he spoke.

"Hidy, Orby," Daddy said. "I reckon you've come for the pig?"

Orby nodded.

"Sissy, run around back and get your pig."

I went behind the house where my pig stood, looking so small and afraid under a pen oak. I knelt beside him and patted his head.

"I'm sorry, Headache," I said. "Sorry about sending you away from the best home you could ever have, away from the ponies you love to run around with and away from me. There ain't no kid in the world gonna love you like I do. But I reckon that's just the way life is sometimes. The things that are so much a part of your world one day, are completely gone the next, with nothing left but a memory and sometimes you feel guilty cause that memory starts to feel like a dream and you wonder if it ever happened at all. Good-bye, my little Headache. Good-bye."

* * *

On Christmas morning, Josh David was the first to awaken. He squealed with delight as he ran through the house, then plopped himself beneath the Christmas tree. He tore into the gifts he believed Santa had brought him. Momma took pictures of him that morning and of Carol Lee and Zelphie as they played with their new dolls, changing their clothes and making them dance to music on a new pink cassette player.

Lou Annie posed with her new clothes on for the camera and Willie held up his plastic monster truck, complete with big wheels and a battery operated motor. And Momma took a picture of me as I painted a picture of brown kittens against an orange background with my new set of poster paints. Yet, the day seemed long and hollow. We didn't go to Granny Eastridge's for Christmas. The worst part about that Christmas Day was that Jerry Wayne wasn't there to tease everyone, or to give me a gag gift. How I wished for a box of rocks.

I walked down by the pond that afternoon. I passed the pigpen, that old haunted truck, and the cross Jerry Wayne and I had put up, and Rusty's grave. I paused there long enough to whisper, "I love you" to the memory of my little brown dog. I stared up at the oak tree that had inspired me to write poetry and thoughts of beauty. Now its leaves were few and brown. It never lost all of its leaves, no matter how bad a winter we got.

When I came to the pond, I sat down on the bank, feeling the cold ground through my pants. My parents had given us the best Christmas they could, but their tears were just below the surface, their pain still so fresh that I could practically smell it in the house. I hugged my knees, buried my face against them, and wept for all the Christmases to come without boxes of rocks wrapped in shiny paper.

That winter stole something from me. Day after gray day, I sat and stared out the window, unable to draw or paint or sing. Whatever the winter took from me was small in comparison to what it took from my parents. I think it robbed them of their youth and of their hope. Sometimes at night, when my door was closed and my lights out, they thought I was asleep, but I could hear them talking in the kitchen over their nightly coffee. One night, Daddy asked Momma why she had told Jerry Wayne he could go swimming after he had said he couldn't.

I could tell Momma was crying by the way her voice shook. "Are you saying that it's my fault Jerry Wayne drowned?"

Daddy didn't answer.

Then Momma said, "If you hadn't yelled at him, he wouldn't have driven off mad that day."

I closed my eyes and bit my bottom lip. Daddy blamed Momma. Momma blamed Daddy and they both blamed themselves.

"Honey," I heard Daddy say. "I have repented before God of my sins and I am forgiven of what I done. Now you need to-"

"I don't want nothing to do with a God that'd let my Momma die and take my boy," Momma cried. I heard her stomp out of the kitchen.

I crept out of my bed and peeped through one of the many holes in my door. Daddy was sitting at the table, staring at his coffee cup. I pushed the door open, went to him and put my arms around him.

"What're you doing up, Sis?"

"I just had to go to the bathroom," I lied.

"Get the flash light off the television," Daddy said.

I walked into the living room, took my coat off a nail behind the front door, then turned around and picked up the flashlight.

"I love you, Daddy," I said. "I love both of y'all." I wanted to tell them that I wished they wouldn't fight anymore, that Jerry Wayne wouldn't want them to fight, and that it wasn't anybody's fault, not theirs, not God's, not anybody's, but somehow the words wouldn't come.

I opened the door and crept out into the night. It was the second day of January and very cold. There were no clouds in the sky and the moonlight was so bright that I really didn't need the flashlight. I looked up at the lone oak tree growing near our house, its black branches stretching their naked arms across the big white moon.

"God," I said. "Why did Jerry Wayne die?"

All I could hear was the rustling of wind in the dry grasses of the fields surrounding our house. I stood quietly. I couldn't tell where the wind came from or where it was going. I couldn't count the stars or understand how a night so stark and cold could be so lovely to look at. "Some things are just bigger than us, I guess," I said to myself.

Inside, I returned Daddy's flashlight to the television, hung my coat up, and stood in the doorway of my parents' room. Daddy was in bed now.

"Good night," I said.

"Good night, honey," Momma said.

"Night, Sissy," Daddy said.

"Good night," I said, and then hurried off to bed.

* * *

About the middle of the month, Clint called me and said his momma wanted to meet me. He said his Momma wanted me to come up and have birthday supper with them. It was Clint's birthday. Momma said I could go and I got real excited.

I picked out the nicest pair of pants I owned and wore a loose white blouse. I thought I looked really nice. I pulled my hair, now well past my shoulders and dark at the roots from where I hadn't been out in the sun in a while, back with combs.

I hadn't fixed up for my first date with Clint, but now I was meeting his momma. That was different. I wanted her to say that I was pretty and that I had good manners. I wanted her to say what a fine girl I was.

Clint came by and picked me up about three o'clock.

"Now, watch your manners," Momma said from the door when I got into the car.

Lou Annie stuck her head out the door. "Don't chew with your mouth open."

I closed my car door and mumbled, "I don't chew with my mouth open." I so hoped Clint's momma would think I was refined.

When I got in the car, Clint said, "Chippie, Momma's not used to having people over and she don't get out much, so you can't pay much attention to some of the stuff she says. Okay?"

"Okay," I said.

"And Uncle Eugene, well, he was a young man in The Depression and has lived by himself for fifty years. He's not quite normal in the head. So, there ain't no telling what he might say. Still, he's a part of my life and I want you to meet him. Just don't get mad if he says something stupid. Okay?"

"Okay," I said, a little more nervous than before now.

Clint lived barely two miles up the road from me; right at the very top of Briar Ridge, we turned down a gravel road that went on for another mile or so past acres of rolling wooded hills with ponds and little white houses scattered about.

"Who all lives here?"

"My aunts and uncles," Clint said. "My family has lived here for over two hundred years. All this land belongs to the Kurtsingers and nobody gets to live here unless they're one of us."

"Wow," I said. "It's beautiful. Reminds me of the place down Walkup Holler where I grew up."

Clint's house sat at the end of the road. There were chickens in the yard and cows in a field on the right. On the left, there were two white horses fenced in. I knew they had to be rich. Only rich people could afford to own chickens, cows and horses. Plus, they actually had white siding on their house, not tar paper.

A little girl, about four-years-old, ran out to meet us. She was less than waist high to Clint and wore her dark hair cut like someone had turned a bowl over her head and cut around it. She had the same eyes as Clint and thick lips. Her face was as round as a plate and her nose was nearly flat.

"This is my little sister, Leeler."

"I think your grandma must have been a mail order bride from Korea," I said to Clint. He looked at me blankly.

"Your little sister is beautiful," I said. "She looks like a porcelain doll."

Clint's Mom met us at the door. She was the skinniest grown woman I had ever seen. Her waist couldn't have been over twenty inches around and her legs, sticking out from her checkered, sea-foam green dress, were smaller than my arms. Maybe the wide white plastic belt she wore made her waist look even smaller than it was. The dress was a summer sundress with spaghetti straps, but she had put it on over a long sleeved T-shirt with flowered designs on the sleeves. The artist in me was already screaming to fix her hideous outfit, but I wanted so much to make a good impression. I had come to realize that some people didn't care too much about how their clothes looked and others simply had no sense of style.

She wore her hair in a style from the fifties. There were tight curls on the top and then the bottom came down to the chin with more curls. And her lips were bright red, just like Damien's momma's always were. She, too, had the almond-shaped eyes, and she had humongous white teeth that showed even when her mouth was closed.

"Momma, this is Chippie," Clint said. "Chippie, this is my momma, Fannie."

"Chippie? Well, I have told Clint that was such an ugly name for a girl."

I felt queasy. "My real name's Nochipa."

Fannie turned and walked into the kitchen. I noticed immediately that her head bobbled when she walked, her skinny neck stretching forward then back, then forward again. Clint and I followed her, the little girl on our heels.

Clint helped her put Leeler in a high chair. I had never seen a four-year-old who still sat in a high chair, but I did realize that all families did things differently.

"Where are your brothers?" I asked Clint.

"Hunting with Hayden," Fannie answered. Hayden was Clint's father. "Liable to be out all night."

"They hunt at night?"

"Coon hunt, fox hunt."

"Oh," I said.

"Have some chicken," Fannie said, passing me a purple ceramic bowl. I set the bowl in front of me and reached in to fork out my chicken. It was swimming in grease. We drank tea with our meal.

"Thank you for having me up here to eat," I said. "It was nice of you to cook for me."

Fannie looked at me. Then she looked at Clint. "Clint," she said. "This girl is as fat as a butterball. Why'd you go and get such a fat girl?"

Fat? Me? I had never been called fat in my life. True enough, in the months after leaving eighth grade, I had quit running every day and I had gained some weight, but I hardly saw myself as fat. Then she talked on and on about how the Pablos had such a bad name in the community. During this time, she also puffed on a cigarette, leaving a red lipstick ring on the filter.

Clint didn't say anything. He just sat there. I don't think he thought there was anything wrong with the way his momma talked.

Later we went into his bedroom so he could show me his record collection. He had posters of girls in bikinis on his walls and rock stars on motorcycles.

"Momma hates these posters," he said. "But I hang them up anyway."

"I think your momma hates everything and everybody," I said.

"No, no...she likes you," he said. He tried to sound reassuring, but he wasn't.

"Likes me?"

"Yes, if she didn't like you, she would have asked you to leave or something. I'll show you something if you promise not to laugh."

"All right. I promise."

He opened a drawer and pulled out a comic book. "I collect comics."

"Why is that funny?"

"Momma says it's a foolish waste of money."

"That ain't what my mom says. She says it's foolish to smoke. If you buy something, like a book, you have something to show for your money, but if you smoke, you just burn your money."

"Don't your Daddy smoke?"

"Yep, and Momma says we'd have money if he didn't." I laughed. "Might as well roll a dollar bill up and set a match to it, she says."

"Your mom's cool. Momma fusses when I buy records and comic books."

I opened a comic and began looking at it. "The artwork in these is beautiful."

He put his hand on the comic to get my attention. "You are the first person in my life who hasn't laughed at me for liking these and you are the only person who has ever taken the time to notice the pictures or say anything about them. Thank you."

"I just got one question," I said. "Why are all the women wearing these spandex bikinis? Real women don't dress that way."

"Well, they're super heroes. Super heroes aren't supposed to dress and look like real people. They're super." We talked a while longer, then he took me to meet his Uncle Eugene, a hermit who lived on the hill above Clint's house.

Uncle Eugene met us at the door in a straw hat and bibbed overalls. Tobacco juice ran out of corner of his mouth and his eyes were red and glazed with cataracts. He mumbled when he spoke and I could barely understand him. I listened closely.

"That's one of them Palo's," he said. I noticed he didn't get my last name right. "This here girl's an Indian, Clint. Her granny lived down yonder in the colored house for years. Indian, I tell you. Her great grandpa, Big Horse Rodgers, was an Indian. He shot a man one time for taking his sister off. I always liked him, even if he was an Indian, but then that littlest girl of his went and married that Joe Willie Palo. Them Palo's all going to Hell 'cause they tie their dogs. Ol' man Jim Palo, ol' Mexican, thinks he's a preacher. He never was no preacher. No preacher'd tie his dog. No sir-ree...plus he don't feed his mules...lets 'em get skinny. If you ask me, Clint, I'd say get shed of this girl right now. She's got Palo blood and that means she's got witch blood in her. Them Palos was always witches."

Jim Pablo was my Grandpa's little brother. He was the color of coffee beans and had cotton white hair. Great Uncle Jim's English was not good, but his heart was. He lived in a four-room house without electricity and still practiced many of his father's old ways. Yet, he believed God had called him to preach. So, on Saturday mornings, he would hitchhike a ride into town, stand on the courthouse lawn, and preach. Uncle Jim couldn't read. So, he just preached what he thought was right, and he would preach it until tears were streaming down his face.

"Besides that," Eugene continued. "This girl's ugly. She's got a neck like a giraffe."

"Take me home, Clint," I said.

Back in the car, Clint said, "I told you not to pay Eugene no mind, Chippie. He's just like that. He never leaves his house, never. Eugene wasn't treated right when he was little and spent most of life away from people. He ain't never been around people, especially women. He don't know how to talk to people."

"Clint, I don't know how you turned out to be half way normal."

"They just worry about their good name," he said. "Eugene says a man's name's the most important thing he's got."

I shrugged. "Momma says your own dignity, pride in yourself, is the best thing you've got. You can be from a messed up family with a trashy name. A person can't help what house they're born in, but they can help what they do with their lives."

Clint had grown up two miles up the road from my house. My father had been born in his grandfather's colored house. His father knew my grandpa and all his siblings, yet in some ways he might as well have really come from Mongolia or some other distant place. Everything my momma said, his said the opposite. Everything my daddy did and the way he acted, his was the opposite. Yet, Clint and I had long discussions on religion, music, and literature. Clint wasn't like any boy I knew. He studied and read. He watched television preachers and actually remembered the things they said.

I would lie awake at night wondering what it would be like to love somebody and have them love me back, like on television. Sometimes I even told myself that my loving Clint was just like a fairy tale or a great story. Whatever the case, I did love Clint Kurtsinger.

Chapter Twenty

We had more snow than usual, but it never stopped the mailman, so I wrote Eloise a letter and sent it to Texas. I told her all about Jerry Wayne drowning and how I felt bad that I'd waited so long to write her about it.

I also spent some time talking on the telephone to Deanna. Now, it was about this time that Deanna's folks announced to the congregation that they were moving. A week later, Deanna was gone and I was pretty sure I'd never see her again. Two weeks after they moved, I got a letter from Deanna. Her momma, thirty-two-years-old, was dead. She died of breast cancer. I remembered all the times Deanna had said she hated her momma. I cried for my friend. Even with her poor little momma lying cold in the ground, she went on and on about whether Jesse had already found another girlfriend or not. Maybe that was her way of coping with her momma's death, but it seemed life had been unfair to her quiet little mother.

Jesse came up for Friday night suppers with Clint. It was cold but we would sit on the car hood anyway, looking up at the stars and talking. It wasn't just Jesse and me. It was all of us, Clint, Willie, Lou Annie, and Jesse's little brother, that we called Birdboy.

"Do you miss Deanna?" I asked him that Friday night.

Jesse shrugged. "Chippie, you know I never really cared much for her. I just went with her 'cause you asked me too and 'cause she had big hooters. Them's the only reasons."

I sat silently for a moment, realizing something that made me sad. I didn't miss Deanna either, not much. I only missed her hanging onto me and my cautioning her against acts of stupidity, but I didn't miss talking to her or doing things with her, because in truth, Jesse was the only thing we had in common.

My Aunt Darla Eastridge had sent me a new brown coat just after Christmas. It wasn't really new, but it was the nicest coat I'd ever owned. It struck me at mid calf, was belted at the waist and had a satin lining. Made of soft tan wool, this hooded piece of art was trimmed with a cocoa yoke. At night, I would fold it up and place it in the cupboard I used for my closet.

One night, a sound from my cupboard woke me, a squeaking, scratching. I lay there for a moment, stunned and afraid to move. Then I had a terrible knowing of why there was squeaking coming from my closet.

"Oh, God no," I whispered. "Please, anything but that."

Moonlight, which was very bright, reflecting off the thin blanket of snow outside, lit my room to dawn proportions. I crept out of bed and carefully opened the cupboard door.

There they were, a mother mouse and a fistful of little furless pink bodies. Maybe newborn mice would have been fascinating or cute to me on any other occasion, but I felt as if I had been betrayed and violated by nature itself. Of all the rags in our house, why had this mouse eaten away the back of my new coat? It was nothing now, nothing but a rat's nest. I was angry, not in a rush of blood to the face and lashing out kind of way, but in a cold methodical get even kind of way. That coat was the nicest thing I had ever owned and my Aunt Darla had given it to me. It symbolized something. I didn't know what. Whatever it was, it made me mad to lose it. I couldn't just smash the mice. There would be too much blood to clean up. I might get sick and vomit. Besides, the noise of it would wake everyone. Then the image of a brown grocery bag came into my mind. I tiptoed into the kitchen and pulled one from the space between the refrigerator and wall where Momma kept them.

Back in my room, I raked the coat and mice together into the bag. I rolled the top down and stood, wondering what to do with them. Then I thought of the stove in the living room.

I tiptoed over the kitchen floor, linoleum cold against my bare feet, and into the living room. I knelt by the stove and opened the hot door with a poker. I shoved the bag in and closed the door. That was the first time in my life that I had purposely killed anything bigger than a wasp.

I crept back to my bed feeling neither justified nor guilty. I felt nothing. I merely hoped the mice would be gone completely by morning. I crawled back into my bed, pulling my covers up. My sheets were still warm from my body heat and I welcomed that warmth. I closed my eyes but I did not sleep. I listened for the sounds of squeaking mice or some kind of screeching cry. None came. Then I thought what if they didn't burn up and what if Momma opened the door and found those half-burned mice in the morning? Would melted mice make her sick at her stomach? I wrestled with these thoughts a long time. I wanted to go back in the living room and check, but what if the mice hadn't burned up yet? What if I saw them on fire and heard them sizzling when I opened the door? Would I puke?

I don't know when it happened, but I did fall asleep. The next morning when I awoke I could hear Momma in the kitchen and the minute I opened my bedroom door I knew that she had already been stirring the fire. The kitchen and living room were cozy warm.

"Want me to put some wood on the stove?" I asked.

"No, it's plenty hot in here already," Momma said. "There were a lot of coals this morning and the fire was real easy to kindle up."

I almost laughed with relief. My coat had burned. The mice had burned and nobody save God and I would ever know about it. I figured the two of us could work it out when I got to Heaven if he wanted. It's just that it seemed to me that if David could slay a bear for killing his sheep, it should be all right if I burned mice for eating my coat.

* * *

It was February when a popular girl named Sharlett Brown put her lunch tray beside me. I had known Sharlett back when I'd gone to the town school before and she'd always been kind to me, but we had never really hung out together. But that particular day the lunchroom was already crowded by the time she got in there and the only seat left empty was beside me.

207

"Can I sit here?" she asked.

I looked up. She stood there, about five feet ten inches tall, olive skin with light freckles, and jet black hair cut in a cute boyish style just above her ears.

"Sure," I said.

I thought how Sharlett looked just like her mom who often came by the school to pick her up early in the afternoons. I had heard girls in the bathroom talk about Sharlett's family before. Her momma was a gorgeous Italian named Katrina who'd moved here from Indianapolis, Indiana, to marry Sharlett's daddy who was nothing but a plain old country boy, born and raised on a little farm just south of Tugman's Holler. But he had money or, at least, it looked like he did. They lived in a big brick house on several acres of the prettiest farmland around. They had five acres of yard for Sharlett to ride her motorcycle on.

"I hate beans," Sharlett said. "Do you want my beans?"

I shook my head. "No, I can barely eat the food on my own tray. I don't eat much."

"I can tell," Sharlett said. "God, you're so thin. I'd give anything to be that little."

"Why?" I said. "You're just about the prettiest girl in this high school."

Sharlett smiled. "You mean that?"

"Yes," I said. "I'd love to have a complexion like yours and cool hair like yours."

"Say, I'm having my sixteenth birthday party this weekend. My mom and dad say I can invite a few friends." She laughed. "So, would you like to come? I think my parents would like and approve of you. They are very picky about who I can bring to my house. But I just know they will love you."

"I would love that," I said. "If my mom and dad let me go."

On Thursday, I dreaded seeing Sharlett. I wanted to go to her house so badly but when I told Daddy that I was invited to her house he said, "No, Chippie. Those are rich people. They'll get you up there and make fun of you, of us."

She was as heartbroken as I was by Daddy's decision. Late that afternoon, I was helping Momma with the super dishes when I looked out the window and saw a shiny red pickup truck coming across the field, not up the road, to our house. Momma and I both ran out. It was Sharlett's dad and right there beside him was Sharlett.

My dad waited for him to cut the engine off then he said, "What can I do for you, Mister?"

Mr. Brown got out of the truck and Sharlett hopped out, too. He shook hands with Daddy. "I'm Thomas Brown and this is my girl, Sharlett. Me and the wife have always tried to protect Sharlett from bad influences. She's been telling me about this girl of yours, going on over what good manners she's got and how she shows respect toward people and, well, I'd be beholding to you if you let her come to Sharlett's birthday supper tomorrow night."

My Daddy didn't know what to say. Mr. Brown

made it sound like my daddy would be doing him a favor by letting me come.

"I believe a man ought to bring his kids up right," Mr. Brown said. "We make Sharlett get to bed by nine and she never stays out late. She tried to be friends with several of the girls from the country club but, truth be told, money don't take the place of plain, old fashioned, good upbringing."

"Well..." Daddy said.

"Oh, come on, honey, let her go," Momma said. "Chippie's a good kid."

"I don't suppose it would hurt anything," Daddy said. "Just this once."

But it turned into more than once. Daddy and Thomas Brown found they had a lot in common, despite the fact that Thomas was a successful farmer and business owner who had more money than Daddy ever dreamed of seeing.

I couldn't believe that a girl as rich as Sharlett would want to be friends with me, who lived in a shack covered in tarpaper and pinned her underclothes together with safety pins. Yet Sharlett and I loved the same things and we could talk for hours. We loved great stories and poetry and Nancy Drew. We loved walks in the woods and telling ghost stories. We liked the same movies and both of us loved to dance.

Sharlett and I would spend most of our time in her basement. She had her own furniture down there and her own telephone. Sharlett's life was like the kids on television. She had nice clothes and never wore hand-me-downs. She knew about classical music and old movies. She was the most interesting person, boy or girl, that I had ever met.

She also had a record player. She would play Barbara Striesand and Barry Gibb records. Then we would put on her satin dresses and dance. Sometimes we did partner dancing. She was always the man, because she was bigger.

Her momma would call us upstairs to watch John Wayne movies after supper and her daddy would have us rub his feet with lotion. He bragged on what good hands I had and said I should grow up to give massages for a living. Even though he was gray haired and gruff, he was kind to me and always managed to say something funny. The best thing about Sharlett was that she loved all my little brothers and sisters. She was kind to them and treated them as she would have her own.

Sometimes I think Clint was jealous of us. Every once in a while, he'd say that he thought I loved Sharlett more than him. I assured him that I did love Sharlett very much, but I loved her in a different way. Between school, chores, being with Sharlett and with Clint, the days went by fast.

One Friday afternoon, Sharlett and I made plans for me to come to her house on Sunday as her parents had a party at a local doctor's house to attend on Friday night and I needed to do something with Clint on Saturday night.

"My dad will come up and get you Sunday around eleven," she said. "Then we can ride my motorbike in the afternoon and maybe go down to the creek. You can stay all night and ride the bus home from school on Monday."

"I think my mom and dad will be okay with that," I told her.

She smiled. "Good. See you Sunday."

I got on my bus and looked forward to a fun weekend. I would go to the movie with Clint that night, sleep late on Saturday, and go to Sharlett's house after church on Sunday.

However, when Saturday came, I woke up early enough to watch cartoons with my brothers and sisters. That's what I was doing when the phone rang.

"Hello," I said.

"Chippie, it's Maylene." Maylene was the Brown's housekeeper, whom I had come to know from my staying there.

"Honey," she said, then stopped. I could hear her sobbing over the phone. "Thomas Brown's dead," she finally said.

I felt like a bumblebee had just stung me in the head. "What?"

Her voice quivered. "Sharlett's daddy is dead, sweetheart. The funeral's Tuesday afternoon. Miss Katrina wants to know if you'll come stay with Sharlett. She's having a tough time of it."

"What?" I was numb, couldn't gather my thoughts. "I mean how? How did it happen?"

"Came home late from a party down at Doctor Taylor's house last night. Closed the garage door but fell asleep in the car before he turned off the engine. At four in the morning Katrina got worried about him that he hadn't come home. She called the Taylors who said he'd been gone for hours. That's when she got ready to get in the car and go out to find him. When she turned on the light in the garage, there he was. Car still running, him slumped over the steering wheel, dead."

"Oh, no," I said.

Momma walked into the room, wiping her hands on a dishtowel as I hung up the phone. "What is it?"

"Sharlett's daddy, he's dead."

Momma just pulled me to herself. "I'm so sorry, baby."

Another period of numbness followed. I stayed a few days with Sharlett, but her eyes didn't laugh anymore. Katrina said she couldn't stay here in this little town in the middle of nowhere. She said she couldn't stay in that big, old house, that her husband's presence was everywhere. A week after Mr. Brown's death, Sharlett's momma put the house up for sale, furniture and all. She and Sharlett packed their clothes and moved back to Indiana. I knew that I would never see Sharlett Brown again. I sat on the cold ground behind the old rusty truck and cried the day Sharlett left. I kept thinking that maybe a person only gets one soul friend in a lifetime. If so, mine was an Italian girl with brown freckles.

About a week later, I went to feed my cat, Tom, and found him stiff. He had taken sick and died from pneumonia. I had been too caught up in Sharlett's moving and doing things with Clint to notice just how sick the little fellow was. I buried him down in the woods beside Rusty's grave and made him a cross out of wood from our kindling pile. I had become so accustomed to things dying that I was ashamed at my lack of shock and sadness. After I buried him, I went to watch a movie with Clint.

Chapter Twenty-One

The last snow of winter came in March, two weeks after Daddy bought an old sow pig from the forklift driver down at the mill. Somehow slopping the hog was still my job.

Clint came over. We couldn't take my little brothers and sisters sledding down the hill behind Tiny Elmer's oil garage because the snow wasn't deep enough. A snowfall deep enough for sledding was a rare occurrence. We usually only got one or two such snows in a given winter. Clint and I sat in my room listening to the record player and talking about nothing in particular.

"Want to go for a walk?" Clint said.

I shrugged. "Sure. We can go down to the pigpen and check on the old sow, and then we can bring Momma an armload of wood while we're out."

We told Momma we were going out to feed the hog and bring in some wood. She liked that idea just fine, since we could never have too much wood packed up to the house.

"Slop bucket's in the corner by the 'fridgerater," she said.

Outside, the air stung my nose as we headed off across the backyard toward the woods. Clint offered to carry my slop bucket and I let him. It was nice to have somebody offer to help me. Nobody ever helped me slop the hogs. That chore was mine and mine alone. Of course, I never complained. I usually welcomed the chance to get out and have a few minutes to myself. I did my best thinking when I was doing my chores.

Along the path through the woods, our feet left muddy prints in the shallow snow. The old sow was glad to see her slop coming and started grunting the minute we came within sight.

"I haven't thought up a name for this old hog yet," I said.

"Your family's the only one I know of that names their hogs," Clint said.

"Ain't nothing wrong with naming your pigs."

I set the slop bucket down and walked over the hill just a bit, to where I could look down on the pond, half frozen over. I gazed out on the next hill, a solid white mound, untouched by tracks. "It sure looks beautiful when it snows." My breath came out white, like I was puffing a cigarette.

Clint put his hand on the back of my neck. "Sure is." Then he turned me around and started to kiss me.

"It's cold out here," I said. "What if our faces freeze together?"

"Our faces ain't gonna freeze," he said, and then commenced to kissing me again. He kissed me just like men kiss women on the movies. I imagined that must be about the best kissing in the world and since I hadn't done much other kissing, I was pretty sure that Clint knew all there was to know about kissing. So, we kissed a while longer. Then Clint started to undo my pants.

I put my hand on his and said. "No, don't do that."

"I love you, Chippie." He whispered in my ear, gentle and kind, like I was a kitten and he didn't want me to run and hide. "This is what people do when they love each other. Now I know you love me, too. I've waited a long, long time to be with you. We've been going together for months and months."

I moved my hand. I did love him.

After he went home, I went into my room. I thought and thought about what had happened. Then a horrible notion came to me. What if I got pregnant? It would kill my momma and daddy, especially after losing Jerry Wayne.

I loved Clint, but I loved my parents, too. And how would I take care of a baby? I was just a kid myself. I had never felt such fear in my life. I had never felt such guilt. Then I heard Daddy holler, "Sis, want to go up to the Church of God with me tonight? They're having a woman preacher. I'd like to hear her."

Daddy was fascinated by women preachers, because he'd been raised that women couldn't be preachers, yet he always found them to be more energetic and 'fired up' than men preachers.

"Yeah, Daddy, I'll go."

That gave me an excuse to get out of the house, to take a bath, get my mind off what had happened for a moment. I heated a pan of water on the stove in the kitchen, and then took it into my room so I could wash. There was no heat in my room, so when I took off my clothes, goose bumps stood out all over me. I looked at my naked body in the mirror and was ashamed of what I saw.

Clint loved me and I, him. How would he feel if he knew how badly I felt over what we'd done?

I wore my best outfit that night, a black skirt and vest with a white blouse. I looked my best on the outside. As we went to the meeting, just Daddy and me, I let him do all the talking. He didn't seem to mind.

I sat through the preacher's sermon, watching her, noticing how she looked and moved and spoke. She was a short woman, no taller than I, with long black, gray-streaked hair that she wore pulled back in a gold clasp. She was large busted and had big hips, but her waist was a tiny thing with a wide leather belt. She spoke in a loud robust voice and ran all over the church house as she preached speaking in tongues often and calling people out to prophesy to them. She preached on people trying to hide their sins from God.

At the end of her sermon, she gave an altar call. People went up and knelt down. She prayed over them and they got up shouting and speaking in tongues. Then she saw me, standing like a little shadow, beside my daddy.

She came to where I stood and put her face up close to mine. "Little girl, you need to be saved?"

I was so nervous I thought I'd pass out. "I'm already a Christian," I said. My nervousness must've made my words come out in a whisper.

"What?" she boomed in her loud voice.

"I done been saved," I said. "Last year."

Then she smiled and put her hand on my forearm. "Then be sure to live it, honey." She turned and went on calling out other people and praying for them.

My daddy was so into the meeting, so caught up in it. He had tears in his eyes. The only time he smiled anymore was when he was in a meeting, and then he smiled through tears and talked about how he'd see Jerry Wayne again in Heaven, in the sweet by-n-by.

I was as quiet going home as I had been coming. Daddy talked about Heaven and Jerry Wayne and seeing Jesus in his right eye all the way home. He told me how he had gone up to the graveyard and prayed with his left hand on the tombstone.

"The ground shook, Chippie. It shook and then I seen him, standing in the corner of my right eye. It was the Lord Jesus himself. He told me that everything was gonna be all right by-n-by."

"That's amazing, Daddy," I said. But I couldn't say any more to him about it. All I could think of was how terribly I had sinned. I had failed God and my parents. The only person I'd made happy was Clint and he didn't have to worry about getting pregnant.

I was thankful that we got home late. I whispered a quick good night to my parents, pecked them on the cheek with kisses, and scurried off to my room like I was going to bed, but I didn't. I changed into my pink nightgown and read my Bible. As I read it, tears splattered my pages until I finally just laid my face in it and cried. I was a bad person.

I had to make things right. I knelt at the foot of my bed, my chest hurting from my guilt. I had sinned. Not only that, it still hurt. My body was sore from it. What would Granny Eastridge think of me if she was looking down from Heaven, and Granny Pablo, who was the purest woman to walk the earth since Mary herself, and Jerry Wayne, oh God, could Jerry Wayne look down and see what a horrible thing I had done?

"Please, God, forgive me," I said. "I'm so sorry..." I choked on my sobs. "I'm so sorry. I wish you'd never made me a girl."

Then I remembered that the mother of Jesus had to be a girl or else Jesus never could have been born. "I'm so sorry, God. Forgive me for thinking those mean things about you. Forgive me for what I did with Clint."

All the fears rushed at me again. What if he had gotten all he wanted? What if he never wanted anything to do with me again? There was a butcher knife under my bed, the one with a knick in it, which I had once promised Lou Annie I would use to protect her if anybody ever tried to break in on us. I could get that knife out and stick it right through my heart before anybody knew what I'd done.

But what about my parents? They had hurt so much over Jerry Wayne. It would kill them to lose me, too. And what of my sweet little brothers and sisters? And of Clint? How would he feel, knowing the only girl he ever loved had gone and killed herself? Besides, everyone knew that suicides went to Hell. Then I remembered a woman in the Bible named Hannah, who made God a vow and kept it.

"Lord," I prayed. "I beg you. Please don't let me be

pregnant and please let me marry this boy to set right this thing I have done. I promise you, God, if you don't let me marry this boy, then I will never marry. I will become a Catholic and be a nun. I will dedicate my body to serving the Lord and never look at, think about, or touch another boy for the rest of my life. And I mean it."

I got up from the foot of my bed, knowing what I had to do. I had to get Clint to marry me before something terrible happened, and I would never tell a soul in the world what had happened between us. If by chance he wouldn't marry me and I did get pregnant, I would just disappear. I would not stay here and hurt or shame my family that loved me. I would run away.

In the coming weeks, I discovered I wasn't pregnant. I said 'thank you' a million times to God. Clint came around more and more. I told him that I wanted to be a good Christian and he said he did, too. He kept telling me that I was the only girl he had ever been with and that he loved me. He even said he wanted to marry me, but was afraid because he didn't think he had enough money.

We would sit in the car after supper and talk. He talked about the end of time and the Antichrist. He spoke of the coming mark of the Beast. We talked about music and his comic books. I even dreamed about the end of time. So, I told him my dreams. They were convincing and sometimes frightening dreams.

Yet, each day, my fear grew worse. I begin to believe that I had no control over anything in my life. I couldn't stop Jerry Wayne from dying. I couldn't keep Sharlett's daddy from dying or her momma from moving her away. I couldn't take away my parents' unending sadness of losing their son, and now, I couldn't even keep myself from wanting to be with a boy, something that would kill my momma and daddy if they knew.

There was one thing I could control, my own body. I decided I would lose weight until my body was perfect. I could control that. I would not get fat. At school, I didn't eat lunch and at home, I told Momma I was too full from school. If Clint and I went to Fannie's, I pretended I had a stomachache. The pounds began to come off. I didn't have a scale but my clothes were looser. I liked being little and no matter how hard I tried, I didn't feel perfect enough. Every time I looked in the mirror, I could see big pockets of fat. I just wanted things to be the way they were when I was little.

I took a summer job at Briar Ridge Elementary School as a student janitor. I scrubbed toilets, mopped floors, washed out the coal room, mowed the yard with a push mower, painted the seesaws. and most days, I ate one meal, usually an egg or a banana. If I went over that, I'd sneak to the bathroom, stick my index finger down my throat and make myself vomit. Momma got really worried about how skinny I was getting. My clothes kept getting looser and looser. I told her that was just because my work was so hard. That was all. I started wearing baggy things to hide myself.

Clint's momma had said I was fat and she was right. I was fat. By the time I entered my junior year of high school, I hadn't had a period in two months. I was just ceasing to be a woman, and that's exactly what I wanted. All my clothes hung on me and I had to belt my pants to keep them from falling down. Still, none of my friends seemed to notice or comment on my size, so I figured I must still be pretty big.

Jesse spent more and more time at our house. He went to the movies with Clint and me. He even drove us in his big brother's car. He often invited us to come to the pool room and shoot pool with him. I was so terrible at shooting pool. My cue ball would leave the table and bounce on the floor. I was afraid of hitting someone in the head with it. But neither of the fellows with me seemed to mind. They just laughed that I was so awful and kept trying to teach me to play better. However, their efforts were in vain. I was born to be the world's worst pool player.

I awoke one Saturday morning and came through the living room in my nightgown. Jesse was sitting on the couch, talking to Momma who was in the kitchen fixing bacon and eggs. I know my mouth dropped open as I started back through the kitchen to my bedroom. I wasn't used to people seeing me in my nightie.

"Morning, Chippie," he said.

I stuck my head back around the door lentil into the living room. "Why are you here so daggum early?"

He laughed. "Mammy sent me up here to borrow some sugar and I got to talking to your momma. Hey, want to see my car?"

"You mean your brother's car?"

"No, I mean *my* car."

"You got a car?"

"Yeah, come out here and look at it."

I started out the door, then remembered I was in my gown. I laughed. "Um...let me change my clothes first." I ran back into my room, scurried into some jeans and a sweatshirt, stuck my feet in some sneakers and tied my hair back. I didn't bother combing it. Then I dashed back into the living room.

Momma shook her head and laughed.

"All right," I said, "let's see this here car of yours."

"A 1975 model," Jesse said. He grinned and spread his hands like a game show host. "Ain't it pretty, Chippie?"

It was long and black, trimmed in shiny chrome. I smiled. "It's gorgeous. Where'd you get it?"

"Bought if off my Uncle Dan. He's started himself a car lot up right down there next to where your Granny Eastridge used to live."

"Wow," I said. "It's got an eight track tape player and a radio."

"It's got a heater and an air conditioner, too," Jesse said. "Hey, get in and I'll take you for a ride up to Briar Ridge Schoolhouse and back."

"Okay, let me ask Momma."

Of course Momma didn't care but cautioned me not to be gone long, because when my siblings got up, they'd eat every bite of breakfast and she said she wasn't cooking a second time. I didn't care. I looked for ways out of eating anyway.

Jesse's car rode pretty smoothly, and he cut the

engine as he pulled into the parking lot at the school. He had his basketball in the trunk, so we shot a few hoops, then sat on the car listening to rock music.

"Chippie," he said, but he never looked at me. "I need to tell you something. Now don't say nothing until I'm done. I know you and Clint are serious, but I got to tell you this. I love you. I've loved you ever since you brought your skinny little butt into Mr. Sizemore's eighth grade room and plopped down in front of me. I know that you don't love me, but still, I had to tell you. I know that you and me ain't meant to be together. You're meant for big things, bigger than Swamp Holler or Briar Ridge, bigger than this whole town. But if you wake up one day and discover that Clint's not the guy for you, that maybe you'd rather have an old truck kind of boy, or a distant cousin, just remember where I live. I ain't proposin' or nothing like that, I'm just saying that I'll always be here iffen you need me." He took a deep breath, "'Cause I'm your cousin and that's what kinfolks do, they take care of their own. Right?"

In that moment, I didn't care about Jesse's long greasy hair or his mismatched clothes. It didn't matter that he had more sun freckles on his nose than a blue tick hound. Jesse's eyes were filled with sincerity. If I hadn't already been with Clint in a man and wife kind of way, if I hadn't already promised God what I'd do with my life, then maybe, just maybe I would tell Jesse...but, the dye was cast and the stones were set. My life plan was laid out. I had made a vow and I was going to fulfill that which I had promised.

"Right," I said. "But, Jesse, no matter what, we *are* still kinfolk and you know kinfolk can never be more than what we are."

"I knew you'd say that," he said. "Things like that don't matter in my family, but I understand that they do to yours." I took his hand in mine and for a long, long time we just sat there as we had done on the steps at school after Jerry Wayne died. Something had changed between us that morning and somehow I knew that even if Jesse married someone else and I married Clint, both of us would always think about sitting in the car holding hands from time to time.

That night, Clint came to the house. We sat in the car and started talking. "I know you've been with other boys." He said this out of the blue. He looked at me like I was the devil.

"What? You're the only person I've ever been with."

"And you never did it with nobody else?"

"No, of course not. I'm not that kind of girl."

"No, I know you're not. I'm sorry. It's just that Eugene says Jesse's going to steal you from me. So, I got to know right now. Do you love Jesse?"

"Yes," I said. "He's been my friend for a long time and he will likely always be my friend, and if you can't handle that, I'm sorry."

"Eugene says all women are evil and deceptive. He says Jesse's in love with you, that he can see it in his eyes. He says you'll run off with the first man that comes along."

"What does he know? He's an old coot that's never

been married. How can he possibly know anything about women or anything else?" I could feel the anger rising up inside of me. "Look," I said. "I'm tired of fooling with your momma and with Eugene. I'm tired of them putting me down because of my last name and I'm tired of people treating me like garbage just 'cause I'm a girl. So, here's the deal. You either marry me or stop coming to see me. I can't go on living like this, worrying every day that I'm going to end up pregnant or that my parents are going to find out I been lying to them. They've been through too much already."

Clint gripped the steering wheel, "Momma don't-"

"I don't give a flying monkey's butt what your momma says. Now what's it going to be?"

"I only got a thousand dollars in the bank, Chippie. That ain't enough to start a married life."

"It's more money than I've ever seen in my whole life and my daddy ain't never had more than a hundred dollars a week. So, we either get married or we call this whole thing off. I can't go on like this anymore."

"I love you, Chippie. I love you more than my own life and I can't lose you. If you broke up with me, I'd kill myself."

"I ain't breaking up with you. But-"

"I prayed my whole life for a girl to love me. I can't believe you love me. I never want to lose you. Make me a promise, Chippie. Swear it to me. Swear you'll never leave me, you'll never run off with somebody else."

I looked at him for a moment. "I got no plans of running off from you. I keep my promises, too. So, yeah, I promise."

"All right then. Let's get married. Screw Eugene. He don't know nothing."

"Amen," I said.

"Momma's going to be mad enough to ring the head off a rooster," Clint said. When you want to get married?"

"How about next March? The first day of spring?"

CHAPTER TWENTY-TWO

Clint sat in our living room chair. I sat on the chair arm, Momma on the couch and Daddy in a chair behind the stove. It was now February, and the weather was warm enough outside that we only needed a little fire in the house to knock off the chill.

I picked at the duct tape on the couch arm next to me. Our couch and chair had duct tape in several places. Since the furniture was orange vinyl, the gray tape showed up like measles on a pale face kid.

"Quit picking the furniture, Chippie. It's already in bad enough shape," Momma said. "Now, what do y'all got to tell us? Though I'm pretty sure I already know. You're wanting to get married, ain't you?"

I nodded. "Yep."

Clint started his practiced pitch. "Mr. Pablo, I love Chippie, your daughter, and I want to marry her."

Daddy was quiet for a minute.

I jumped in. "Daddy, Momma was just fifteen when you married her. I'll be seventeen in just a few months. Clint and me can't go on dating forever."

"I just don't want you running off, Sissy. It don't seem like you're as old as you are."

My parents had eloped when Momma was fifteen and Daddy was twenty-one. They went to Tennessee but nobody there would marry them on account of Momma being just a kid. Then they went on to Lafayette, Georgia where Daddy lied to a judge and told him Momma was knocked up.

When they got back, they stayed at Grandma and Grandpa Pablo's. Granny made Momma feel like one of her own girls and told my daddy that she loved her like a daughter and thought she had the prettiest black hair she'd ever laid eyes on. But Grandpa Eastridge was so mad that he took to packing a pistol so that if he saw Daddy out somewhere he could shoot him. He then had the marriage annulled and took a warrant out on Daddy.

The sheriff came down to the mill and arrested Daddy while he was at work. He had to go to court for kidnapping a minor. And it was only by Momma's pleading and begging her daddy that he finally dropped the charges and didn't send my daddy to prison for kidnapping. The following September when Momma was sixteen, she and Daddy eloped again. She told Grandpa Eastridge that he could annul her marriage as often as he liked, but he couldn't make her quit loving Daddy. Grandpa gave in, but he never liked Daddy and he didn't keep that fact a secret.

"You can marry my girl if you promise me one thing," Daddy said. "You won't move her off from here. Don't go taking her to no California nor off down to Georgia. Don't take her out of this county. This here's her home and all the people that are going to love her most in life are right here. I want my kids close to me 'til the day I die."

"That's right," Momma said. "We ain't losing our little girl, we're just gaining a new son."

I thought Clint would cry when she said that. He

wasn't used to people being so accepting like my parents were. There was room in Momma and Daddy's hearts for a hundred kids.

"It don't matter if you're married or not, Sissy. You're always going to be our baby girl. You've always got a home here," Daddy said. He took a draw on his cigarette and blew out a ring of smoke. "So, where you aiming to live?"

"Down at the end of the road in Tiny Elmer's empty house. We done talked to him about it," Clint said. "He says the rent's thirty-five dollars a month."

Daddy nodded. Tiny Elmer's spare house was a four-room box house at the end of our road. It had been empty for twenty years. Both my parents smiled.

"Why, that'll be just like being in the next room," Momma said.

Before Clint left that day Momma was already looking through boxes under her bed for extra curtains and Daddy was telling Clint the best people to buy a rick of wood from.

Telling Fannie and Clint's daddy wasn't so easy. Well, Clint's daddy was easy. He just grunted and walked out the door to shave. He had a car mirror wired to a hickory tree out in the front yard where he kept a cup and some lathering cream. He would stand there and shave in the front yard.

Fannie put her hand on her head and sat down. "Oh lordy, Clint. She'll be pregnant in two weeks. I am too young to be a grandmother and just think about it. People are going to talk about us. Our good name'll be ruined what with you marrying a Mexican."

I clutched Clint's arm.

"I love her, Momma."

She drew on her cigarette, then pulled it out, red lipstick all over the butt. "Who's going to take care of me, Clint? You know I'm poorly. I can't take care of Leeler all by myself. I need you to carry in the wood and do the dishes. Who's going to help your daddy in the tobacco and stay with Eugene at night?"

"You've got a husband and another son," I said.

"They don't care nothing for me," she wailed. "They'd rather coon hunt and chase women on the ridge. You can see how he is. Look at him out there. He don't care that Clint's running off and leaving us."

"Momma, I'm just moving two miles down the road-"

"Yes. And off the ridge," she said. "Ain't nothing good ever come out of Swamp Holler. Why couldn't you get a girl from the ridge?"

She wanted Clint to stay there and be her slave for the rest of his life or else marry some well-to-do girl from up the ridge who'd make her look good in the community and whose family's money might rub off on her. Well, I'd show her. I was just as good as any of her high-falooting big shots up on the ridge.

"I'm getting married, Momma," Clint said. "And that's all there is to it."

Fannie blew out rings of smoke from another draw on her cigarette. "You'll come back home. Just wait until you get hungry, because I'm sure she's too stupid to cook."

I wanted to hit her, but I didn't. I just took in a deep breath. If this was going to be my mother-in-law, then I was going to have to be able to take all of her racial slurs and outright assaults on my family and my person without physically hurting her. I would just clam up around her and let her words bounce off me, kind of like Grandpa Eastridge had always let Granny's temper tantrums slide off from him.

When I told Momma how Fannie had acted, she said I had to understand that Fannie felt like Clint was abandoning her, like he owed her something for raising him and now he was giving all of his devotion to someone else. She said a lot of women were like Fannie, afraid to let their kids grow up because they were terrified of being alone someday.

So, despite Fannie's opposition, Clint and I were married on the first day of spring at three o'clock in the afternoon. Our wedding lasted fifteen minutes. Clint borrowed Daddy's only suit because his father, who was only five feet, four inches tall, had nothing to fit him.

Momma made me a white wedding dress out of Swiss dot material. The simple dress gathered at the waist and had lace three-quarter length sleeves. I had no veil, so I wore blue flowers in my hair. Clint bought them for me at the florist. My bouquet cost twelve dollars and was made with blue silk flowers.

The preacher at the Methodist church only asked for twenty dollars to do our ceremony and the lady who played the piano said she'd do it for free because we were nice kids. Clint's brother was our best man, and I wanted Lou Annie to be my bridesmaid, but Fannie had a fit.

I was hiding from Clint in a Sunday school room. Momma said he couldn't see me in my wedding dress. She was in there fixing my hair and Lou Annie was putting on the jacket to the dress Momma had made her for the wedding.

Fannie came into the room, her curls piled on her head, her lips painted red, and wearing a red dress with a shiny black belt and shoes. A woman in her mid-twenties came in right behind her. I knew from pictures that I'd seen that this was Clint's older sister who had run away from home when she was sixteen.

The young woman had a face identical to Fannie's, minus the smoke wrinkles above her lips. Her long brown hair hung past her waist and she wore a blue dress.

"This here's Earnestine, my oldest girl and-"

"I want to be the bride's maid," Earnestine said.

Momma froze. Lou Annie turned away from the mirror.

"But Lou Annie's-"

"Look," she said. "I'm Clint's sister, his older sister, and I'm going to be the bride's maid." She put one hand on her hip and stuck the other hip way out. She flipped her hair back.

I shot a glance at Lou Annie who looked as if she would burst into tears. "Lou Annie's my bridesmaid."

Earnestine took a cigarette from her purse and started to light it up.

"You can't smoke in here! It's a Sunday school class," I said.

"Look, little missy. I can smoke wherever I please. I don't care nothing about this church. Ain't nobody here cares nothing for me. Now, I'm going back out the door and when the music starts, I'm coming in as a bridesmaid."

"Lou Annie's my-"

"Well, we can just have two bridesmaids," Momma said. Then she smiled. "After all, baby, it's your wedding day and people should get along on their wedding day. You'll remember this day for the rest of your life."

As soon as Fannie and Earnestine went out the door, I turned to her. "Thank you, Momma. But I tell you what. Lou Annie's my bridesmaid, and that Earnestine's just some tag along that wandered in the door. When my wedding's over, she'll head back up to Ohio or wherever she came from and leave Clint and me alone. No wonder she ran away from home. Her and Fannie are both so mean, they can't stand each other."

Momma laughed. "I'd say that's more than likely the truth." She kissed me on the cheek and gave me a hug. "I love you, Chippie. You look beautiful. Now, it's time for the wedding so I got to get on back out there and take my seat. You and Lou Annie get on around there to the church house door where your daddy's a-waiting on you."

She went out into the sanctuary. Lou Annie and I went out an outside door of the Sunday school room that led into the parking lot. We walked along the side of the church to where Earnestine stood at the front door, finishing up her cigarette and waiting on the music to start. She gave me a malicious grin, then stomped her cigarette out right on the church porch.

Daddy waited by the bottom step and took me by the arm. He didn't say anything, but I could tell that he was proud and, for a moment, I felt like crying. Even though I would always be his baby, I could never be a little girl again, if I had ever been one at all.

As soon as Lou Annie stepped up on the porch, the piano music started. 'Here Comes the Bride' drifted through the closed doors. Those doors opened as if by magic, yet I knew there were two men from the church opening them.

Earnestine took off down the isle, and then Lou Annie followed her. Finally, Daddy and I walked in. Clint waited at the front of the church with the pastor. Clint's seventeen-year-old brother, Ray, stood beside him as best man.

The music stopped. The pastor read some vows to Clint. I was so nervous I didn't really know what all he said. "I will," Clint replied.

Then he read some vows to me. "I will," I said.

Then the minister said, "Who has the ring?"

Ray had it, but it wasn't one Clint bought me, because Clint couldn't afford to buy me a ring. It was my

Momma's ring, the one she had worn when she and Daddy got married. It was too little for her now. A size six, a whole size too big for my finger, but I figured maybe I could wrap a bit of tape around it after the wedding.

I had no ring for Clint and neither of his parents had anything to share with us. In fact, his mother had made it perfectly clear that we need not ever ask her for money because how could she help us when she needed help herself.

We both said, "With this ring I thee wed."

Then the preacher said, "You may kiss the bride." So, Clint kissed me and the pastor pronounced us 'husband and wife.' We turned and walked down the isle, everybody cheering and coming after us.

For our wedding, Momma and Daddy were out twelve bucks, because that's how much it cost to make my dress. And Clint's Momma was out for a box of cake mix and some icing. That's all she could afford.

Outside, Clint's car was covered in shaving cream because Willie, Birdboy and Jesse had gotten a hold of it during the wedding. They tied tin cans to the back bumper and wrote 'Jes Maryed' on the back windshield.

Clint and I got in our car and drove to town just so we could go around the square, honking our horn, like all married couples do. Then we came back to our four-room house down the road from Momma and Daddy for our wedding reception. We cut our wedding cake, a lemon cake with white icing. At least, Fannie wanted to do something. And she kept asking everyone how the cake tasted. Of course, all my relatives took on over how delicious it was.

I fed Clint a bite of cake and he fed me, while the families photographed the ritual. Then we opened presents from our neighbors, church members, and relatives. We received a blanket, pillows, a toaster, a can opener, pinto beans, a laundry basket, vacuum cleaner bags (for the vacuum sweeper we would one day have), and a sand bucket for the well out back and a water bucket.

Clint's boss gave us a table and chairs. My uncle, Dody Eastridge, gave us a little black and white television that he picked up at the Tuesday night barn sale. He came in and set it up for us. At first, there was no picture but Uncle Dody smacked it hard on the top and the picture came on.

"Now listen, you little turdheads, this here's how it works. You got to lay something heavy up on top of it to make it work. Hey, Butterball, run out yonder and get me a big old rock or something."

He was talking to Lou Annie. He always called her 'Butterball.' She went out and found a rock to lay on our television and sure enough, it came in fine, except for the little black streak that ran across once every four minutes.

"Well, thank you, Uncle Dody," I said.

"Danged little idiots," he mumbled and walked out the door.

That was as much affection as Dody Eastridge was ever going to show anyone in this world. Those words of his were his terms of endearment.

After all of the guests had gone, Fannie stood by the front door, putting her coat on, even though it was seventy degrees outside. "I don't need to be catching no cold," she said. "It wouldn't take nothing for me to get pneumonia and have to go to the hospital. You know I ain't healthy. I probably won't live long. Ain't nobody cares enough for me to stay home and help me out. Now here," she dug through her purse and pulled out a pack of condoms. "Here, Clint. You use these here rubbers and, Chippie," she said, giving me a small card. "Take this down to the health department first thing Monday morning. I got you an appointment. Lord knows we don't need you having me no grandkids. I ain't old enough for that. And you ain't got sense enough to take care of no kids."

Then she left. I was more than glad to go to the health department. But I was sure Fannie wasn't doing it to help me because she wanted to look out for me. Fannie hated me and couldn't stand the thought of having a Pablo for a grandchild.

On our wedding night, it stormed severely. Clint suggested we go to his Momma's house to wait out the storm because Eugene had a cellar. So, we spent part of our wedding night riding out a storm at Fannie's house, listening to her gloat about how Clint would always need his momma. His little sister had cried all afternoon because some girl had stolen her big brother. So, I spent the stormy evening doing all I could to make her like me. I fixed her hair, painted her nails, and told her stories.

Chapter Twenty-Three

The next morning after Clint and I got married, we went to church. I vowed that I would be a pure and honest woman for the rest of my life. And I was a woman; after all, I was married and would have to pay all my own bills. Monday, I caught the bus and went to school. Everything was the same, except I had a new last name and got off the bus at a different house, my house.

My house had four rooms. Each of the rooms was connected to the next by a door lintel. There were no doors in the house at all, save the front door and the back door. I hung a curtain between the kitchen and the back bedroom, and then I hung one between that bedroom and our room. Between our bedroom and the living room, I hung no curtain and I didn't hang one over the kitchen door either.

The living room was baby blue with a big picture window. That big window had blue and white curtains that came with the house. Momma gave me red curtains for the door window and the other window in the room. Someone gave Clint and me a black couch and a red carpet for our living room. So we had a couch, a chair, the little television from Uncle Dody, a coffee table and a wood stove made from an old oil drum.

Our bedroom was gold. The room already had paper shades and thin white curtains. I loved them and left them there. In that room, we had my bed, the same bed I'd slept in since the day I was born, we had a dresser that Tiny Elmer let us use and an old wardrobe that looked like it came straight out of a C.S. Lewis novel.

In our sunny yellow kitchen, there was a row of windows, then a lone window on the west side of the room. In that room, we had a stove, which only had two working burners. On top of the stove, we had a toaster oven that Clint's boss gave us. We had a wooden table that the previous tenants had left in the house twenty years ago, a refrigerator from 1955, four chairs, wooden and wobbly, a white aluminum cabinet and another woodstove, made of sheet iron. It was better than the oil drum stove because it was made from a sheet of iron heated to extreme temperatures, then bent into a round shape. Clint's daddy bought that for us as a wedding gift.

The last room in our little home was a blue bedroom that had no bed. We had no furniture left for that room, so Clint put his comic books in there. He had hundreds, for he had been collecting since childhood, despite his mother's constant griping about him wasting money. He also kept his little brown bench press in there, a barbell, two dumb bells and an old feather tick, in case we had company. I covered the feather tick with a crocheted afghan that had belonged to Granny Eastridge.

The first day I had off from school, Fannie had Harlin bring her down to the house. She and Clint took me to the health department where I underwent the most humiliating afternoon of my life, getting examined by a nurse, but when I left, I had enough birth control pills to last six months.

After school, I would help Clint mow gardens. I also helped him do farm work on the weekends for local farmers. I helped Clint's daddy, Harlin, unload cattle feed one afternoon. I climbed up on the wagon and handed the feed sacks down to Mr. Kurtsinger, who had never done more than grunt. He rarely spoke.

On this particular afternoon as I handed him a bag of feed, he took it and sat it on the ground. "Clint," he said. His voice sounded like cellophane when you wadded it up. "This here is the hardest working, strongest girl I've ever seen. If you ask me, she's a good one; lifted this bag of feed like it weren't nothing." Then he smiled at me.

My heart soared. For all of his wife's complaining and apparent dislike of me, my father-in-law was fond of me.

Some roads, once you start on them, are just plain hard to get off of and that's how it was with me and not eating. For some reason, being married made me want to waste away more than ever. It's not that I didn't love my husband. Truth be told, sometimes I would get to thinking, what if Clint got killed down at the mill where he took a job and I'd burst right out in tears, afraid of being a sixteen-year-old widow. All during the months of April and May I'd come home, kill the 'waspers' out of my kitchen windows and go right to studying on my homework.

If Clint was thirty minutes late, I'd get to worrying that maybe he'd been killed and nobody could get a hold of me because we didn't have a phone. I sat right there and did my lessons with tears splattering the ink on my pages. I kept telling myself that I was being silly to keep thinking of the bad stuff that could happen, but bad stuff happened to Granny Eastridge and to Jerry Wayne. I knew there was no magic door that a person could lock to keep sorrow from moving right in and making itself at home.

I got out of school in May and spent the whole

summer working for people in tobacco. When I wasn't in a tobacco patch somewhere, I was hoeing out my garden or cleaning my little house. At night, I was always so tired I couldn't stay up past ten-thirty to save my life, even when Clint so wanted to watch Solid Gold and see who had the latest hit records out.

Momma had signed us up on food stamps, because she worried that we'd go hungry. Therefore, we had enough to eat, but I didn't eat. Clint did love me, but he and his momma both made it plain that my cooking wasn't right. In fact, a lot of things I did weren't good enough. But there were two things I could do better than anyone. I could make good grades in school, perfect grades, and I could have a perfect body, as skinny as a model or an actress. It was my own secret victory. I didn't have control over any area of my life. I belonged to other people, but my will over my own body belonged entirely to me.

Our first summer together came to an end, and in September we celebrated my seventeenth birthday at his parents' house. Fannie made me a cake then gave me a card and three dollars as a gift. For Fannie that was a lot, and for me it meant that just maybe she was beginning to like me at least a little.

That fall I entered my senior year with enough credits to graduate in December, which I did. When January came, I did not get up and go to school. I got up and went to work for Mrs. Rose Downey Rutledge who was in need of a house girl. I cleaned her house twice a week. The other three days I worked on the farm for her husband, an ex-military man everybody called Captain Abe.

Ms. Rose was in her mid fifties and had gray hair. She easily weighed three-hundred-fifty pounds and simply could not get around well enough to do the tedious parts of her house cleaning, like climbing on a ladder to dust shelves or getting down on her knees to shine the wooden baseboards. She kept her house immaculate, which kept me working and earning my three dollars an hour.

Now Captain Abe was as strict as Ms. Rose in other ways. He walked as straight as a floorboard and his hair, though he was pushing sixty, was as black as crude oil. He spoke in a deep voice when he did speak. He never asked me to do a thing; he ordered me!

Ms. Rose always cooked a big meal and would try to make me eat. I would only pick at my food, then first chance I got, I'd throw it all up. I know the gagging was yucky, but it was the only way I could think of to keep Ms. Rose off my back and not end up fat as she was. I could see right off what good cooking and good housekeeping did for women. It turned them into little fat balls that waddled around picking up for their husbands.

What I didn't count on was that Ms. Rose would call Momma and talk about how poorly I looked. One day in March, Clint and I went up to visit Momma and Daddy. It was rainy and cold. We all sat in the living room talking the way grownups do when Momma up and said, "Chippie, honey. I heard of a thing called anorexia and I'm worried that you've got that. You got to start eating more."

No. I gripped the chair arm. I could not do this. This control over my body was my comfort, the only thing that enabled me to go from day to day. I could not get fat. I could not. I wanted to be perfect and in this one area I would be.

I don't know why tears came but they did. And I don't know why I shouted, but I did, and I shouted at my momma, the person I loved most in this world.

"I can't, Momma, I can't. I will die if I get fat. I can't get fat."

I burst from the room, running out the front door. I ran as far and as fast as I could. I ran down the path to the hog pen, past the pen and on. I kept going. I don't know how far I went into the woods or how long I stayed. I only know that I came to a creek, swelled by rain, and followed it. I sobbed and sobbed, as if some dam I didn't even know existed had broken.

I eventually came out across the road from my own house. I went in and changed my wet clothes, then I just sat down on the floor behind the wood stove and hugged my knees.

"God," I said. "I'm horrible. I'm a horrible person. I don't even deserve to live. I wish it was me that died instead of Jerry Wayne. Look at me. I am fat and ugly and can't cook right. I can't do anything right." I looked around the living room where my paintings sat propped against the walls, without frames. I could never afford frames. I couldn't even afford real canvases. I just painted on whatever I could— wood, cardboard, old pieces of furniture I found in the landlord's garbage pile. Those paintings weren't good enough. Once I had tried to sell one to a Pentecostal lady up the road for just five dollars because Clint and I needed extra money but she wouldn't buy it.

Clint came in the door. His face went red when he saw me. "Chippie, I hope you're proud of yourself. Your sick Momma's been standing out in the rain calling for you," he said.

I hadn't realized Momma was sick.

"She fainted while we were out there looking for you," Clint said. "You better get back up there and let her know you're all right."

"Momma fainted?"

"Yeah," Clint said. "She was only out a few minutes, but your daddy's done got her in the car. They're on their way to the hospital."

I felt so bad about Momma being sick that I ran right out the door and got in the car. Clint came out behind me and drove me to the hospital. Momma was in the ER waiting room when we got there. I told her that I was sorry and that I'd try to eat better and take better care of myself. We sat with Momma and Daddy until the doctor called her in. She told us to go on home, that she'd tell us what he said when she got home.

That night, we went up to the house. Momma still looked poorly, but she told us that the doctor said she was just run down, that she needed to take it easy and relax. She then wanted to play a game of Rook and drink a good cup of coffee. No matter what had happened in our lives, a game of cards, late night conversation, and a cup of coffee made it all better.

The following week, I was in the grocery store when I spotted a magazine with a muscular woman on the front. It was two dollars. That was a lot of money for me, but I could not take my eyes off that woman bodybuilder. She had beautiful dark hair and wore a red bikini. Her face was as close to perfect as anything I'd ever seen and her body looked as strong as a man's. Below her picture were the words, *Rain's Secrets to a Successful Workout*. Her name was Rain, a beautiful woman with a beautiful name, yet she was as lean and strong as a man. I bought the magazine. After that I read and reread her articles over and over again. She had written inspiring words about balancing her body, mind, and spirit. Rain became my mentor, my hero, my guide, yet she never even knew I existed.

CHAPTER TWENTY FOUR

Lou Annie sat on my couch drinking coffee. She loved nice things so she drank out of my prettiest teacup and held her pinky out when she sipped. "This is the way rich people do it," she said.

I laughed. "Well, rich people don't sit on a couch held together by wire and duct tape when they drink, do they?"

"You got to use your imagination, Chippie." Then her face grew solemn. "I wish that I could imagine Daddy happy. Things ain't never going to be the same at home again. And I ain't talking about you marrying Clint. Daddy has hated me ever since Jerry Wayne died. I don't know what I did, but he's not the same to me. You know what happened yesterday? We went up on the hill to the store. And you know how that old woman, Meredith Goodin, in there is always saying that people are going to hell for wearing shorts?"

"I wear shorts in her store all the time."

"Yeah, but she don't notice you 'cause you look like a little girl. But I went in there to pay for Daddy's gas and she said, 'You're too big to be wearing them tight short breeches out in public. It ain't right at all how you young girls show your bodies off nowadays.'

"Well, Daddy overheard her through the screen door. When I got back out to the car he said, 'Lou Annie, you ain't coming with me no more if you're going to dress like a whore.'"

Lou Annie sat her cup down, her eyes big and round in her pale face. "Can you believe he said that to me, Chippie? My own daddy calling me a whore."

"Oh, Lou Annie," I said. "He didn't call you a whore. He just-"

"It don't matter," she said. "He don't like me. He would never say a word to you about the way you looked or dressed, but I'm fat, Chippie. And he is ashamed to be seen with me. I look like the Eastridges and my own daddy is ashamed of me, 'cause ever time he looks at my face, he sees Grandpa Eastridge's face. He treats me like I'm the one who did him wrong all those years. Well, it wasn't me. I never hurt nobody. And you know what? I'm going to do what I please with my life whether Daddy likes it or not."

I grieved inside when Lou Annie said those words. Yet with every visit home, I could see the growing tension. There was a rift between my father and my little sister and neither seemed able to see the beauty in the other. I knew Daddy loved Lou Annie, but the two of them saw the world through different eyes. Soon afterwards, Lou Annie started dating Rocky Delano, a boy from town.

Rocky was a dark-haired boy with olive skin and black eyes. He was also in and out of trouble all the time for minor things. He drove a Trans Am and smoked whenever he pleased. I don't know if Lou Annie was truly smitten with him or if she just dated him because he was everything my daddy didn't like in a boy.

Late one afternoon when Clint and I were up for a visit, I helped Momma wash the dishes. I washed. She rinsed. I noticed that Momma was far too quiet and that she kept staring out the window. "Momma," I said, "Is there something wrong?"

She sighed. "Yeah, a couple of things. Did you see Carol Lee out in the yard playing?"

"Yeah. I think so."

"You didn't smell of her," Momma said.

"Smell of her? Why would I want to do that?"

"Chippie, Carol Lee and Willie got to playing tag this afternoon. She did the dumbest thing. To get away from Willie, she climbed up that old bed rail that your daddy left propped up against the outhouse. She got on top of the outhouse and kicked the rail away. Willie said she was standing up there jumping and hollering, 'can't catch me now' when all at once the roof caved in."

"Say what? She could've been killed."

"Oh, it liked to have scared Willie to death. He ran in here and got me. I dropped the meatloaf I was cooking on the floor and ran out the backdoor, my heart beating so fast. I thought she was kilt. When I reached the toilet I flung open the door and there was no Carol Lee. I heard her hollerin' and I looked down the hole. There she was in shit and liquid up to her chin, treading like she was in a swimming pool. The garden hose was laying about three feet from the toilet door. I grabbed it and threw it down the hole. Carol Lee took hold of it and me, Willie, Josh David, and Zelphie pulled her out. There she was crying and screaming, scared half to death, and I couldn't even hug her to comfort her. I got sick from the smell and threw up."

"Oh, Momma, that's terrible, but is she okay?"

"She's covered in scratches, cuts, and bruises, but nothing's broken as far as I can tell. I sprayed her down with the hose, then made her take a bath in bleach water. It's a miracle I suppose. I mean the roof just happened to give way right over the hole part and the skinny little thing just fell straight through and shot right down through the hole. I have told your daddy so many times that the toilet hole was so wide a person could fall in and he kept saying that it wasn't."

"Did y'all take her to the doctor?"

"No, not yet. We're going to wait to see if anything swells. I hope and pray she's all right. Can you even imagine what we'd tell them at the hospital? Who would possibly believe it? Of course all they'd have to do is smell her. She still stinks to the high heavens."

As I passed her a plate, I said, "What's the other thing? You said there were a couple of things."

Momma took the plate and shook her head. She bit her lip like she was trying to keep from crying. "Chippie, Lou Annie's pregnant."

I almost fell down. "Does Daddy know?"

Momma nodded. "Oh, he knows. He threatened to kick Lou Annie out of the house. I told him if he did, he'd have to kick me out too."

My parents fighting? I wanted to burst out in tears right there on the spot. My parents didn't fight, not the parents who raised me. I looked at Momma from the side, her black hair, her smooth porcelain skin, and I realized that my Momma was young. She still had the face of a girl and she had been married since she was fifteen. For some reason, I wanted to hold Momma and let her be the child. She had not been one in a long time and now, at thirty-seven-years-old, she was to be a grandmother— a grandmother without gray hair or wrinkles. Grandmothers should look old. They shouldn't look like schoolgirls who've had to work too hard.

That night at home in bed, I turned my back to Clint and let silent tears wet my pillow while he slept. The very thing that I had feared had happened to my sister. I had been terrified of bringing shame, guilt, and pain on my parents. Now Lou Annie was living my nightmare.

The next thing Lou Annie did was get her driver's license, something I had not done, something Momma had never done. Lou Annie decided that she was going to take herself to the places she needed to go, mainly to the doctor's office. Of course, Momma was going with her. Momma had been seeing her doctor on a regular basis, then all of a sudden, she up and quit. She said she would be fine, that she needed to be there for Lou Annie and didn't have time to be fretting over herself.

Momma's decision bothered my daddy, but he never would talk about it. He just stayed angry at Lou Annie a lot and could hardly say a peaceable word to her. Daddy would come home from the mill and they would be gone. Lou Annie would take Momma to do the laundry in town.

"Momma," she'd say. "There ain't no need in you

having to use that old wringer washer and working so hard. Let's you and me take them clothes to town and wash them." They'd often get groceries afterwards.

Zelphie and Willie would be looking after Josh David and Carol Lee. Zelphie was nearing teenage years and could cook, wash clothes, clean house, and change diapers. Zelphie had taken care of Granny Eastridge when she was only ten and was an exceptionally bright and level-headed child who happened to look like Momma's little twin. Still, Daddy would be upset. He had always come home to a hot meal and a steaming cup of coffee. He had always sat at the table and talked to Momma about his day, but often times now, Momma wasn't there.

One day while Clint was at work and I was off because the rain kept Captain Abe from doing any pressing farm work and I had already cleaned Ms. Rose's house twice that week, I lifted weights in front of the mirror, noticing the muscles in my arm.

Then I felt a strange thing, almost like someone had laid a hand on my shoulder. "So, this is what the hand of God feels like," I said to myself. "Okay, Lord, Momma's right. Help me." I whispered. "Momma has always loved me, even when it seemed like the whole world didn't like me. I swear to you that if you will help me, I will never gag myself or throw up on purpose again." I thought of how Momma and Daddy were hurting over Lou Annie getting pregnant. And I thought of how scared Lou Annie must be, her only fifteen-years-old. A dam of tears broke inside me and I cried for my family.

CHAPTER TWENTY-FIVE

For Lou Annie, having the car Jerry Wayne left behind and a license not only allowed her the ability to take Momma places, it made it possible for her to go out with Rocky and meet new people any time she wanted.

Daddy tried to get Lou Annie to marry Rocky, but instead of marrying that boy, Lou Annie broke up with him, swearing she would never marry anybody she didn't love. It was plain to me for sure that Lou Annie only went with him because she was mad at Daddy in the first place.

Lou Annie's independence brought Myrtle Jean Cooper into her life. Myrtle came from Greensburg and was the daughter of a traveling Pentecostal preacher.

The first time I saw Myrtle was when she walked down to the house one afternoon with Willie to borrow a cup of sugar so Momma could make some chocolate gravy pudding. She was tall and thin with fine features and alabaster skin. Her hair hung past her waist in black waves, but was dry and frizzy.

She had grown up wearing long skirts and had never worn makeup. At seventeen, she did everything she could to go against her raising. She wore a blouse so low that if she bent over, her breasts came spilling right out of it and her pants were as tight as her skin. She wore makeup, and lots of it. Her eyelids were moss green, trimmed in thick lines of eyeliner and made heavy with mascara.

I'm not sure how she hooked up with Lou Annie, but she did. And she just kept coming around; no matter how many times Daddy told Lou Annie that she wasn't nothing but a strumpet. In fact, the more Daddy protested, the more Lou Annie had her over. It seemed to me that the one who was most captivated by her was Willie, who had just turned thirteen. He followed her around the house and yard, jabbering at her and teaching her how to ride our ponies.

Clint was still at work, and I was planting beans in the little dirt patch beside my house one afternoon when I looked up and saw Zelphie crossing the road into my front yard. My little sister had grown up to be a beautiful, slender twelve-year-old.

"Chippie," she called before she reached me. "S-s-somethin awful's happened."

I dropped my hoe, "What?"

She was out of breath and had clearly run all the way to my house. She started telling me but was stuttering so bad I couldn't understand her.

"Slow down, Zelphie, and tell me."

"W-w-willie's in b-b-bad t-t-trouble. Him and Myrtle done g-gone and robbed Mr. George's house. Momma said he m-might go to jail. She's home crying 'bout it now."

"Why would Willie rob Mr. George?" I asked.

"It wasn't really him that did the robbing. It was M-Myrtle. Her and Willie went over to the store to get them a pop. On the way back across the field, Myrtle noticed Mr. George wasn't home and that he left the bathroom window open. She told Willie to watch and see if anybody was coming while she crawled inside to look around. Willie told me that she said she just wanted to see how an old man lives, but she found a jar of money under his bed and she took the whole thing. Had thirteen hundred dollars in it."

"Where's Myrtle now?"

"Up town in the j-j- jailhouse. Somebody over at the store was getting in their car and seed Willie standing by the house and seed her come out the window. I reckon they went back inside and called the police.

"The cops went out and got Myrtle this morning at home and put her in jail. The sheriff just now left the house and told Momma that Willie might have to go to c-court if Mr. George presses charges again him. I'm scared to death, Chippie. And Momma is crying. Lou Annie keeps saying she can't believe Myrtle would do that to her, but she did. She g-got Willie in so much trouble. And Daddy, he won't even talk to Lou Annie. He's behind the house, down by the toilet, just keeps staring out into the woods and saying 'Lord, Lord.'"

My little sister put her arms around my waist. "Come up home, Chippie. Everybody will be better if you come to the house. 'Cause you stay calm all the time."

"All right," I said, then took Zelphie's hand. We crossed the road together. "Everything's going to be all right, Zelphie. Don't you be scared now, you hear?"

When we reached the house, Momma met us at the door. I could tell she had been crying. Her face was red and her eyes were puffy. Willie was sitting in the orange

256

chair in the corner, his head down, long dark hair hanging down over his eyes. Willie had taken to wearing his hair long and it was well past his collar now.

Momma said, "Chippie, you heard?"

"Zelphie told me."

"We're waiting on the sheriff to call or to come back," Momma said. "They don't know yet what they're going to do. We don't know if George's going to press charges or not."

I went in the kitchen and put on some coffee water for Momma. We sat at the table and drank coffee. Lou Annie came into the kitchen and sat at the table, too. I could tell that she'd been crying. Her belly, though she was far along now, didn't stick out half as much as most pregnant women's do. I suppose that if I hadn't known she was pregnant, I would just think that she was a big girl.

"Momma," she said. "I ain't never hanging out with Myrtle again. I didn't know she would steal, and I didn't know that she'd get Willie in trouble like that."

Momma set her cup down and looked at Lou Annie. "I'm not blaming you, honey, but if Willie goes to jail over this, I don't know what we're going to do. This family's been through too much. Chippie, go check on your Daddy."

"Okay, Momma." I got up and went down to where Daddy was standing beside the outhouse.

"Sissy," he said as I stood beside him. "I've done lost one son. I just can't bear to lose another one." There were tears in Daddy's eyes. "I have always loved every one of you babies."

"Lou Annie doesn't think you love her."

He bit his lip and shook his head. "Lou Annie is hard-headed. Once she gets a notion in that head of hers, there ain't no getting it out. I just wanted her to be a decent girl, but now she's done gone and got herself knocked up, a disgrace...but you know I love her. Ain't nothing ever going to change that."

"She needs you to tell her that."

"All I can think about right now is what's going to happen to Willie."

The sound of crunching gravel and a car motor drew us to the front yard where the sheriff's car sat in the driveway. The sheriff got out and motioned Daddy over. Mr. George got out of the passenger door.

Daddy nodded toward the house. "Go on in the house and get your momma. Keep the kids inside until we get done talking."

I did as he asked.

After a few minutes, Momma stuck her head in the door and said, "Willie, come out here. The sheriff wants to see you."

Willie still didn't look up, nor did he say a word. He just got up and went out to the sheriff.

Lou Annie and I watched them out the living room window. Zelphie, Carol Lee and Josh David watched them out the bedroom window; all of us were nearly holding our breath, wondering what would happen to Willie.

Then we saw Daddy wave at the sheriff and Mr. George pat Daddy on the back. Then the two men got back in the police car. Momma, Daddy, and Willie came toward the house. We waited for them at the front door.

"Well," Momma said when the door opened. "Willie ain't going to jail."

"Mr. George didn't press charges," Daddy said. "He's a good man in his own way I reckon. He says it'd be a shame to send a boy to jail over not having enough sense to watch the company he keeps."

"Willie's not going to jail?" I asked and some of my brothers and sisters did, too, all at once.

"Nope," Willie said. "I ain't a-going to no jail."

"George got his money back before Myrtle could spend it and since Willie is only thirteen and really didn't know she was going to steal the money, well, Mr. George feels that he was really kind of innocent. Still, the sheriff says if he ever gets in trouble again, even just a little, he'll probably go straight to jail." Daddy put his hand on Willie's shoulder. "But you ain't going to get in no more trouble are you, son?"

"I ain't aiming to," Willie said.

"What about Myrtle?" Lou Annie asked.

Daddy pulled off his hat and gritted his teeth. "She's got to go before the judge, but one thing's for sure. That girl ain't never setting foot in this house again."

I spent the whole afternoon with my family. Momma and Daddy had a cup of coffee together at the kitchen table after the sheriff left. They talked. I went with Lou Annie into Jerry Wayne's old bedroom. She had moved in shortly after I got married. Momma and Daddy had fussed about it. Daddy felt like nobody should touch any of Jerry Wayne's things, but Momma said that Jerry Wayne would have wanted to share with his brothers and sisters, just like he always gave his hand me downs to me. So, Lou Annie and Willie divided his shirts between them. And Lou Annie moved into his bedroom and took to driving his car.

We sat in her room on the bed. Even though it was just the last weekend in April, it was plum hot outside and Lou Annie ran a fan in her room to keep cool. Lou Annie propped herself up on a pillow at the head of the bed. I sat on the foot, one leg on the bed, and one on the floor.

"My baby's due next week," she said. "And I ain't got no idea what to name it."

"Well, you could name it after one of your sisters or you could name it something pretty, like Juliana."

"No, no, that's a normal name. You know I never would name my baby something normal."

"Hmmmm," I said. I stared out the window. A little brown sparrow landed on a bush beside the windowsill. I watched as it settled its little body into a small nest. "How about Sparrow? Momma always says a sparrow stays here in the winter. It braves the cold in hopes that spring will come."

"Sparrow?" Lou Annie said. Then she said the name

over and over to herself several times. "You know, that is a neat name. I never heard of anybody named Sparrow. I kind of like it. Sparrow Dawn."

I smiled. "That's real pretty."

"So if it's a girl, I'm calling her Sparrow Dawn."

"What if it's a boy?"

"It ain't going to be no boy."

"How do you know that?"

"Cause Aunt Suez came up here the other day and felt my belly. She can tell what a baby is by feeling how you're carrying it. I'm having a girl."

"But what if she's wrong?"

Lou Annie laughed. "She ain't never wrong. Granny Pablo taught her how to do it and she ain't never wrong."

"Well, let's think up a boy name just in case," I said.

"All right. All right. I think if it's a boy I'm going to name it Jeremy Wayne, after Jerry Wayne."

I grinned. "I like that, Lou Annie. I sure do like that and I know Jerry Wayne would, too."

When I came out of Lou Annie's room to head home, I noticed Momma lying on her bed.

"You all right, Momma?" I asked. I sat down on the bed and laid my cheek on her back.

"Yeah, honey, I'm all right. I just feel awfully tired

sometimes." She coughed. "And I've got a bad cold, but don't you worry none." I stretched out on the bed beside Momma. For some reason, it felt good to lie beside her like this. I lived a stone's throw from her, yet it seemed like I had been gone away from home for a long, long time, like I could never really go home again. I just wanted to be with Momma in the dark room.

"You know," she said. "Lou Ellen was here this morning, wanting to borrow five dollars in food stamps."

Lou Ellen Pablo, Damien's momma, who was always making fun of me drawing and saying I wouldn't amount to anything. "You didn't give it to her, did you?"

Momma smiled. "I've been talking to the Lord. He spoke to me. I never really believed in God before, but he spoke to me sure as you're talking to me right now. I heard his voice. Me and him worked some things out. And he showed me some things. I did give them to her. I didn't have much, but people got to stick together, Chippie. That's one of the things he showed me. We got to love one another."

I had never heard my momma talk about God in this way before. There was nothing artificial in her voice and I knew that if my momma said God had talked to her, then he had. Other people might have had ulterior motives, but not my momma.

"I know Lou Ellen has her quirks," she went on, "but it ain't easy being in this world, and we got to forgive each other because nobody's perfect. We got to treat people the way we wish the whole world would treat us, not the way the world does treat us. Life is so short,

Chippie. Remember what I used to say when you'd pick flowers on my birthday?"

"You always said that it was a good thing to give people flowers while they're living because after they're dead, they can't appreciate them."

Momma nodded. "I don't hold anything against Lou Ellen. She can't help how she is. And I want you to keep this in mind, too. Idy Jo and Tiny Elmer, they're good people and so is Mr. George. And poor little Lou Annie, she's a good girl. Just got a little mixed up is all, but she's still my baby and I love her. I love all you kids. You're all I have ever wanted in this life."

I put my arms around her again. "I love you, Mommy. I love you so much. I'm sorry if I have ever hurt you."

"You ain't never hurt me. I am proud of you, Chippie. You're a smart girl and a hard-working girl. I believe with all my heart that you can be whatever you set your mind to being. You've got gifts. All I ask is that you use them. Go on to school. Get your education and do something with your life to make this world a better place. And Chippie," she said, "keep on believing in Jesus like you do. Everybody in the family's looking to you. Sometimes you don't know it, but it's true. You're a light. When all the world was dark and Jerry Wayne died and Granny Eastridge died, your little light was shining."

Then Momma told me to go on home and get Clint's supper. She said she wanted to rest her eyes. I could hear Momma coughing when I closed the living room door. I stepped off the porch into drizzling rain and started home beneath a darkening sky.

CHAPTER TWENTY-SIX

Dogwood winter comes in April. It's not really winter, but rather a time when the spring temperatures that have been running in the seventies drop to the forties and fifties. It's a rainy season when the sun doesn't shine for about a week. During this time, it's hard to keep a fire burning.

One afternoon, the fire wouldn't burn; Clint was kneeling down in front of the stove. All at once, he jumped to his feet and just growled, the iron poker still in his hand. Without prior warning, he hit the wall with the iron poker as hard as he could, knocking paint and plaster to the floor.

"I can't do nothing right!" he screamed, then kicked the stove so hard that it scooted near the edge of the tin.

"Calm down and let me try," I said.

He handed me the poker but stood behind me, cussing and ranting. I fought back tears. This wasn't the first time Clint had displayed this strange sudden angry behavior.

"Clint," I said. "I know I promised you that I'd never leave you, but if you ever hit me..." I bit my lip. "If you ever hit me instead of the wall or the car or whatever else your fist finds, I swear I will leave you and I'll never come back."

"I won't ever hit you," he said. "But I am tired of never being able to do anything right. Nobody likes me. Nobody will give me a break in this life. I might as well be dead."

"Don't talk like that," I said. "I wouldn't be here if I didn't love you."

"I can't help my temper. I've always had it. Just ask Momma. Our house was full of holes in the walls. You know why?"

"Why?"

"It's because nobody ever loved me, Chippie. Eugene and Daddy called me green, growing up. Earnestine made fun of me. I used to dream about going to the navy, but I ain't never gonna do nothing."

"I'm sorry," I said. "I didn't realize that marrying me kept you from living your dream."

"Oh, you didn't," he said. "I didn't go to the navy after high school because I was afraid. I'm afraid of everything, Chippie. I'm afraid of living and I'm too scared to die." He shrugged and flipped on the TV, then went in the kitchen and got himself a cola.

I walked over to the front door and looked out. There are those moments when a person recalls some small memory that has been shoved so far back in her brain there should be no finding it, but a smell or sound or sight brings it floating right to the top of her memory.

That's how it was as I stood in the front doorway, looking out at a house down the road that sat on a big hill, looking at the big oak tree in the yard, with its branches spread so wide, looked black. It reminded me of the way the big maple trees looked in our yard when I was very young.

I recalled a day when I was seven. I had been swinging under one of those maple trees in our front yard down there in Walkup Holler, and I was singing. I was singing about angels, which I had never seen but wished I could see in the clouds. So, I pretended the white fluffy clouds were giant angels, looking down, trying to talk to me. Then I heard Momma call my name.

I went running into the house to see what she wanted. I had a terrible lonesome feeling that day. It was like a chill wind had swept over me, though there was not a breeze stirring anywhere. It was the type of thing that Granny Pablo always called a warning from the other side. I had shouted, "Momma, what did you want?"

She had been in the kitchen, churning butter, and humming as she often did when she worked. "Nothing, Chippie."

"But you called me," I said.

She laughed. "No, I didn't. It's just your imagination, sweetheart."

Some imagination. That incident had left me with cold-chill bumps all up and down my arms. And upon remembering it, they returned. Some things never change, like the weird feeling you get when you have déjà vu or when you hear your name being called, but there's nobody there to call it.

"Chippie," someone screamed. I turned and saw Carol Lee running down the road from Momma and Daddy's house.

"Oh God, Chippie! Come quick! Something's wrong with Momma."

"Clint, let's go!" I said.

He stood, "What? I'm watching T.V."

Carol Lee was in the yard by the time I got out the door and Clint, sensing now that something was really wrong, switched off the television and came out behind me.

Carol Lee was crying. "Momma won't wake up. She laid down for a nap. I went into the bedroom and found her sitting on the bed with her head in her hands like she always sits when she has a bad headache. I said, 'Momma?' but she didn't say anything back to me. I went over there and shook her. She still didn't say anything or move. Oh, Chippie. I think she's dead. We can't get her to move or talk or anything. Hurry-"

"Get in the car," Clint said.

``We rushed to the house and found all my brothers and sisters in the back bedroom gathered round Carol Lee and Zelphie's bed. Momma was sitting on the side of the bed with her head in her hands, just as my little sister had described.

"Oh, Momma, Momma," Willie kept saying as he shook Momma's shoulder.

"I came in here to ask her something," Carol Lee said, "And I found her like this. I think she's dead." All the kids broke out bawling.

I got down on my knees and shook her, "Momma,"

268

I said. She didn't answer.

I looked up at Zelphie, "Where's Lou Annie?"

"Gone to get Daddy," Zelphie whimpered.

"Call an ambulance," I said to Clint.

Willie said, "Lou Annie's done called it."

Clint went into Momma and Daddy's room and looked out the window. "Ambulance just went up the highway," he called.

Just then, we heard the front screen door slam. Daddy and Lou Annie raced through the house. Daddy fell on his knees beside Momma, crying uncontrollably, "Oh, baby," he said. "Oh, honey."

He pushed Momma back on the bed and tried to give her mouth-to-mouth, but he didn't know how. None of us did.

"Lou Annie," I said, "the ambulance passed up our house. Call the station again."

Lou Annie did just that and in a while, strangers in uniforms rushed through the front door with a stretcher. They came into the bedroom where Momma was. The first thing they did was give her CPR, but their results were no better than Daddy's.

Then they eased Momma off the bed and over onto the stretcher. She was as limp as a rag doll and looked so little and faraway lying there, like some part of her had left. We all watched as they loaded Momma in the ambulance.

One of the drivers, a fat man with a light brown beard, said, "Mr. Pablo, you can ride with her, but just one. That's all that's allowed."

Willie, Josh David, and I got in the car with Clint. Zelphie and Carol Lee got in Lou Annie's car and we followed the ambulance to the hospital.

Outside the emergency room, we waited for about forty-five minutes. Then a nurse told us there was a chapel where we could pray. The chapel was a small room, about ten feet by ten feet with an orange-carpeted floor and pale green walls. There was a big wooden cross on one wall with an altar railing running beneath it and there were six wooden pews, padded with more of the orange carpet and a roll top desk sat in the very back of the room.

All of us, from Josh David to Daddy knelt at that altar railing and prayed. I heard Carol Lee, beside me, sniffling and crying. She said, "Please, God, please don't take my Mommy."

Daddy stood up in the corner, eyes turned upward, "Oh, God, if a life must be taken, take mine instead of hers."

I couldn't pray. I couldn't cry. I couldn't feel. I did not know how to pray this time. I did not know what to say or ask for. I felt as if there was something beyond my understanding at work, some wheel of fate that had been set in motion and would not stop turning until it was meant to do so. I heard myself whisper the only words I could remember, the words Jesus prayed when he knew he was going to the cross. "Let your will, not mine, be done." Nobody heard me whisper that prayer, nobody but

God. As soon as the words left my mouth, I knew. Momma wouldn't be going home with us. Her journey in this world was done, her mission accomplished. The doctor walked in. We all stood. Daddy went to the back of the chapel.

Dr. Robert had known our family for a long time. He just stood there, his face almost as pale as his white hair. Then he shook his head. "I did all I could." Daddy crumbled right over a chapel pew. My little sisters broke out in wails and Dr. Robert had tears streaming down his face.

"She was too young," he said. Then he laid his hand on my daddy's back. "I tried to get her to go to Louisville for treatments, Joseph. Adult onset acute leukemia is so…so…" He left off speaking for a minute and bit his lip, fighting back his tears. "She wouldn't let me admit her because she didn't want to leave her babies, especially the grandbaby that's on its way. I'm so sorry." After a minute more, he put his hands in his lab coat pockets, turned, and walked out.

Some moments in life are vivid and clear. Some are a blur. The moments after discovering my momma was dead from a disease she had kept secret from her children are like a photo taken with too much flash in my brain. There is only a blob where there should be a picture.

A nurse must have called the rest of our family, because Uncle Dody and his wife were waiting at Grandpa Eastridge's house when we got there. Grandpa Eastridge sat at the kitchen table like he always had, wearing his gray work shirt and the old felt hat that covered his blue-gray hair, a ceramic coffee cup in front of him. Momma had once said that Grandpa Eastridge would drink a cup of coffee even if he were being blown away by a tornado. It was true. No matter what, he drank coffee. And now, at Momma's death, it seemed that cup was the only thing holding him in the world. He clutched it as if it were his lifeline and looked at it as if he were talking straight to it. Then he broke right down and cried. "My little girl is dead." I don't think he said much after that. I didn't know Grandpa Eastridge could cry, but he could and he did.

We stayed there that night. Clint and I slept upstairs in an old antique bed that had been a part of Granny Eastridge's house for as long as I could remember. Of course I really didn't sleep much at all. I lay in bed fully dressed, staring out into nothingness most of the night. It did not feel real. Nothing seemed real. I kept thinking I would wake up and everything would be back like it was before we ever moved to Briar Ridge, back when we lived on the farm and a person could smell Momma's cobbler pie clear across the field, and when I played beneath the old pear tree, and Momma hung Christmas garland on the banister rails. But morning came and the nightmarish existence was still with me.

Aunts and uncles came from everywhere-Arkansas, Tennessee, Louisville, Bowling Green, Somerset, and Lexington. Pablos came and Eastridges came. They drank coffee together, ate together, and shared stories. They talked in loud voices of old times and about all the wonderful things Momma had done and said to each of them. The Eastridges got to talking about what it was like when they were growing up and I saw them in a way that I had never seen them. I saw them as Momma's brothers and sisters, people who had played games and pulled crazy stunts.

Aunt Poodle Bug told about the time that a teenage Uncle Dody and a friend cut eye holes in refrigerator boxes and walked around the town square, trying to snatch a lady's purse. They all laughed as they relived the time Uncle Sammy Eastridge climbed on top of Granny's roof to sneak a smoke, but accidentally caught his britches on fire. They lived next door to a schoolyard, so about fifty kids saw my uncle's bare bottom that afternoon as he stripped out of his burning pants. Every one of them had a tale to tell about Momma. I saw them, as they might have been when they were children, and they seemed much like us.

We had a three-day wake for Momma, who had nicer clothes in her death than she had ever worn in her life, because again like when Jerry Wayne died, people felt sorry for us and pitched in. She looked like a girl lying in that pink coffin, in her pink dress and without a wrinkle on her pretty face. Her hair, black as charcoal and her flawless pale skin, made her look as if she were a china doll, instead of a real person who had given birth to seven children and loved them with her last breath.

The funeral parlor overflowed with flowers and with people. Old neighbors from when Momma and Daddy first married came. People Momma had known as a girl came. Cousins came. Ladies from the Nazarene church came and from the Methodist church, too, even though Momma had never been a member at either place. Idy Jo and Tiny Elmer were there. The teachers from Briar Ridge school came and from the high school, too. Everybody hugged us kids and told us how sorry they were. Some of them would look at little Josh David and hurry out with handkerchiefs over their noses. I don't think I ate more than one bite for the whole three days, though the food at

Grandpa Eastridge's house was stacked two layers deep on the table from where friends and neighbors had wanted to do something to help.

There was so much crying during the funeral as some ladies from my church sang 'Unclouded Day' and 'Sweet Beluah Land,' then a minister stood and read Psalm 23. Then the preacher from my church stood and spoke kind words about Momma. He told how little Carol Lee had confided to him that her Momma had just two days ago said she had accepted the Lord and was ready to go home should he call. He went on to say that according to my Daddy, Momma had known for two weeks that she had leukemia, but she wouldn't let herself be put in the hospital for she didn't want to be without her babies that long and knowing she might die anyway, she wanted to die at home among those she loved so much.

I sat there just thinking about Momma, about how she was so unselfish. I knew the reason she wouldn't go to the hospital. She was afraid Lou Annie might go into labor and have no one there to be with her and tell her everything was going to be all right. In a way, Momma had given her life for Lou Annie's baby. I thought about how I once heard a preacher say that the greatest love was a love that would lay down its own life for the sake of another.

Well, if Momma wasn't going to Heaven, then nobody in the whole history of the world would ever go, because Momma was living love. That's all she was. The minister preaching her funeral went on, naming off the things people had told him Momma had done to bless their lives, little things that she did just because they were a part of who she was.

Momma was buried the first of May, fourteen months after Clint and I were married. The sun shone that day and there was not one cloud in the sky. At the graveyard, birds were singing like all was right with the world, but those birds were lying. People filled that cemetery with so many cars there was nowhere for some of them to park. I held onto Clint some of the time, to my little brothers and sisters some of the time. Lou Annie, her belly sticking out with a baby that was already a few days past due, stood by Momma's coffin and cried until they got ready to put it in the ground and my Aunt Suez had to pull her away. But then Lou Annie broke loose and pulled a red rose from Momma's casket flowers. "Something to show my baby," she said. "Something to show my baby."

CHAPTER TWENTY-SEVEN

After the funeral, we all went home. I went to my little green shack on the side of the road and my brothers and sisters went to that ugly tarpaper covered shed we had called home. Only it wasn't home anymore. It was a little shack that had lost part of its life when Jerry Wayne died and the rest of it when Momma died. It was gray and ugly. It reeked of poverty and death. Every time I looked at that house, I thought how beautiful our lives had been before we came to this place. Now Daddy lived with Carol Lee, Willie, Lou Annie, Zelphie, and Josh David in this wooden box of sad memories.

I spent as much time up there with them as I could, but Daddy didn't talk. He only sat in his chair and stared out into space, crying. Sometimes he took long walks. There was so much pain in that house and without Momma there, nobody could ease it. I was helpless to help anyone.

One Friday, Clint was at work and I was just home from setting tobacco. I had barely finished my bath when Daddy pulled into the driveway with Lou Annie and Aunt Suez in the car. The baby was coming and he had to get her to the hospital in Danville. Lou Annie wanted me to be there when her baby came. So I left a note on the door for Clint and jumped in the car.

Daddy and I remained in the waiting room while Aunt Suez went in with Lou Annie. We waited a long time, Daddy praying that Lou Annie would not die in childbirth.

After hours that I forgot to count, a nurse came out

and said, "Mr. Pablo?"

Daddy stood, so nervous that his hands were shaking. "How's my girl?"

The nurse smiled. "Your daughter's fine and you are grandfather of a healthy baby girl, Sparrow Dawn Pablo."

Daddy looked up and closed his eyes. "Lord," he said, "You've taken my wife and my boy, but now you've given me a granddaughter." He wiped his eyes. "Momma always said that when one life is taken from this world, another enters to replace it."

Not much later, we saw Sparrow Dawn through the big nursery window. She lay in a white bassinet, shaking her pink fist at something we couldn't see. Her wide eyes were bright blue and her hair, a mass of white silk, just like Lou Annie's.

I wanted to call Clint to tell him that we were all fine, but I didn't have change. I tried to call collect to Fannie's house so she would give him the message, but when the operator got her on the line, I heard Fannie on the other end, "I won't accept no collect calls."

"Tell her it is from her daughter-in-law," I told the operator.

"I won't accept," Fannie said.

"I need her to tell Clint the baby came and everyone's okay," I told the operator. Still, Fannie would not accept. Then I got down right mad and said, "Well, tell her that she's a selfish, stingy woman that only worries about herself and what little money she has." I hung up the phone. There was a sinking in my stomach. Clint's world and my world were so far apart. I didn't know where tomorrow would find us, but for the first time in a long time, I could rejoice in life and hope.

About a week after Sparrow Dawn came into our lives, Uncle Dody Eastridge stopped by.

He sat down on the couch and I fixed him a cup of coffee in the kitchen, "Chippie, your curtains match," he hollered through the door.

I brought his coffee into the living room. "Yeah, they're all the same color."

"I'm surprised at how well you keep this house, being so young and all."

"Thank you," I said.

He picked up his coffee. "Don't be like your momma."

"What do you mean?"

"You married so young," he said. "Don't start having a house full of babies and never make something of yourself. Go to school, Chippie. That's what she wanted for you kids. That's what your Granny Eastridge wanted, too. They both had high hopes for you."

"Granny Eastridge had high hopes for me?"

He nodded. "For all of you kids. Especially you and..." He looked down. "Jerry Wayne."

He sat his coffee cup on the table. "Did you paint all of these landscape pictures?"

I nodded.

"They're good. Can I borrow a few? I'd like to show them to a friend of mine who works at the college."

About a month later, I received a letter from the college, inviting me to bring my art portfolio to the director of the Art Department. The art professor had seen my work and wanted to see more. She was impressed with my grades and there was the possibility of a scholarship.

I was ecstatic. I called Uncle Dody from Daddy's house and thanked him.

"Chippie," he said. "You're a smart girl. I want you to do something with your life. Don't wind up a barefoot, pregnant little hillbilly like your Pablo cousins and like…" He almost said Lou Annie, I could tell. "Just make something out of yourself. Your momma always believed you'd be the first Pablo ever to go to college. Don't let her down."

I didn't like the way he viewed Lou Annie, but I had never imagined I could go to college. That was something rich kids did. Up until this point, I was just proud that I would be the first Pablo to graduate high school.

When Clint found out I was nominated for a scholarship, he got angry. "College! It's just somebody else trying to take you away from me. What makes you want to go to college?"

"It's the chance of a lifetime," I said. "A dream

come true. Don't you see? I was meant to do this. I can feel it inside."

After he pouted for a day, he up and said, "Well, if it makes you happy, go for it. Who knows? One day you might be a rich and famous artist."

On the appointed day, I put on my purple overalls, pulled my dark brown hair, which now reached half way down my back, into a ponytail and gathered my best art pieces. Clint drove me to my interview on the local college campus.

Century-old brick buildings sat beneath ancient oaks and pines atop a long hill. The campus lawns were trimmed so that not a stray blade of grass poked its head up past the sidewalk. There was mulch around every tree and flowering shrub.

A cobblestone walk led from the parking lot to the admissions building, a big old southern estate type edifice that looked like it belonged in *Gone With the Wind*. The building had a high porch with steps leading up. A solid copper handrail ran down the center of the steps, which led to the shady porch, surrounded by big white columns.

I thought of how my house and Daddy's house could both fit inside that building with plenty of room left over and I wondered about what it was like to work in such a beautiful building, with its many tall windows.

"Wow," I said as Clint and I got out of the car. "This place looks just like a scene from a movie."

Inside the admissions building was also impressive. Three flights of stairs wound their way around its polished floors and our voices echoed off its old wooden doors, stucco walls, and high ceilings.

After filling out my admissions paperwork, we asked directions to the Art Department and found it was in a building on the far side of the campus. The art building had rows and rows of windows so that light spilled into the big open room, bathing everything in sharp shadows. We waited there for the director. I put my hands in my pockets to keep them from trembling. I had never been more nervous about anything in my life.

"I've never been to a college before," Clint said.

"Maybe if I go now, you can go after I get out and get a good paying job," I said.

He shrugged. "I don't know. I don't think I'd like to go to college."

We heard the sound of someone approaching just before a tall, thin lady with cropped blue-gray hair walked in. She was dressed very manly in navy slacks and a V-neck sweater vest with a long sleeve white blouse under it. She wore glasses and almost no jewelry, save a watch and wedding ring.

She extended her hand, "Hello, I'm Jean Austin Randell, the art instructor."

Jean Austin Randell, what a refined sound that name had. It was the most eloquent name I had ever heard. And what a refined lady she seemed to be with her perfect grammar and manicured hands.

"I'm Nochipa," I said, "but everybody calls me

Chippie."

The corners of her mouth turned down, but she wasn't frowning. I could tell by her eyes that she was smiling, smiling upside down. "Well, if your mother named you Nochipa," she said. "Then I will call you Nochipa."

I smiled. She said my name right. "This is my husband, Clint."

"Husband? Good Lord, child. You don't look a day over fourteen. I hardly think you need a husband. But I know how things can be here. I did grow up on Briar Ridge."

"Briar Ridge?" I couldn't believe it. This lady, this eloquent, well-groomed, college professor was from Briar Ridge?

She laughed. "Is that so hard for you to believe?"

Clint and I answered in unison. "Yes."

"Nochipa, a person can be anything she wants to be in life. It doesn't matter who she is or where she comes from. You kids have married so young. You'll need to work hard to take care of each other and you'll always have a special bond. Now," she smiled upside down again. "Let me see this art portfolio of yours."

I took a deep breath and handed her my portfolio, homemade from a brown paper grocery bag. She removed the first drawing. Then another. After each piece, she said. "Mmmm."

She spread my work out on the table and looked at each piece. "Yes, yes," she mumbled to herself then pulled her glasses down over her nose, squinted, and looked at the pictures more closely. Then she pushed her glasses back into place, crossed her arms in front of herself and turned to face Clint and me. "Nochipa," she said. "I am going before the scholarship board this Thursday night. Now, there have been several applicants for this scholarship, but I am going to recommend that you receive it."

"Oh, thank you, Mrs. Randell," I said. "Oh, thank you!"

"You are a very talented young woman and if you are as hard working as you are talented, then you need to be in college. I have been a teacher for fifty years, since I was nineteen-years-old and I can recognize a gift when I see it."

Clint and I were so excited that we went straight to Fannie's house.

She was washing dishes and smoking when I told her. Her cigarette lay loosely on her lips and I wondered how she kept ashes from falling in her dishwater. She wiped her hands on her red-checkered apron.

"College?" She took her cigarette in her fingers and blew smoke out her mouth. "Ain't that going to cost money?"

"I might be getting a scholarship," I said. "For my drawing."

"What do you mean?"

"She means the school's going to let her go the first

two years for free if the College Board approves her."

Fannie laughed. "That ain't going to happen. They give stuff like that to rich people. Besides, all that time Chippie's in college, she could be making some real money. The sewing factory's hiring. Now there's real steady work." She put her cigarette with its red ringed butt in the ashtray on the table. "You get on there, Chippie, and you can start making money for you and Clint right now."

I had learned that it was just foolish to try to talk logic with Fannie. No matter what I said, she always saw only one viewpoint, her own. It turned out that she had already set me up a job interview over at the factory for the following afternoon.

Clint took off work early to take me to my interview. The factory was a big rectangular brick building behind a high fence. It had a big parking lot with one scrawny tree growing up out a patch of dirt in the center. The only windows in the entire building were in the front office where a lady with curly hair sat behind a desk. She wore a lot of makeup and was chewing gum.

"Can I help you?" she asked.

"I'm here about a job interview," I said.

She looked me over for a second. "Honey, I'm sorry, but you have got to be at least sixteen to work here."

"I'll be eighteen in a few months," I said. "I am Nochipa Kurtsinger. I have an appointment."

She looked at her appointment book. "Yes, I see."

Then she pulled an application from her desk drawer and handed it to me. "Just fill it out at that table over there."

I did and gave it back to her.

She stood then and I could see that she had been sitting in that chair everyday for so many years that her bottom had taken on a sitter-like quality. Her hips were huge in proportion to the rest of her and the wide white belt she wore only accented the feature.

"Right this way," she said. I followed her through a door out into the factory where rows and rows of sewing machine sat with long faced women operating them. We then went into another small room.

"Have a seat," she said. She took a wooden board that looked like some sort of game from a shelf. "Put the pegs in this board as fast as you can," she said.

"Does this test my IQ?" I asked.

She laughed. "Your IQ's not important. We just need to see how fast you can put the pegs in the holes."

Somehow the whole notion of this building with its gray, windowless walls and long-faced women made my hands shake. I felt sick to my stomach, like I wanted to throw up. I put the pegs in the board, but I dropped several of them as I did. My hands visibly shook.

Clint and Fannie were waiting in the car.

"How'd you do?" Fannie asked.

I shrugged. "I don't know. I might not be smart enough for this job." I was sarcastic with her all the time and she couldn't even tell it. She probably thought I truly doubted my intelligence.

Fannie beamed. "Oh, I hope you get it, Chippie. This is a job to last a lifetime. You can put some money back with a job like this."

Clint smiled at me. "What do you think, honey?"

I shrugged again. "The building's got no windows."

That Sunday afternoon I sat in the sun behind my house. Clint had a chair nearby under a shade tree, reading a book. He laid it down. "You think anymore about working at the factory?"

I had my eyes closed, just letting the sun shine on my face. "I ain't working at no factory."

"You're not even going to consider it?"

I sat up. "Clint, I'd rather die now and get it over with than spend the next twenty-five years in that room without windows. Those women got nothing besides that factory. They got no dreams. You should've seen their faces. All the light and life in them has been drained right out until they're nothing but robots, getting up every day before daylight, working in that boring place all day long then coming home to cook supper for their husbands and kids. I don't want to live that way. I can't live that way. I need to do something that's going to make a difference, a real difference, in people's lives. I don't want another soul to die too young, like my momma. If I have to go to work in that factory, I might as well put on a striped suit and go to prison, 'cause that's where I'll be."

"So, you're not going to work in the factory? Even if you don't get the scholarship?"

I lay back in my chair and closed my eyes. "I'll starve to death and rot before I work in some old sewing factory. I wasn't made for that place and I'm not going."

"We need the money, Chippie."

"We needed the money you spent on that record the other day, too."

He flung his book down on the ground. "Chippie. If a man can't buy his comic books and albums, the things he likes, he might as well be dead. I'm tired of people always putting me down."

"I didn't put you down," I said. "Just making a point. You work at the mill and you work hard, so you buy what you want with your money, even if we don't have food on the table."

"Well, the electric bill's paid," he said.

I nodded. "All I'm saying is this. If you can spend your money on things we don't need, then I can go to college in hopes of a better future." I looked at him seriously. "Clint, I've prayed and prayed about this thing. I have to go to school. I just have to."

"Why do you say you have to do it?"

"Sometimes a person just has to do something because it's what she was born to do. I was meant to go to school and I have to do it."

"Then I'll stand behind you on this. I do believe in

you, Chippie."

I went to him and kissed him. "Thank you, Clint. Thank you so much."

Two weeks later, I received a notice from the college in the mail. I was the recipient of the art scholarship as well as a merit scholarship. My tuition was paid for. The college, due to my low income and good grades, was also offering me the chance to work part time as a janitor to pay my traveling expenses.

I would clean dormitories between classes, before and after school. Clint and I worked it out so that he would drop me off on his way to the mill everyday, even though it was an hour before my first class. I would sit on campus benches until something opened or in the student union building.

But college wasn't until August. It was still May. I had the summer ahead of me to work in tobacco and for Ms. Rose. I knew the money I earned wouldn't be much, not enough to help me through school, but just maybe, I could buy a car. First though, I had one very important night ahead of me, high school graduation. I still needed to walk through the line and receive my official diploma.

CHAPTER TWENTY-EIGHT

"Will you take a picture of me and Leeler?" I asked Fannie the day before my graduation.

I stood on her porch, wearing my cap and gown. She wasn't keen on my going to college but was bound and determined that no wife of her son would appear in front of hundreds of people in a graduation gown that didn't fit right. Therefore, she hemmed and ironed my gown, then trimmed my hair.

Clint's little sister stood beside me that afternoon as she snapped our photo.

"I did a good job on that gown," Fannie said afterwards. "Didn't I?"

"Yes, you did," I said.

For it was true. Fannie was a real hand at sewing; nowhere near what Momma had been, what with her making wedding gowns and all, but Fannie was a heap more handy with a machine than I would ever be.

She smiled at me a little, but it was a smile sure enough. "Now, Chippie, go get that gown off before you tear it."

Graduation night was hot and the high school parking lot was so full that Clint drove around and around, trying to find us a good spot. Once inside, he got with my family and went on to find a seat. I went into the bathroom, put on my cap and gown, and fixed my hair. Then I waited in the cafeteria with the other graduates where teachers helped us line up in the proper order. The wait was long and hot, but finally someone shouted. "It's time."

The cafeteria doors swung open and we marched single file into the gym where we sat on folding chairs near the stage. On two sides, bleachers surrounded us. A basketball goal hung down in front of the stage and another one hung at the back of the room.

The principal introduced the speaker. I didn't even catch his name. His words were long. I couldn't pay attention to what he was saying. My mind was wondering over what I would do with the rest of my life.

When the speaker eventually sat down, the principal called out the names of the valedictorian and salutatorian, both lawyers' children. Then he called off the name of college scholarship recipients. He called several names. Students stood and the auditorium exploded with applause. Then he called my name.

When I stood, I looked, for one brief second, up into the stands where I saw Daddy standing, too. He had his teeth set, gritted, like he was nervous and worked up. No, that wasn't it. He was proud, doggone proud. And I felt that somewhere, maybe straight above me, Momma was standing, and Jerry Wayne was with her, his eyes lit and his thumb up. There beside him was Granny Eastridge, stretching her neck and trying to see, because she was short, even in Heaven.

As I walked to the stage for my diploma I looked out over that gymnasium. It was packed, yet the only faces I could see were the faces of Pablos and Eastridges, brown faces and white faces, the faces of my family.

I worked in tobacco the summer after I graduated and got so brown that I looked like I was from India. I worked every day except on Sundays and when it rained. From sunrise until dusk, I worked, eating my lunch on a wagon by a barn or on a porch. Then in July, a Pentecostal preacher from Russell Springs came to an empty field on the very top of Briar Ridge. He put up a circus tent and held meetings every night for a month.

Meetings started at seven o'clock. Farmers came in their work clothes and so did the mill workers. I always went home and put a dress on first. Granny Eastridge had told me so many times that a woman ought to wear a dress to meeting.

Every night, the service started with the Rainwater Sisters, a twin duo from somewhere in East Tennessee. The sisters, Millie and Martha, were well into their seventies and still had coal black hair. I was pretty sure they dyed it. Nobody that old could have hair that black, at least nobody I ever saw. They were Cherokee and both as skinny and knotted as old fence posts. Neither sister had ever married. When they were young, they had dedicated their talent to spreading the Gospel of Jesus Christ and since they didn't believe in women preachers, they had taken to singing his word all over Tennessee and Southeastern Kentucky. Their names were known all the way from Casey Creek, Kentucky to Knoxville, Tennessee, on down into Cherokee, North Carolina.

The Rainwater Sisters would sing several lively tunes like "Jesus on the Mainline" or "God is Good," then the Pentecostal women would take to dancing, shouting, and shaking tambourines. It wasn't just the Pentecostals that came to the meeting; it was the Baptists, Methodists and Nazarenes too. Although they disagreed on doctrines like dancing and speaking in tongues, they all agreed that Briar Ridge was crawling with sinners that needed saving. Therefore, the whole Christian body of Briar Ridge was behind Brother McClair's efforts. The tent was crowded every night with two to three hundred people, a large percentage of them new converts.

When Brother McClair preached, I felt like Jesus himself would come walking into the tent at any second or that the rapture might take place and only the righteous would be taken up to Heaven. When he preached, goose bumps stood out all over my body.

"Hell's hot and Heaven's sweet," he'd say. "And the Lord Jesus, his children shall meet. Y'all get ready now, 'cause He's coming for the saints, not the ain'ts. If you're living in sin, then give your life to Christ right now, before it's too late. Jesus loves you." Then he would throw his hand into the air and shout as tears rolled down his face, "Jesus loves you!" He would bring his arms into his chest and bow his head and in a hoarse voice, he'd whisper just loud enough to be heard, "Jesus loves you. Why don't you come? Look how many people are here tonight. Do y'all know why you've come out? I'll tell you why. It's 'cause you're hungry. You're hungry for something you can't see with your eyes. There's a hole inside you that nothing seems to fill. You can search the whole world over, but ain't nothing going to fill that hole except knowing there's a God that loves you enough to become one of you and die for you. Oh, sinners, why don't you come to Jesus tonight?" He'd bury his face in his hands then solemnly say, "Millie and Martha, y'all come on, girls."

The Rainwater Sisters would take a stand in front

of the portable organ, played by a big woman with hair to her knees. They called her Sister Juanita.

"Just as I am, without one plea, Oh Lord, I come. I come." Martha and Millie sang in their thick alto voices. They sang so loud, I was sure a person could hear them all the way down to Meredith Goodin's store. Their voices went right through the tent walls and ran up and down the road for a half-mile each way.

I had made my mind up that I didn't want to miss a night of it. I came in one afternoon. Clint was drinking a coke and watching rock music videos. He looked up when I told him and said, "Chippie, them Holy Rollers is of the devil. Momma said all they do is shout, roll, scare little kids to death, and show their rear ends. I'm a Methodist. My Grandpa Jefferson Grant Lee was a Methodist circuit rider and my daddy is a Methodist. I was born one and I'll die one. I don't want you hanging out with them Holy Rollers no more."

"Well, then, if you won't take me. I'll walk. You ain't making me stay home."

Clint kicked the coffee table. "I swear, Chippie. I ain't losing you to a bunch of Jesus freak hippies. They've done brainwashed you."

"Well," I stiffened. "If you think I'm brainwashed, why don't you come to the meeting with me and see what kind of soap they're using?"

The next night, he went.

Fannie went, too. Her curiosity got the better of her. She sat in the backseat, smoking as we drove to the meeting.

"Chippie, roll that winder up. The wind's messing up my hair."

"Gosh, Momma, it's too hot to roll the window up," Clint said. "And it's window, not winder. Hicks say winder."

"I wore curlers in my head all day, so my hair would look decent," she said.

I sighed and rolled up the window. About three minutes later, Fannie said, "Chippie crack that winder a little bit so I can blow my smoke out."

"Good grief, Momma," Clint said. "You just now had her roll it up."

"Clint, tomorrow I need you to take me over to the department store. After work come up to the house and get me. I need to get some *ar-tickles*, and your daddy's too stingy to take me."

"What?" I said. "What's an ar-tickle?"

"*Ar-tickles*," she said. "You know...*ar-tickles*."

"What's an *ar-tickle*?" I said again. "What's one look like?"

"Oh, Chippie," Fannie said. "Don't act dumb. An ar-tickle can be anything. Here's the ones I need, some batteries for radio, some material to make a waist for the baby." She meant Leeler.

"What's a waist?"

Clint said. "It's a stupid blouse. Momma, call it a

294

blouse or a top. Nobody says waist."

She ignored Clint. "And I need some *asp-par-reens*. Chippie, roll that winder up some. Wind's a-messing up my hair."

"Momma!" Clint said. "I'm dying of heat over here."

"What are *as-par-reens*?" I asked.

"Aspirins," Clint said, annoyed. "She means aspirins, Chippie!"

"Oh," I said.

About that time the tent came into view. We were early but a crowd had already gathered. Fannie put her cigarette out the minute she got out of the car and freshened up her red lipstick.

"For crying out loud, Momma," Clint said.

We waited for her to finish, then walked toward the tent together.

Brother McClair preached about how the Holy Ghost was the Spirit of God on the earth, left here to connect people with their Father in prayer, just like a telephone line connects a long lost child with its parents. Then he said that the Spirit had a language all Its own, that It knew all languages.

At the close of the service, he invited anyone who wanted to receive the Holy Ghost to come on up. I went up there and let them pray for me until I mumbled something in another language.

Clint and Fannie were fit to be tied on the way home.

"I thought you were a Methodist," Clint said, through his teeth.

"I am," I said.

"Chippie, you ain't going to be going round talking in tongues all the time, are you?" Fannie asked. "There ain't never been no Holy Rollers in our family before, and I hope you don't start acting like them."

"I'm not a Holy Roller," I said.

"Then why'd you go up?" Clint asked.

"Because I want to know everything the Lord has for me," I said. "I want to do something for God with my life. I promised my momma I'd keep following Jesus and that's what I feel like he wanted me to do."

"Hmph," Fannie said, blowing smoke out the window. "I been a Christian my whole life and I ain't never felt like the Lord wanted me to do anything, most especially speak in no tongues."

The next morning, I awoke before Clint and slipped out of the house. I sat on a white bench my dad had made me beneath the willow tree in our backyard. There was a morning mist rising and it hung in the air above a pond size mud puddle.

I remembered how ashamed Clint had been of me at the tent meeting. "Is this thing real?" I asked.

I remembered something Granny Pablo had once

said. "The earth is the Lord's, Chippie. He made us and all that's in this here world was made by him."

I slipped from the bench and knelt on the damp ground, placing my palms on the grass, something I had done many times as a small child. It was the way Granny Pablo taught me to pray. I felt a gentle current flow through me. "The earth is the Lord's and the fullness thereof," I whispered. "The water, the sky, the air, the mossy rocks in this yard, Lord, You made them all and You made me, too. What would You have me do with my life? Show me, Father. Teach me."

It didn't matter if I couldn't explain my experiences to Clint or to Fannie. All that mattered was that I knew the Spirit inside me was alive so I gave voice to it and let it sing out. A song poured forth from me, some ancient language my mind could not understand, soft and light, like the rising fog and beautiful to my ears. I felt I was soaring.

It wasn't like the wild hollering at the tent. It was just a simple knowledge that God was real and that He cared about me. I knew that I would have the courage to go to college, to succeed at it and to make a change in my life. I looked up and saw to the southwest of me a large hill, hazy and blue in the distance, rising up beyond Briar Ridge. "I will lift up my eyes," I said. "When the world tries to push my head down, I will lift up my eyes unto the hills where my help comes from and my help comes from the Creator of Heaven and Earth. When everything in this world tells me to set down and quit, I'm going to stand up and just keep on standing up."

The day before college started, I went with Fannie, Clint and his little sister to pick up apples at an orchard in

Casey County. Lou Annie had always loved to pick up apples so I invited her to come with us and bring little Sparrow Dawn in her stroller. What a beautiful September day it was. The smell of ripening apples was poignant. The sun streaked gold through the branches of the trees. Each of us had a grass sack for apples. The rough texture of the strong burlap felt reassuring in my hand.

As I often did, I got lost in my own thoughts while the rest of the world fell away from me. All around me hills rose up, closing us off from the rest of the world. This valley was a realm unto itself and what lay beyond the hills was something else, someplace I had never been, just like college. In twenty-four hours, I would leave and go beyond Briar Ridge, beyond the world I knew. Lou Annie pushed the baby stroller over to where I was.

"What are you thinking about, Chippie? Going to college?"

I shrugged. "Yeah, I guess."

"You ought not be sad that you're going off to college."

"Lou Annie, do you remember how it was when we left Walkup Holler to come to Briar Ridge? Remember how we sat by the old well pump?"

She nodded. "Yeah and we talked about how we didn't want to move."

"I reckon sometimes we've got to move on," I said. "Sometimes life just takes us where we're supposed to be, like you…" I looked down at Sparrow Dawn. "Sometimes what seems like an accident is just what needs to happen to bring a person's heart where it ought to be."

"You mean like the way me having a baby made Daddy realize that he can't lay down and die because Momma and Jerry Wayne are gone?"

I nodded. "Sometimes I get scared about going to school, Lou Annie. Nobody in our family's ever done it before. I get scared that I'll go out in the world, beyond what we see here and the girl I am, the person I used to be, will get lost out there. I'm afraid that one day, I'll wake up and look in the mirror only to see a stranger looking back at me. Yet I have to follow what's in my heart. I feel like I was born to do this thing."

"One day," Lou Annie said, "You're gonna be a famous artist, Chippie. I feel it in my bones."

I took Lou Annie's hand. "I always wanted to be an artist, and that's good, but it's not enough. I have come to believe God put each of us into this world to walk our own road and that if we just listen to His spirit inside us, He'll guide us on the right road. Lou Annie, I was wrong. The day our momma died, I thought it was a spiritual thing to just pray "let Thy will be done," but now I know that it wasn't spiritual, it was just ignorant. It ain't God's will to take a momma away from her babies. What happened to Momma wasn't right. She ought not to have died so young. I can't bring Momma back, but there is something I can do. Lou Annie, I can be a warrior."

"You're gonna join the army?"

"Yeah, but not the kind that shoots a gun. I'm going to be a doctor. Cancer killed my momma and I aim to spend the rest of my life making it pay. I aim to do two things with my life. I'm going to tell every soul I meet that God loves them and then I'm going to do everything I can to cure their sicknesses.

"I need to do something that matters with my life. Lou Annie."

"A doctor," Lou Annie said, then she chuckled. "You'll be a good one."

It was late when we got home from the orchard but I talked Clint into taking me up to the cemetery where Momma, Jerry Wayne, and Granny Eastridge's graves all lay side by side. He sat in the car while I walked over to their tombstones.

"Jerry Wayne," I said. "This is the last time I'll be coming up here. I wanted to tell you that I aim to make you proud of me. Granny Eastridge, I know you weren't much for saying 'I love you,' but I did and still do, so I just want you to know that I'm going to college. And, Momma, I'm never going to bring flowers up here because you told me not to. You didn't believe in that sort of thing and I'll hold true to your wishes. You told me I could be anything I set my mind to, so I've decided what I want to do, and I think you'd be pleased."

The wind blew my hair across my face and I sniffled. I hadn't realized I was crying. I looked over the rows of graves and my heart felt so light that I began to sing, "He set me free, He set me free, glory to God. He set me free." I walked toward the gravel road leaving the cemetery. "He set me free, oh glory to God, He set me free.

EPILOGUE

College days quickly turned into years. In those years, my little brothers and sisters became adults. Lou Annie finally opened that restaurant she dreamed of as a child and married a boy from Ashland. She has never had a big name singer in, but Sparrow Dawn grew to have a lovely singing voice and performs every weekend.

Carol Lee never became a magical cartoon character who ran around handing out exploding gifts, but she is the head chef at Annie's Loft. She changed her name to Carolee and has been married and divorced twice. Still she remains happy and full of fun. However, to this day she will not go near an outhouse. She is always taking in foreign exchange students and college kids hang out at her house for she gives motherly advice along with a delicious peach cobbler.

Zelphie married a boy from Harlan, and has three children. She is a fine electrician. Every year, for Christmas, she gets tools, gloves, and coveralls from her husband. She also developed a good head for numbers and business sense. Nobody can talk a deal or save a buck quite like Zelphie. For the most part, she has stopped jumping over furniture.

Willie's break-in incident was not his last brush with the law, but after his rocky teenage years, Willie is a top-notch carpenter. He has four children. They still come around for Christmas dinner where Little Josh David, who now weighs about two hundred fifty pounds, plays his guitar and entertains the whole family with his music. Josh David is a rock musician who has never married because life on the road is not conducive to marital relations.

Jesse married my cousin from Arkansas. They have three children. I email him often and he emails me back, misspelling most of his words, but that's Jesse. He no longer wears mismatched checkered pants or hunts for snakes in the creek. Jesse is a fine mechanic and wears jeans and T-shirts. He has a tattoo of a Senorita on his right arm.

Upon graduating college, I won an internship position at a hospital in West End, New York. Clint and I traveled there and spent about a week. He fell in love with the city and it was in his heart to stay there, but I felt like the streetlights stole the stars and the noise stole the sounds of nature, sounds I couldn't live without or maybe the simple truth was that I knew it wasn't God's place for me. I came back home to Kentucky, did an internship in a local facility and eventually opened up my Oncology practice in a coal mining town where I still live.

I have a daughter of my own now, but that almost didn't happen. For a while, Clint left me. He was angry that I left New York. One morning, he told me that he was going back. I didn't try to stop him and we didn't exchange any harsh words. He just left. I guess I knew it was coming, but each night as I said my bedtime prayers, I called Clint's name before the Lord, praying that his eyes would be opened.

He was gone about a year; then one evening when I came home from the clinic, he was on the couch waiting for me. He told me how he had driven a taxi and lived in a smelly apartment building below a drunkard who peed out the window every morning.

I guess the best thing he told me was that New York

wasn't much without somebody to share it with and that after a while, the noise and the smells and the people started to close in on a person. He thought he loved the city, but without his family and the people who cared about him, the city was just another place. I suppose that meant he loved me more than New York. We started over and our marriage is better than before.

During our second summer in the mountains, he took one of the Wayfaring High School seniors for an admissions interview at the Asbury campus. Clint came back with admissions papers of his own. He eventually obtained a degree in History and landed a job as a professor at a small private college about a half an hour from Wayfaring.

Fannie was proud when I became a doctor. She taught me to sew and we spent summers canning tomato juice and pickles. I learned to play the dulcimer and we sang folk songs together. Three years ago, she died of a stroke. Eugene is almost a hundred and still lives in the house where he was born.

Uncle Dody Eastridge struck it rich and lives in a mansion up around Lexington. Aunt Darla married three more times and is now divorced. She still lives in Memphis and gives tours at Graceland.

I never saw Sharlett Brown again.

Daddy never remarried. He lives near me. We talk on the phone and visit often. We are planning a trip to Mexico in the fall, to the village of his grandfather's birth.